HEXUAL AWAKENING

ALSO BY ANDREW FORREST BAKER

MORE FROM THE HEX'D SERIES

HEX MAGIC : BOOK ONE

GREAT HEX : BOOK THREE (COMING SOON)

NOVELS

THE HOUSE THAT WASN'T THERE

LESSER GODS & DEMONS

SHORT STORY COLLECTIONS

WE TREMBLE AS WE SINK

ROAST

HEXUAL AWAKENING

ANDREW FORREST BAKER

PARLVAREE PRESS

Parlyaree Press
Atlanta, Georgia
www.parlyaree.com

Library of Congress Cataloging-in-Publication Data
Names: Baker, Andrew Forrest, 1980, author.
Title: HEX MAGIC / Andrew Forrest Baker
Description: First Edition | Atlanta : Parlyaree Press, 2024
Identifiers: LCCN: 2023923232 | ISBN 9781961206076 (paperback)
Subjects: LCGFT: Novels
LC record available at https://lccn.loc.gov/2023923232

Design by Parlyaree Press
Imagery liscensed from Adobe Stock.

Front Cover/Title Typeface is Rosella Solid.
Interior Text Typeface is Baskerville, designed in the 1750s by John Baskerville and cut by punchcutter John Handy.
Interior Ornaments from Espiritu, LTC Flourons, & Bodoni Ornaments.

Paperback ISBN: 978-1-961206-07-6
Ebook ISBN: 987-1-961206-08-3

To Sean.
To Seven.

ANDREW FORREST BAKER

HEXUAL AWAKENING

HEXUAL AWAKENING

ANDREW FORREST BAKER

CHAPTER 1

"Where do you think you're going?"

I froze in my tracks, lifting my hands slightly at my sides to show they were empty. The last thing I needed was some trigger-happy guard tossing bullets—or worse yet, spells—in my direction. My breath seized in my chest as I heard my partner's voice in my ear telling me to "abort mission." It was kind of like a spy movie—one where I had an earpiece and an anxious tech guy waiting in a van nearby to direct me through the maze of hallways as I maneuvered my way through the enemy HQ.

Except Cernun's voice was just an echo of his warnings from the past two weeks telling me not to do this. And I was far from a spy. The correct term was *witch*, though I'd been called several other not so sweet names over the years. I was storming the enemy's headquarters though. But I was invited. Sort of.

"I-uh… I'm a guest of Learco Clarke," I stuttered, turning slowly as I spoke, hands still raised and empty. *No sudden moves,* they promised.

The guard's face was flushed when I finally made eye contact. It could have been for me—I may have been a little bit famous in some circles—but it was probably because I'd mentioned his boss. As the head of the Southeastern Division of the Moral Authority of Witches, Learco's name held some sway.

"Mister Cullen!" he demurred and apologized.

Maybe it was about me. I guessed my name held some sway too.

"Darragh," I insisted as I smiled at the young witch, preferring the first name basis my farm upbringing had taught me would create a sense of immediate equality and compassion.

In my opinion, people were just nicer without the force of honorifics. Plus, I always avoided the gendered and property-centric language of mortals when I could. Someone might be a "Lord of the Land" in the eyes of the state, I guessed, but nature was her own and could not be owned.

The guard was cute. A solid jawline, perfectly shaven, and surprisingly plump lips. A sharp curve to his nose, probably from an old football match. A bit of well-carried weight beneath the black of his uniform. He was a young witch from a good family—as were nearly all MAW agents—working to make his parents proud by policing and intimidating his own. I didn't have a very high opinion of the organization. Though, in fairness, my partner and I had been dating the guy in charge. And great sex always magneted a moral compass, shifting due north to a cardinal direction I hadn't thought to pursue before.

"I think I may be a little lost," I lied, shrugging my shoulders and attempting my best *silly me* smile. "I'm supposed to be meeting Learco for lunch."

I'd only been to the MAW's Atlanta HQ twice before, so it was a believable story as far as the hall monitors were concerned. I'd actually been a bit disappointed the first time I came. In my mind, I'd always pictured something more—magical. A castle straight out of Camelot. Or a warded gingerbread house that appeared as a Great Oak Tree in the middle of Piedmont Park so that only those in the know would walk inside. Or some high tech, powered version of the control room on one of those FBI shows Cernun liked to watch on television. Instead, it was a sea of identical cubicles, and hallways with beige carpeting and beige walls, and ID scanners to use the elevators nestled in a nondescript office building along a Buckhead corridor. Even the Magical Artifacts & Antiquities Museum had a more fantastical vibe, and it was built inside an old drug store in a strip mall.

"Mister Clarke's office is on the sixth floor," the guard said. "I'll happily escort you."

"Oh, no. That's quite al—"

"It's my job, sir."

Well, fuck the Fae.

Cernun was not going to let me hear the end of his correctness. My plan to slip into the archive room unnoticed would, of course, not go unnoticed. I shrugged, and smiled, and hoped Learco would understand.

"I take it you couldn't wait to see me."

Learco smirked from across the restaurant table. The twist of his mouth highlighted the forever chap of his lower lip. He knew I found that irresistible. The rest of him wasn't so bad either. Tight bantu knots clung close to his scalp and drew attention to the fullness of his deep brown eyes. Those eyes, flecked through with golden strands that mimicked the color of his aura when his magic manifested, drove me wild with their secrets. He held his thin, broad shoulders with a regal ease. I smiled as I imagined the diamond nipples on his toned chest, the gentle sparring of curled black hair there, and the undulation of his eight pack beneath his tailored red suit. When he saw me looking, the blush that highlighted his cheeks gave his rich, ebony skin a slight tinge that matched the pinot noir in his glass.

"Thanks for covering," I frowned. "And I'm sorry."

I hadn't wanted to keep my mission a secret from him, but with the politics at play within the organization, I'd thought it better to give him plausible deniability in case the worst happened. Which it almost did.

"I'm not even going to ask what your goal was," Learco sighed, "though it doesn't really take a crystal ball to guess it has something to do with the archive room, a certain leader of the Fomóraiġ, and that shipment of unedited Shadow Books we got in two weeks ago."

I thought it was cute that Learco referred to Books of Shadows as Shadow Books. It made me giggle a bit each time I heard it. His family had sent him to Atlanta from the Caribbean for school when he was fourteen, but that island lilt and phrasing still clouded his tongue with its sensual fire. It made for fine conversation. And hotter times in the sack.

"You know I have a team of spell cast scholars searching the archives for any mention of the Dark Fae or cross-world travel," he said, relaxing his shoulders a bit with my laughter. "If the Moral Authority of Witches has anything on Balor or his kin—anything real, that is—I will find it."

The truth was, we'd found plenty of stories about the Fomóraiġ—hell, I'd grown up with my Grandma talking about Balor and Bree and Conand as if they were kin—evil kin you didn't want to invite to Sunday Supper, but family nonetheless. But the folk tales were as unreliable as they were entertaining. Generations of telling had taken the kernels of truth there and elaborated upon them until the magic became mystifying again. After meeting Balor himself, I imagined a good number of the embellishments came directly from the Fae. All that said, it was nearly impossible to delineate the truth from the fiction and harder still to determine what magical routes wouldn't consume me, Cernun, and Learco in their power when we tried to make good on our deal.

I frowned but nodded at Learco's promise, defeated as I fished a french fry from my plate and dragged it through the peppered ketchup there. I knew he was on top of things as far as the MAW was concerned, but I also knew how much the organization liked keeping secrets in order to police the witches of the world, and I wouldn't put it past them to keep secrets even from their own. Plus, without being able to tell them *why* he was searching for the information, it was too easy for Learco's scholars to miss something important. Besides, magic had a lot more freedom and nuance to it than the Moral Authority and its scholars were willing to admit to, mostly because they'd spent centuries trying to erase and deny those aspects.

I was spiraling again.

"It's been five months since we made the deal with Balor," I whispered, keeping a cheerful expression on my face for the nearby diners as I sipped a not great but serviceable Old Fashioned from the nearest sit-down to the MAW HQ. It wasn't comparable to Aunt Paulina's, but not too much in the city was. "We aren't any closer to figuring out either a path or a loophole to the bargain we made. It's all made me a bit... itchy."

"We have three years."

"Two and a half now."

"We have two and a half years. Plus a month." Learco's genuine expression warmed me as he furrowed his brow in compassion. "You, me, and Cernun. The three of us together, we can figure this out. I know I've not known you for long, Darragh Cullen, but I truly believe there is nothing the three of us can't do.

When we work together."

It was the kind of sappy Learco was known for—at least as far as Cernun and me were concerned, though I imagined he was quite different in his role as the leader of the Southeastern Division of the Moral Authority—and I fell for it every time. I let my shoulders fall, for real this time, as he sent his aura out to caress the edges of my own. It was comforting, feeling the quick vibration of his energy pulse against mine, and I grinned as I reached to massage him with my own power. We swelled there at the table. I imagined a few new things the three of us could do.

"Pardon me, Mister Clarke."

I winked as our foreplay tease was interrupted by the latest of Learco's assistants. He'd gone through eight since his last real assistant, Samara Byrne, had plotted with my former protégé to strip us of our powers in order to reignite a line that had never been magical to begin with. It was obvious he had trouble trusting those he let into his circle.

This one was cute though, in an "I really want to please you" sort of way. His posture screamed of a formal upbringing, but his eagerness to please said he had disavowed the money of his youth and rent was coming due on his Atlanta apartment. Not forced to wear the sleek black uniform of the other MAW agents, he'd chosen a semi-casual light blue button up that fit his weight well, accentuating his broad chest and full stomach in a flattering way. His hunter green slacks clung to his thick thighs, accentuating the bulk of his cock at the crotch, and the bold paisley pattern dancing across his boat-large boots let me know the bulge was not a lie. I appreciated the view of his full ass as he leaned in to whisper something into his boss's ear.

Learco's eye twitched a bit with the news he was given, but overall he kept a stoic expression. The calm, casual demeanor with which he held himself was part of what made the man so good at his job. It was also one of the things I liked to taunt to the wild side during more carnal situations.

"Thank you, Rafael," Learco smiled as the assistant rose back to attention. "If you could wait outside while I say goodbye to my companion, I will join you shortly."

Rafael nodded, first to his boss and then to me, before he made his way to the door of the restaurant. Learco scrunched his face apologetically.

"Is everything okay?" I asked.

"Is it ever?" Learco shrugged. "Sorry I have to cut this short."

"Don't be!" I smiled as I reached my hand across the table to cup his. "This was an unplanned and unexpected excursion."

Learco's eyes darted over his shoulder to catch Rafael waiting outside the front windows. The new assistant held a casual stance, but even I could see the urgency and agitation swarming beneath his countenance. Learco's face softened as he turned back to me.

"See you tonight?"

"Definitely," I smiled brightly, then sank back into my chair as he made his way to the exit.

I watched the men pile into a black sedan idling at the curb and frowned into what was left of the food on my plate. I hated lying to Learco, even if it was by omission, but it was easier for him to believe my attempted infiltration of the MAW's archives room was about the Fomóraiġ. *That* he could get behind, and he would not be forced to "do his job" toward someone he cared for. Besides which, dabbling in ancient and forbidden magics had enough danger to it without getting my new lover involved.

"How'd it go, babe?"

Cernun's wicked smirk told me he already knew the answer as I bungled through the door of my apartment. I'd inherited the place—and the magic shop below it—when my Uncle Gardner had decided to retire to Key West with his husband, and, like any good Guncle, left it all for his queer nephew. It was a great living quarters—spacious with large windows and blond wood floors, a floating island kitchen that made meals and spell work easy, and an open living room with a large screen TV I never watched for longer than fifteen minutes. Cernun, Learco, and I had never really gotten the "and chill" part of the phrase down. Although, according to the sales associates at the magic shop, we had it exactly right.

Beneath the majestically woven rug in the living room was a beautiful, inlaid pentagram Uncle Gardner had placed with his own two hands in the 60s. The five-pointed star was a perfect six feet in diameter; and the dark, lush walnut he used looked brilliant and almost black beside the light oak flooring. Like a grounding point, Spirit pointed due north at all times. I liked knowing it was there beneath my feet.

To the side of the living room, my bedroom featured a king size four poster bed that never felt cramped and a newly renovated bathroom. After three years of waiting for the other spell to drop, I finally figured the boon the shop received from my being The Guy Who Exposed Magic to the World was somewhat solid. And if things did crash, at least the rainfall, walk-in shower, or the antique claw foot tub that was perfect for lavender scented bubble baths, could keep me going. I was lucky it all fit without magic.

I was also lucky I'd inherited the building from my uncle. One of the last original shops on our newly hip block of Atlanta—well, us and Aunt Paulina's—the Herbal Emporium Xpress, or HEX for short, had served witches and mortals alike for over seventy years! Rising rents would have driven any other shop specializing in dried herbs and candles out of business ages ago. But, thanks a bit to a little notoriety in the witch community, alongside a fascination with real magic from the humans, I'd managed to keep up with the property taxes and made the shop somewhat of an institution.

"Did Learco text you?" I asked, a bit embarrassed as I plunked down on the couch beside Cernun.

"Haven't heard from him. I just figured it would be a bust. I told you it was a bad idea."

His pale blue eyes were sympathetic as he spread his muscled, tattooed arms to let me nestle into his broad chest. His thick hand clutched my shoulder warmly, and I swiveled my head to stare into the abyss of his darker than black hair.

"You really should tell him what you're doing," he sighed.

"I know," I grumbled, sure he was right once again. "But I can't."

"You keep saying that," Cernun chuckled, "and maybe it'll make it true."

I sighed heavily then breathed him in deeply before pulling back to look him in the eye.

"Learco has enough on his plate," I explained. "A brand new relationship with two of the hottest witches this side of the Mississippi. Plus dealing with our dealings with Balor. Running the Moral Authority. Not to mention the covert faction within the MAW that wants him gone and me dead."

"Samara's been dealt with."

"But she wasn't working alone," I insisted. "I'd bet my power on it. And you know what I'll do to keep that. And you."

Cernun frowned and ran his hand through his hair. His bicep bulged as his palm reached and rested on the back of his neck. Faerie fuck, he was a beautiful man. My eyes traced the curves of his skin evident beneath his tight black tank top all the way down to the thick, heavy bulge in his pants. I licked my lips as I sent my aura out to trip against his, teasing him as my energy pulsed warmly along his own.

A low growl escaped his throat as his energy rose to meet mine. His lip twitched into a grin, but he wagged a finger between us.

"I still think he'd want to help," he said.

"This thing with him is so new," I pouted—gracefully, I thought—as I pulled back on my aura and slumped against the couch. "I can't just go up to him and tell him, on top of everything else, that one of the guys he's fucking is seeking MAW-banned spells from the archives. That puts him in a really awkward situation."

"Better said to his face than done behind his back," Cernun sighed.

I knew he was right, but I didn't want to accept it. Though my first attempt at changing the subject away from my subterfuge failed, maybe the second wouldn't. Cernun was a horn-dog after all.

"I can think of a few things I'd like to do behind your back right now," I moaned.

"I'm being serious," he said. Still the smirk on his lips, the sultry squint to his eyes, told me he knew was I was up to. And he certainly wasn't opposed.

"I am too," I purred.

My aura pinned his with a sudden jolt of power, and I watched as he trembled in pleasure. Squinting, he sent a pulse back through me that made me gasp.

"We're not done talking about this," he said.

"I know," I smiled, and I kissed him.

His soft lips parted to welcome my tongue. The taste of

him sent my senses into overdrive. I swung my leg over his lap to straddle him as our auras wove an intricate tapestry around our bodies. Hungry, my tongue traced the rough stubble of his jawline to the sweet, soft spot on his neck that drove him wild. He gasped as my teeth brushed against his skin. The welcome combination of hard and soft, of push and push harder that was our sex enveloped us in ecstasy.

My fingers found the bottom seam of his tank. Smiling, my palms pushed their way across the undulations of his abs, trapped between his skin and the cotton, until they cupped his pecs. I let my thumbs massage his nipples, flicking playfully as they hardened, while my fingers toyed with the rough expanse of hair that spread over his tattoos. My tongue worked along the tendons in his neck as our auras mingled to heat the air around us. It was heady and wonderful and just what I needed on a hazy Tuesday afternoon in February.

His growl rumbled through his throat, vibrating my mouth there, as his hands gripped my back and pulled me closer still to him. I felt his cock throb against me, pulsing hard against the fabrics between us, wishing to be freed, but liking the anticipation all the same.

My own breath caught in my throat as his lips met my neck, and I moaned as my head rocked back. As he worked his way downward, his hand reached up and pulled the collar of my shirt aside. I bit my lip as his teeth met my shoulder, nibbling at the constellation of freckles there and promising more to come. My fingers wove through his hair, twisting and turning through his gentle curls in the same rhythm our auras made around us. I dropped my chin, letting the scruff of my three-day beard prick along his cheekbones as he lifted his face for our lips to meet once more.

Kissing Cernun was always intense, and magical, and almost

as hot as the sex itself. Almost.

His gruff grunt sent a shiver down my spine as his fingers wrapped my hips and lifted me slightly into the air. His eyebrows raised as he twisted his body alongside mine until my back met the cushions of the sofa, and he angled seductively above me. I craned my neck against the pillows, burrowing in there and watching as Cernun lifted his tank above his head and tossed it to the floor. I moved quickly to follow suit with my own shirt, throwing it aside to join his just as his palms found my shoulders and pushed me back down to the couch. I smiled at his smirk, gasping slightly as he ran a hand down my chest and across my stomach, then gripped and pulled at the waistline of my pants. The sudden burst of air—the freedom inherent in it—made my shaft jump and pulse with the same intensity it had when the pressure of Cernun's body laid upon it.

I reached for his belt buckle but had barely made it when the breadth of his chest met mine, warm and strong, and our lips joined together once more. My hands slipped around his back, and I pulled him against me while my tongue explored the spells his lips contained. He tasted sweet, like honeysuckle fresh from the flower, full and present and intoxicating. He'd told me once I was more earthy—fresh, like thyme—and the taste of us combined was like magic in itself.

I moaned as our bodies pulled into each other. Our auras wove electricity through the air of my apartment. Every inch of me was awakened and intensified. Pleasure pulsed through me with such single-minded euphoria, I barely even registered when he pushed off his jeans to join our shirts on the floor or shifted my own pants down my thighs.

Still on top of me, he extended his body to reach for the bottle of spare lube we kept hidden in a wooden box on the side table for when occasions like this arose. The view was amazing as his chest and abs—colored with stories of his past—moved like a movie above me. I wet my lips and teased the tip of his cock as it throbbed just beneath my chin. Cernun froze there, thighs tensing and hand still gripping the lube as I took as much of him into my mouth as the angle would allow. My hands gripped his ass to guide him further, relishing the teasing touch, but he stayed firm in his position. He had other plans for how this was going to go.

I kept him in my mouth as his torso twisted and his slick hand wrapped my shaft. Both cool and warm at once, the lube glistened as he massaged it along my cock. He squeezed more onto his fingertips and reached to wet himself. My eyes met his just as they rolled back into his head, finding the pleasure in his own fingers as he readied himself for me. One hand gripped my chest as his other surrounded my dick, steadying it as he lowered himself slowly onto me. We both inhaled sharply as the head of my cock entered his hole, our breaths caught there as I allowed him to control the rate of penetration. Both his palms met my shoulders as his head rolled back, exposing his neck and his chest and his sex. He looked beautiful there, stretched above me as our bodies joined like our auras.

Our thighs met, and we froze there. The magic of our connection pulsed through the air like a spell on the verge of being spoken. Intent and need followed longing and ecstasy. I throbbed within him as he pulsed around me. Just when I thought I couldn't take it anymore, he moved, rising slowly and pulling me upwards until our lips met. I wrapped my arms around him, clinging to his skin like it was all I'd ever wanted. In that moment, it was. IIe was. We were.

The rhythm of our auras matched the measure of our bodies: perfect, well-timed, and holding us there in suspended animation. In that moment—in most moments—Cernun was the whole of my world, and I knew I was his.

He came, warming my stomach with the sticky spasm of his orgasm. I smiled as he continued to rock on top of me, skin meeting skin until I released inside of him. He shivered as our lips met, our kiss sensuous and slow as he lifted himself from me and snatched his tank top from the floor. I used it to wipe down as he padded his way to the bathroom.

The water pattered against the porcelain tiles as Cernun spun the knobs on the shower. I smiled as I sank into the couch. The morning may have started off rough, but the afternoon was shaping up quite nicely.

"Don't think this means you get an out on our conversation," he called with a gasp as the water hit his skin. "I know you think you're protecting Learco, but lying to him about what you're doing for Mads, even by omission: it's going to fuck you in the end. And not in the good way."

I inhaled deeply as reality set back in. Cernun was right. No matter how I tried to spin it. But if I told my new lover I was doing a deep dive into MAW-forbidden spells for my new sales associate Madison, I'd be putting him and our budding relationship into a precarious position. At best, he'd be forced the choose between whatever was happening between us and his job as the head of the Southeastern Division. At worse, he'd think I'd been using him all along. And he could flame me for both.

I sighed as I tossed Cernun's tank top back into the pile of clothes, then swooped it up to toss the load into the washing machine. I slipped behind the shower curtain to join Cernun beneath the hot water.

"You're right," I whispered as my lips met his shoulder and he lathered up his hands for me. "I'll tell him the truth."

And I would.

I just didn't say when.

CHAPTER 2

The Herbal Emporium Xpress had been unapologetically magical since long before our kind had been exposed to the world. A quaint shop on a popular street just east of downtown, its countertop stone and gem displays dazzled as the overhead lights shone off the polished rocks, and a library-card-catalog-like system kept back stock close at hand. Dried and fresh plants, procured from some of the finest farms around the world—including the one still run by my mom and dad—kept me connected to the land I grew up on and added an earthy, fresh aroma to the air. Hand-dipped spelling candles hung by their wicks from walnut pegs beside shelves of wood carved figures of gods. Pan with his goat legs and eponymous flute; Oshun, wrap painted yellow, with her Abẹbẹ fan and her peacock; The Green Man with his oak-leaf face and the mischievous glint in his eye.

I'd never been a god-bound witch myself, preferring nature as the source of my power and the heart of my intent, but after coming face to face with Balor, one of the mythic Dark Fae of old, I had to admit that maybe the gods were more than just the short-hand names for focus I'd believed them to be. Still, a part of me told me that creatures who called themselves gods rarely were, no matter how much power they possessed. I really hoped that part of me was right. Otherwise, when we made good on our deal to release the Fomóraiġ into the world, we were in for a whole mess of trouble.

Adjoining the god statues was a fine collection of books Madison had brought in using the connections they'd made working the gift shop at the Magical Artifacts and Antiquities Museum. I'd always wanted a bookstore element in the shop, but the MAW policed what could and could not be sold. Maybe I could ask Learco for approval. After I told him the truth about why I was sneaking around his Buckhead HQ. Ugh. Still, several of the leather-bound journals were perfect for starting new family Books of Shadow as knowledge of spell-craft grew in this new, unbound era. Because it was growing, whether the MAW sanctioned it or not.

Cast-iron cauldrons of various sizes were displayed beside the central cash wrap with stock on hand in the backroom for customers to take home immediately. Rare and more potent herbs and stones were beneath the glass countertop alongside spelling salts, sigil chalk, and a small selection of oils and incense for witches on the go who didn't have time to craft their own. The lower shelf housed athames, scrying mirrors, and table scarves designed to gleam on any altar.

Freshly showered, I made my way down the stairs from my apartment into the stock room where Stacey had a collection of yarns and hides and fabrics spread across the wooden surface of Uncle Gardner's spelling table. I cringed a little when I saw the messy display. I'd never been able to hide any emotions from my face.

"Oh, sorry, boss," Stacey blushed sheepishly as she reached to gather her materials. "I thought it'd be okay to set up here if I cleansed it real good after."

"Don't worry. It's fine. I'm—I'm glad it's getting used."

It wasn't Stacey's fabrics that bothered me, it was the table beneath them. Don't get me wrong; it was gorgeous. A beautiful white ash hand-carved and crafted by my uncle, it was the perfect height and size for any number of enchantments. I'd used it often throughout the years since Uncle Gardner had left me the shop and moved to Key West with his husband, but, for the past five months, I hadn't been able to touch it. It laid dormant and unloved at the edge of the stock room like the obsidian mood rings I'd ordered in bulk when that trend was still happening. The thought I'd once imagined having "spell school" around it for the community made my stomach churn.

Stacey nodded and frowned as her fingers traced the wood beneath her fabrics.

"Do you still see Aiden when you look at it?"

"Sometimes," I confirmed in a soft sigh.

Aiden was the very first employee I'd hired on at HEX, and I used the spelling table in my weekly magic lessons with him. Well, I had before he and his father betrayed me and tried to pull the power from not only my veins, but Learco's and Cernun's as well. Which I should have expected from a Gowdie. His non-magical ancestry had a rich history of power grabbing and tattle telling. Hell, his most famous relative, Isobel, had turned herself into the Church in 1662 to be flamed while yelling tales of midnight masses and animal transformations just so she could feel like a real witch. The burning had given them placement in the annals of witch history, but I doubted there was ever any power there.

I still shuddered when I thought about it. I guess it didn't help that some of her accusations were the basis of the secret research I was helping Madison with and the very thing I was keeping from Learco.

"This table was yours and your uncle's long before that bastard got his grubby little fingers on it," Stacey said. "Don't let him take your power."

I laughed as I attempted to shake the anxiety from my bones. If she only knew the full truth in her words. But while some of the details had been disseminated, the MAW's redacted telling of that night kept both Cernun and myself out of it.

"You're right," I surrendered, hoping my smile showed I meant it. "As usual. How are the sachets coming?"

Though historically most witches preferred to make their own charm bags—sewing their intent into the container with every stitch—modern spell casting in the city had a much faster pace than it used to, and who was I to stand in the way of progress? Stacey constructed some of the most gorgeous bags I'd ever seen, so I'd commissioned her to make some for the shop. They sold like hot cakes and upped the herb and gem sales alongside them. I paid her outright by the piece and also gave her half the profits from each one sold. It was going so well, she'd soon been able to make it her full-time gig, leaving working the sales floor to Madison and Verne.

"Check 'em out."

She proudly displayed a beautiful array of tiny drawstring sacks, each about the size of my palm. A delicate array of wool, animal skins, and cottons, they were all-natural and patched together with both aesthetic and intent in mind. I could see why they were so popular with both our witch and non-witch customers alike.

"Amazing, as always," I smiled. "I'll let you get back to it."

I took one more solemn look at the spelling table before I made my way toward the sales floor.

"Hey, boss. Wait a sec," Stacey called, then bounded toward me with her hands extended. "I made this for you."

I took the charm bag from her and turned it over in my palm. The purple-dyed leather was immaculately stitched and tied. I sniffed at the opening but didn't dare to release the knots. Beneath the soft scent of leather rose a mossy mix of fresh pine and weathered oak. I inhaled deeply and smirked.

"You trying to kill me?"

"Only if you eat it!"

Stacey grinned and blushed as she joined her hands behind her bag. Her toe shuffled against the smooth concrete at our feet.

"I don't want to overstep," she said, "but I've got a pot or two of aconite on my patio. And, with... well, everything, I thought a protection bag might help."

I beamed as I tucked the sachet in my pocket. The warmth of her intent washed over me.

"Thank you," I said, and I meant it wholeheartedly. "If the Moral Authority let me sell wolfsbane or ready-made spells, you'd be my supplier on that too."

Stacey glowed as she returned to her work, and I slipped onto the sales floor. It was such a sweet gesture on her part. Maybe I wasn't as bad at reading folks as Aiden had made me believe.

Madison's eyes darted hopefully to me the moment I stepped through the door, but they kept their composure as they guided their customer through the ins and outs of herbal potency differentials in burning, brewing, and baking. They had a good grasp on the knowledge and didn't seem to mind explaining it all to a mortal who didn't have the spark to take the potion further than a mild acknowledgement of intent, but I could tell they were dying to ask me how my morning excursion had gone. I felt horrible that I'd have to disappoint them.

"They really ought to charge for those lessons they're giving out," Verne whispered to me when his customer left, and I slipped behind the cash wrap with him.

"And have the Moral Authority shut me down for operating an illegal school?" I chided. "No, thank you."

"Couldn't you just get your new boyfriend to look the other way?" he shot back, and I chuckled along with him as he pulled up the daily sales report for me to peruse.

It was a good day, sales wise, especially for a weekday. Though we weren't allowed to offer any actual spells, much to the chagrin of the mortals who wandered through our doors, with February 14th fast approaching, I'd had a hard time keeping rose quartz, red candles, and dried damiana in stock. Even if we couldn't perform the spell for them, by the Fae, they were going to douse themselves in love goddess oils and call out for the unyielding attention of Paul or Mary or Leonard or Peggy Sue. It had gotten to the point over the years since magic had been revealed that every red candle came with a pamphlet warning the user about the unintended consequences of a love spell gone wrong. The pamphlet was more to cover our own asses with the MAW than out of a fear of the spell working, but it made the non-witch customer all the more excited to call the corners and light the wick.

"Can't go wrong," Madison told the young woman with the sharp haircut and lust in her eyes, and I smirked at the supply of herbs and stones they had bundled up for her already. She wasn't a witch so the spell wouldn't spark the way it would if someone powered performed it, but who was I to judge? Besides, if it gave her an outlet for the emotions that overwhelmed her on top of an appreciation of the natural wonders of the world, everyone was a winner in my book.

"You think you'll be okay if I pull Madison from the sales floor for a little bit?" I asked Verne, side-eyeing him as he tucked away the cell phone he'd surreptitiously pulled out when he thought I was distracted.

"I'll manage," he shrugged. "Plus, Stacey's in the back if I need her.".

If HEX, albeit just downstairs, was my home away from home, Aunt Paulina's was my kitchen by another mister. Or something like that. Located catty corner and across the street, its grungy, rock-n-roll aesthetic and the Fae-may-care attitude of its owner and waitstaff made it a favorite of locals and tourists alike when they were searching out a taste of down-home ATL. Plus, they were home to the best damn burgers and the crispiest fries in town. Mix that with a stellar Old Fashioned and how could I not love the place?

Paul, the owner and namesake, was an old, old friend of my uncle's, but he didn't let age stop him from donning his fishnet tights, pleated schoolgirl skirts, and a generous helping of lipstick and rouge. He smiled from behind the bar when Madison and I entered, then nodded for me to go ahead and claim my favorite booth near the back of the restaurant. His blonde wig had seen better days, but still glimmered in the glow cast from the holiday lights tacked up around the mirrored shelves displaying an impressive collection of whiskies and gins. He'd always treated me well, but now he gave me special treatment since I'd revealed magic to the world on the curb in front of his restaurant a few years prior. The increase in sales for him as magic chasers and looky-lous came through meant a few free Old Fashioned for me.

"Hey, Darragh. Oh! Hi…"

Paul's niece Katrina stopped short as she approached our table. Her blush as she turned away from Madison spoke volumes even though I didn't know the story.

"Hey, Kat," Madison smiled, their own skin darkening until their cheeks countered their blue locs perfectly. "I didn't know you were working tonight."

"Picked up a shift from Jordan," she said. Then, after a long pause added, "Y'all know what you want?"

Katrina's southern twang took me immediately back to my childhood on the farm a few hours south of anywhere in the state. Sweet and lilting, it warmed me to my very core and offered a nice contrast to her closely shorn blonde hair, her khaki cargo shorts, and her militant gaze. Even months after moving to the city, the gruff exterior she'd formed from growing up queer in the country still armored her like a protection spell. It was one of those "necessity" things that became a beautiful calling card of our culture. And, judging by the look on Madison's face, I could tell it intrigued them too.

Their eyes followed her as she nodded to her uncle and swung through the kitchen door to let the cooks know to drop our fries. I had a single eyebrow raised in question when their stare turned back to mine.

"What's going on there?" I prodded.

Madison's face fell. Their shoulders slumped as their fingers traced the condensation rings of drinks long past on the lacquered table.

"Sorry," I said quickly. "We don't have to talk about it."

"We went on a really shitty date," they shrugged. "Like one of those where nothing really went wrong, but then nothing really went right either. It was like we just kept missing each other by a few seconds. We were in the same place, you know, but not."

I nodded. Before Cernun, I'd had a few dates like that myself. Of course, before Cernun, I'd been more concerned about the connections made after the date portion of the evening than what happened in the small talk before.

"I don't think she gets that I'm not a lesbian," Madison sighed. There was a longing in their eyes as they looked beyond me to where Katrina had joined Paul behind the bar. "I may have been AFAB, but that's not who I am. At my core, or whatever."

An understanding clicked into place, at least when it came to the importance of what I was trying to help them with. I could see the pain they carried, shielded and buried behind the bubbling strength that youth and power gave them. I hadn't really noticed it before—or I'd passed it off as the typical malaise of college existence—but the sudden weight of not feeling comfortable in ones' own skin overwhelmed me. Being assigned female at birth because it fit the linguistic narrative of external genitalia didn't take into account the humanity, the soul, of the witch who sat across from me. And to feel betrayed by their body itself, that had to be unbearable. We were so much more than the skin that contained us. My power had taught me that.

If the folk lore was true—if at one point in history witches had actually been able to shift, to supplant our skin and our bones and our minds to become truly one with the natural world, the possibilities awakened for someone like Madison were vast and wonderful and filled with so much hope.

I found it strange that people could wrap their heads around the concept of a werewolf—though, as far as I knew, Weres weren't real—but could not grasp the humanity of a trans person who was living and breathing and existing right in front of them.

A month ago, when Madison had asked for my help in searching out and reviving ancient magics that had long since been lost to us—mostly at the hands of the MAW—I'd honestly been worried about a repeat of my former protégé Aiden. My mind raged with scenes of betrayal and aggression and power grabs played out in little, deadly vignettes. Still, I'd agreed to help because I wanted to believe that people—especially witches—were inherently good. And now, even though I felt horrible in keeping it from Learco, I was glad I did.

I did my best to tame my wandering mind as I pulled myself back to the table, surer now that I was doing the right thing, lies by omission aside.

"Katrina's a sweet young woman," I offered. "She just may need some time to wrap her head around the concepts and the language. I remember how new everything was for me when I first got to the city. You know your boundaries and what is healthy for you, so you should decide where or even if you want to pursue things with her. And, honestly, that's what's fair to the both of you."

They twisted their lips and leaned back against the red vinyl of the booth. Their electric blue locs looked almost purple in the bar lights.

"I guess you're right," they sighed. "I mean, it's a fairly new language for me too. But… When someone tells you who they are… Do you try to convince them they are someone else?"

"Is that what she's doing?"

"It feels like it. The whole date, she kept talking about being a proud lesbian and a proud feminist and moon cycles like my menstruation defines me. And I just kept wanting to scream 'I'm not a fucking woman!' as loud as I could. I wanted to scream, and I wanted to run."

"Heard."

We both turned swiftly to lock eyes with Katrina as she slid the basket of fries and our drinks onto the tabletop. Her trembling lip betrayed the stoic expression plastered to her face. Madison's mouth gaped as they attempted to find the words to save face. Katrina squinted as her mouth twisted into her best customer service smile, telling us both where we stood. Or sat.

"I'll have Kenny take over your table," she said, then scurried off to the kitchen.

Paul shot me a questioning look from behind the bar as his niece disappeared behind the swinging doors. I winced as my eyes shot between Madison and where Katrina had disappeared, and Paul nodded. He slung the bar rag over his shoulder, adjusted the black bra strap beneath his white tank, and sauntered off to care for his niece as Madison collapsed against the table.

"Fuck!" they exclaimed. "I really am hopeless. First Angel and now this. Fucking Fae."

I tried for my best sympathetic smile. Angel, Madison's former crush and best friend, had been dating Aiden—or, more accurately, was being used by Aiden—when he and his father had attempted to murder me and my lovers for our magic. The two of them had been like toads in a cauldron before that, but over the last few days Madison had clammed up whenever Angel was mentioned, so I'd thought it best to leave it be.

"Why don't you take the rest of the night off?" I suggested. "I mean, you're free to hang out there if you want, but if you want to leave, that's cool too."

"I take it that means your archive expedition was a bust?"

"Didn't even make it through the door," I confirmed.

"Well, shit."

They picked up a fry from the basket but didn't bring it to their mouth. I couldn't blame them. I suddenly wasn't very hungry either. I hated seeing them look so sad and dejected. It made me more determined than ever to find the spells we were searching for.

"I guess I'll take you up on that offer," they sighed, dropping the fry back into the batch and downing their vodka gimlet in a single gulp. "If you really think you'll be fine."

"We'll be great," I insisted. "Will you?"

Madison nodded and pulled themself from the booth. Their smile was weak but the light in their eyes wasn't fully diminished as they said goodbye and slipped from the restaurant.

Absently, I squeezed a dollop of ketchup onto the paper basket liner and used the shaker to coat the red in a thick black crust. I used one of Aunt Paulina's famously crispy fries to swirl the pepper through, then dropped it, and focused on my drink.

The warmth of the whisky, even against the ice cube, felt glorious as it washed down my gullet. It'd been one hell of a day, and an Aunt Paulina's Old Fashioned was just what the witch doctor ordered. Paul grinned as he slipped a backup drink onto the table and slid onto the bench across from me.

"How's Katrina?" I asked.

"Hurt and confused," Paul shrugged. "Which is the same damn thing as being young and in love, ain't it?"

"I definitely had my fair share of heartbreaks back in the day," I agreed.

"You and me both," Paul chuckled. "Heck, I still do. But they'll figure it out, the two of them. One way or the other."

I smiled and nodded. It was nice having Paul around. He reminded me so much of my uncle, it was like a little piece of Gardner was still nearby, watching over me. But I knew Paul was looking forward to retiring and passing the place on to his niece. Once he got up the courage to leave his namesake behind.

"I gotta say," I said, "I'd root for the two of them. I think they'd be pretty cute together."

"Maybe," Paul agreed. "Or maybe not the way you think. That's the thing about love, right? It takes all these different forms, and then the trick is finding how it fits in each situation."

I smiled at the beauty—the aged wisdom—in his words. He was right. I'd never been a boyfriend type of witch, but that had all changed when I met Cernun. We just fit together, nearly instantly. And that wasn't to say it didn't take work and evolution, but we had something really special that seemed to come out of nowhere. Or maybe everywhere. It'd changed the way both of us were living our lives, and neither of us had even thought to look back. And then, years later, here we were introducing Learco into the mix. So that was coming with more change and more love and more ways of fitting. Figuratively and literally.

Even if I didn't want to accept it, I knew I needed to tell Learco what Madison and I were up to. I owed him that much. Yes, he was the head of the Southeastern Division of the very organization that had outlawed and hidden the magics I was pursuing. Yes, that slammed him into a sticky, rock hard place between his work and his relationship. But he knew what he was getting into with me, and whatever type of love this was that was forming, it had to have the chance to find the right way to fit. That required honesty. And maybe a quick trick with my tongue to keep him from turning me in to his agents.

Besides which, with his help, I could bring Cernun on board; and I was certain the three of us together could unlock all sorts of magical mysteries. The thought of restoring power to what it once was, before the Moral Authority had watered it down to keep us hidden and subsequently—or supposedly—lost it to history, was invigorating. Especially now that the world knew we existed. Even in the few short years since magic had been exposed, the open use and practice of our power had already strengthened what we were capable of. Maybe Learco and the MAW would actually be excited to uncover some of our ancient secrets. He was adamant he wanted to change the organization from within. What better way to present change than with a shape-shifting spell?

I left a twenty dollar tip and magicked a little heart around it for Katrina to find when she made it back out onto the floor. She and Madison would figure things out, I told myself. And if they were both reacting so extremely, it must have meant something special was brewing there beneath the anxiety. That was a good sign. That was hope. I waved my thanks to Paul and began the short trek back to HEX.

The Winter air was crisp as the sun made its early descent, opting for somewhere warmer to spend its evening. I shivered as I pulled my jacket a bit tighter around my shoulders. Head cocked, I took in the pair of black, four door sedans idling at the curb outside my shop. The last time that had happened, fake MAW agents had kidnapped me and taken me to ritual like a sacrificial lamb. It gave me the heebie-jeebies just thinking about it. So maybe my shiver had more to do with them than the brisk weather. Reluctantly, I picked up my pace as I crossed the street.

Learco didn't smile as he emerged from the passenger seat of one of the cars. He held his hand up in his *I'm-on-official-business* way when I moved in for a kiss. Disappointed, my heart faltered a bit as he cleared his throat.

"Where is Madison Ridge?" he asked. The formality in his voice was strained and haunting, even with his island lilt.

"I sent them home early," I said. "Is everything okay?"

Learco glanced at the agents waiting in the cars. His face sank as he turned to look me in the eye. I could tell he was torn between duty and his affection for me. That was something I understood all too well. He stepped in closer and lowered his voice.

"The magically mutilated body of a young witch was discovered late this afternoon," he confided. His eyes pleaded as they searched mine. "We believe it to be Angel Stewart."

"Holy fuck!" The words flew out before I could stop them. By the Fae, Madison would be crushed. "Are you sure? Do you need

Mads to identify the body? What the hell happened?"

Silence stretched like loss between us.

"We're sure that it's Angel," he said softly, his voice faltering. His fingers found mine as his lips scrunched to form the pained line between wanting to comfort me and having to be the boss. "Her parents broomed in and made a positive ID."

That must have been what pulled him away from lunch today. Fuck. Not only were Moral Authority agents hated by most of witch kind, they also had to deal with the gruesome magic shit the cops didn't want to touch. I wished I could make him feel better. The hurt radiated from his face.

Verne and Stacey tried to look casual from behind the storefront glass as they cleaned and rearranged displays ever closer to the door. Learco shook his head and signaled for the agents in the second car to leave, and the driver of his car to wait. He looked gutted as he turned back to me.

"I can deliver the news to Madison when I see them," I offered. "So you don't have to."

I could take that off his plate at least. After denying countless requests from his supervisors for me to start working for the MAW, it was the least I could do. Besides, he had his hands full with tracking down the killer. Faerie fuck! I couldn't believe Angel was dead. Madison would be crushed.

"We're not looking to inform them of the death," he gulped. "Madison is our main suspect in the murder."

CHAPTER 3

"I can't be such a bad judge of character, right?"

"I don't know. I mean, you picked me, didn't you?"

I smirked at Cernun's attempt at humor, but it didn't stop my pacing through the living room. Shock swirled with a heartbroken fury and pounded through every step I took as if I could somehow force the feelings from my body if I just walked far enough, but I felt the mixture resound back through me every time my foot met the floor. It almost felt like a spell, the way the pain and anger twisted through every thought that entered my mind in rapid succession. I just could not believe, in a city of so many upstanding witches, I was facing another friend taken in by the MAW.

Cernun's lips twisted as he watched me from his perch on the kitchen island. His pale blue eyes squinted in a sympathetic wince, and the colorful tattoos stretched across his furry chest danced as his pecs heaved with each deep breath he took. By the Fae, he was gorgeous. The way the black denim clung to his thighs was almost enough to distract me. Almost.

"Learco's coming over after?" he asked.

"After he black bags another of my sales associates and friends into Moral Authority custody?" I finished sarcastically. "Yeah, he said he'd swing by right before he hightailed it to Madison's dorm with his magic dampeners and torches."

Cernun sighed as he slipped from the marble countertop and stepped in front of my path. His firm grip on my shoulders helped to ground me as he forced my eyes to focus on his.

"He's just doing his job," he assured me. "We both know Learco is not one to act impulsively. If he's taking Mads in, it's with good reason. And if they're innocent, he'll see to it they are not harmed."

"I suppose," I conceded, but I was no less pissed off. Just a little horny on top of it. Fuck, that man knew how to tweak my libido. "He did take you in on impulse though."

"And risked his job to help me escape," Cernun reminded me.

I sighed, somewhat dramatically, as I collapsed onto the couch and let my hand massage my temples. I wasn't sure who to be angrier at: myself for trusting Madison; Learco for believing Madison could commit a crime, let alone kill their best friend; or Madison for potentially doing the damn thing. The "damn thing" being murder meaning that Angel was fucking dead. Now, I was mad at myself again for not even taking a moment to consider what that meant. Ugh. I didn't want to be mad at any of us.

Cernun's feet were soft as he padded his way to the couch. The warmth of his presence loomed over me as he slipped his fingers through my reddish-brown hair and massaged my scalp. He knew I was spiraling, but he also knew his touch would help. I peered up at him with a half-hearted smile of appreciation.

"You're all over the place," he said. "We need to ground you before Learco gets here. You can't blame him for doing his job. You can't blame yourself for something you didn't do. And you can't blame Madison until we know for sure whether or not they did this." The denim stretched taut over his thighs as he squinted to kiss my forehead. "Now, breathe," he commanded.

Like any good witch, I knew how to center myself when the spell called for it. I pulled the air through my nostrils slowly, filling first my lungs and then my diaphragm. I held it there, like magic spindling within me, for as long as I could before my lips parted slightly, and I pushed the air out slowly. I exhaled until there was nothing left inside of me, the breath pulling the currents of my mind along with it, until my brain and lungs felt empty, felt on the verge of collapse; and then I inhaled once more. It was a slow process. And though it did not make anything make sense, it started to pull things into perspective.

The rooty, grassy scent of vetivert mixed with the sweet smell of honey and filled the room. I smiled broadly at Cernun. Leave it to him to brew up a potion of the calming plant to bring me back to the present. A witch needed their earth connection. If he added a drop of chocolate, the whole earthy concoction would be perfect. Though I normally preferred iced coffee, even during the height of the cold months, a warm, calming tea would really sate my nerves.

My smile skewed as Learco slipped through the front door. A haggard expression pained its way across his face—eyes wide but squinted, cheeks taut, and mouth held firm. Even his thick, chapped lower lip which I found irresistible looked thin as he tried to silently communicate his angst. He held out a drink carrier from Brew as an offering. The borage blue cauldron emblazoned on the capped paper cups still bubbled with the spell placed on them, and I knew that the tea inside was still hot.

Cernun kissed his forehead as he pulled the cups from Learco's hands and centered them on the kitchen island. Reluctantly, I pulled myself from the sofa and joined my partners on the barstools. No one spoke as I grabbed my cup and blew through the aperture in the lid until the cauldron's bubble reduced to a simmer. I let the liquid coat my tongue, seeking out the clean, crisp taste of the vetivert and fighting back the grin my lips tried on when the underlayer of dark chocolate found me. Learco remembered exactly how I liked it. He was truly a great guy. And the pain which radiated from his aura spoke volumes.

"I didn't mean to—"

"I'm sorry I—"

We both stopped trying to speak over one another and relaxed a little onto our barstools. I could feel the fear slipping from him as quickly as my own anger was subsiding. The pain was still there though. And the confusion.

"Did you apprehend Madison?" I asked.

It was such a harsh word—*apprehend*—but it was what it was. Learco may have had dreams of changing the Moral Authority from within, but he still had to oversee their Big Brother/Police State tendencies nonetheless. It was important to call it what it was and not succumb to whatever euphemisms the organization preferred.

"They have not returned to their dormitory. Their roommate let us in to look around." Learco's face scrunched as he took a sip of his coffee and stood to grab some oat milk from the fridge. "I'm not going to ask you if you know where they are."

"You kind of just did," I quipped. We were quickly entering standoff territory once again, so I added, "But no. When they left, they said they were going home."

I shook my head. It certainly seemed like Madison may be on the run and that certainly read as guilty to the three of us sat there in my home. My mind replayed their statement from earlier—*"First Angel and now this!"*—on repeat. Maybe the MAW was right. It wasn't looking good. But I still couldn't bring myself to believe Madison would be capable of murdering anyone, let alone their best friend, no matter what issues they were having.

"You really don't think Madison is a murderer, do you?" Cernun asked. The concerned look on his face as he attempted to navigate the murky waters between us warmed me a bit. It made me glad he was there.

"Personally, I can't see it," Learco admitted, tapping the thick paper of the folder nervously. "But I honestly don't know them too well. And our agents found Madison's spell sign all over the scene."

My brow furrowed as my head tilted in question. I'd heard Learco mention spell signs before, and any witch worth their salt knew that all magic left behind remnants of the power used there, but I'd never known it to be traceable to the witch who performed the spell. Besides which, assigning it to one particular witch would require the MAW to have samples of their magical residue in the first place. It didn't seem possible.

"It's something new Leland Hyde is advocating for," Learco answered my unspoken question. "Since all of the magical studies programs at universities require an entrance exam, the MAW has been able to take samples of the residual power left behind by each spell and compile a pretty hefty database for comparison. So now, it's kind of like the FBI's fingerprint system but for witches."

I scoffed. Not only was it yet another new and untested form of control by the Moral Authority, the whole basis of it was problematic and highly unethical. And if Leland Hyde, the MAW's resident cleaner, was part of pushing it through, I had a feeling the worst with it was yet to come.

"So what?" I growled. "My spell sign—as you call it—is all over this place. As is Cernun's. As is yours. If someone dies here, does that mean all three of us get dragged in for it?"

Learco winced. His head dropped as he riffled through his leather satchel with a slow, purposeful demeanor.

"It's true that the spell sign is tied to the witch and not to a particular spell," he sighed. "We have no way of knowing what Madison was casting. But the only other spell sign present was the victim's. And we are certain that magic was responsible for her death."

He slipped a red file folder from his bag and clutched it at his chest. The deep chestnut of his eyes studied both me and Cernun as he steadied his breath.

"I'm not supposed to share these," he admitted. "And you don't have to look if you don't want to see the photographs. It was an extremely gruesome scene."

My breath caught in my throat as bits of reality crashed around me. A young witch was dead. She had been murdered, brutally, in her own apartment right here in Atlanta. And even though I'd only seen her a handful of times when she popped into the shop to bring Madison their lunch or gossip about which boys in her Chem lab she thought were cute, I could still picture the shining sincerity of her features when I'd first met her and Madison at the Botanical Gardens last Equinox. She was gone. And the remnants of who she was were captured in the photographs Learco was offering to share. The gravity of it all, and the pettiness I was throwing at him, clung to my chest like the folder clung to his.

I sighed as I nodded and lifted my eyebrows in question to Cernun. He tried to appear calm as he agreed to view the pictures, but I could tell the whole thing excited him a bit. With all the years he'd spent searching for his birth parents, following clue after dead end after renewed possibility, he fancied himself a bit of a detective. He just couldn't bring himself to work for the MAW, even if we were dating the local leader.

"You're sure?" Learco asked.

I could tell his insecurity lay in what was pictured in the images instead of in breaking MAW protocol by showing them to us. I braced myself for something horrific.

"Let's do this," I confirmed.

He averted his eyes as he slid the red folder atop the counter. His chest heaved as he suckled on his lower lip the way he did when he was nervous. Cernun reached out apprehensively, showing the level of timidity required by the situation, but his hands remained firm as he flipped open the folder and spread the contents across the marble countertop.

My stomach turned. I swallowed hard to force down the bile rising into my throat. The scene on display was disgusting. Every surface from every angle was splattered with red like rust from a particularly humid Summer, like the slaughterhouse once the prized cow loses her milk. It appeared as if she'd exploded from the inside, the way her blood radiated out in every direction.

Angel herself—what was left of her anyway—lay prone and sharp-cornered on her bed. Her features, so subtle and hopeful in my memory, twisted in an impressionist's painting of terror and agony. Mouth agape and eyes wide, all the light and breath removed from her left a dark void of apparent emptiness. It was below her face, though, where the real horror resided.

Ruptures creased the skin of her nude body where bones, sharp and jagged, burst from the wounds. Her right arm twisted in on itself like it had been wrung in circles before it was cleaved in two. Her left thigh curled upwards like the haunches of a great, four-legged beast. Stretches of skin were replaced with tufts of wolf-wired fur or reptilian scales. A close up of her face showed her dark pupils pulled tight to form the slitted eyes of a cat. The whole Frankensteinian chimera of her visage made it obvious her last few moments on earth were excruciatingly painful.

My eyes locked on Cernun's. We were both thinking the same thing.

Shit! The photos made it obvious that someone was attempting to use shifting magics. But even though Madison had tasked me with finding those ancient and buried spells, I couldn't believe they were responsible for Angel's death. They just didn't have it in them. Did they?

Heat rose through my body as I flushed with my conflicting emotions.

"Uh, Learco—" I started, but faltered as I slipped the photographs back into the folder and closed the red cover. I didn't want it to be true.

"You need to tell him," Cernun urged.

He reached a thick hand across the table to cup and stabilize mine. His other moved to intertwine with Learco's. I nodded and reached a hand to Learco's empty one to complete the circle. We had created a safe space, and I knew whatever I had to tell him would be accepted with love, even if the understanding came later. I could feel myself starting to sweat. Was it getting hot in here? I took a deep breath.

"I know I told you my recon mission to the MAW today was about Balor," I said. My eyes locked on his, and I sent out my aura so he would know I was being truthful. "But that was only half of it. The truth is, I've been working with Madison to—"

"Do you feel that?"

I blinked at Cernun's sudden interruption. I'd finally built up the courage to be honest with Learco. I had to see it through.

"Something's not right," Learco agreed, and our hands dropped our circle as we peered around my apartment.

An uneasy feeling—like a malevolent force permeating my wards—seeped into the space around us. The heat beneath my skin flicked to a flame, and I saw the sweat that now dappled Cernun and Learco's brows. Whatever dark magics were at play, they were powerful and intense.

"Fire!" Learco bellowed.

My eyes shot across the living room to find the crimson and amber flames of a small blaze licking its way through the white oak flooring to slither up the doorframe to my bedroom. A quick thought sent a burst of my power out to extinguish the fire. The dark char of ash left in its wake was almost beautiful in a what is and what was sort of way. But I still felt the heat under my skin.

"What the fuck was that?" Cernun asked.

Just as his question met the air, flames leapt back to join his words.

"Faeric fuck!" I exclaimed.

"HEX!" Learco joined.

He was right. The fire must have been coming from my shop below. Fae, fuck it. My store was on fire!

I leapt to my feet as Cernun ran to the sink to grab the baking soda from the cabinet so he could quench the fire the old-fashioned way. I flew through the door and down the stairs to my stockroom so swiftly, I was surprised I didn't tumble pointed hat over feet down the steps. The stockroom was intact, but a thick plume of black smoke snaked its way through the door from the sales floor.

Which meant it wasn't a magical fire. Powered flames tended to produce white smoke if any exhaust at all. Black smoke meant an accelerant which meant human hands were behind whatever I was about to find. Shit! With the right power, magical mayhem could be undone. That produced by human hands required nonmagical means to rectify. Our power alone would not be enough to extinguish the fire. I braced myself for what I was about to see.

"Dammit!"

I recoiled from the heat when I touched the door, shaking my hand and steeling myself to push through. I imagined the worst. My entire livelihood, my uncle's history, succumbed to flame. Candles shaped liked goddesses melting like the evil witches of movies. Tiny bonfires of dried mugwort or blackthorn readied for their stakes, waiting for the poor souls tied there to burn. Wooden figurines puckered and split from the heat, splintering to ash on the shelves. Now I understood why the MAW did not allow any objects sold to be imbued with actual magic. The carnage as the flames triggered them would be unimaginable. Hell, what I was imagining was pretty unthinkable on its own. I needed to see the truth.

A firm hand gripped my shoulder as I began to push forward.

"Cernun's keeping the fire at bay upstairs," Learco assured me. "We've got this down here."

As I nodded, the stinging taste of salt wet my lips. I had not even realized I'd been crying.

"Too much smoke in my eyes," I lied.

Learco smirked affectionately as he pulled his shirt over his head. In one swift motion, he'd ripped the fabric down the center. A quick spell pulled what little moisture there was from the air to dampen the fabric, and he tied it over his nose and mouth. He used the other half of the shirt to wrap around his hands. Even in the midst of disaster, I had to admit how sexy he was. Not only in his always prepared, never dismayed attitude. Smoke swirled around his tight pecs in motions I wished my tongue were performing. His toned eight pack flexed as he steadied his breath, his resolve. His biceps jumped as he tested the door with his fabric-wrapped palm.

"I'll push open the door," he said. "You aim at the flame."

I followed suit with my own t-shirt and grabbed the fire extinguisher. Until then, I'd only kept one because the city required it, but I was grateful it was there. Manmade problems required manmade solutions. My spell work could diminish the flame, but it wouldn't put it out. Not entirely.

"Don't worry," Learco promised, feeling my hesitation. "Whatever is on the other side of that door, we can handle. And we'll get through the aftermath. Together."

He was talking about the damage done to HEX, but I had a feeling he meant a lot more than that. Angel's murder and

Madison's possible involvement in it was about to put us on different sides of the proverbial amulet. It was up to us to not be thrown from it as it spun in the air, Fate herself deciding heads or tails. We both sensed it coming. But his steadfast words felt good on my soul, even if they weren't true.

"Are you ready?"

Once Learco opened the door, I had to act fast. One quick spell to hold back the flames; two hands trained with the fire extinguisher. We couldn't risk the backdraft of fresh oxygen from the stockroom inciting more flames.

"As I can be," I answered and braced the spell on the edge of my mind.

I could hold it there, just barely shy of being an actual thought so it would not be activated until the door swung open. It was a trick my grandmother had taught me ages ago, and not one that every witch knew about or could master. But it came in handy when backwoods, schoolyard bullies would knock the breath out of me in the sandbox. Holding a spell just out of reach so it could be activated with a thought instead of having to calm and conjure could trip a lot of legs in immediate karmic retribution.

Not that I'd ever break MAW rules and use magic directly on a human. Of course I wouldn't do that.

As the door swung open, I readied the aim on the canister and shouted, "*Ná ligtear an t-aer chuige!*"

Though the direct language of the spell didn't matter, my family had always used Irish or Gaelic commands to focus our intent. It helped some witches to speak another tongue, especially one of their distant heritage, when conjuring. The purpose laid in choosing the phrases—needing to translate them and decide carefully which words to use—made the connection to the elements more intense. That was why Learco spoke Yoruba when he spelled; why Cernun's choices were an amalgamation of whom he'd learned the spells from. The words were the guide, not the spell itself.

I'd literally asked the elements not to let the fire be exposed to the air. It was a bit clunkier than it would have been if I'd had more time to think, but it didn't matter. It worked! I watched as the fire shrank away from the thin bubble of altered oxygen surrounding it, burning itself down until I found the source. I spewed the entire contents of the fire extinguisher, watching as the concentrated liquid foamed over the flames and battled for dominance. Once spent, its clang against the concrete floor filled the deafening silence left in the fire's wake.

I pulled the makeshift mask I'd made of my shirt from my mouth and walked onto the sales floor, Learco quick on my heels. It hung around my neck like a bandana, still wet and clinging to my skin as it dripped down my body like tears.

The flames had kissed nearly everything, though the damage was not as intense as I'd imagined. None of the product was salvageable, but I thought I'd be able to save a few of the display tables Uncle Gardner had built himself when he'd opened the store way back in the 60s. I stared at the black soot near the cash wrap where the fire had climbed a column to the ceiling. That was how it entered my apartment above, not by consuming the entire space. Thank the Fae for that. It could have been so much worse.

"Do you see that?" Learco asked.

I followed his gaze to the broken storefront window and then back to the brick and the shattered bottle splayed out in the middle of the floor. The remnants of a Molotov cocktail confirmed what we already knew: this was a human attack, not a magical one. My eyes traced where the bottle had broken and the accelerant had splashed outward, taking fireballs of destruction along when it.

There was that damn smoke in my eyes again.

"Well, shit. I've been in many a dank, smoky room with hot shirtless men before, but never quite like this."

I smirked at Cernun's attempt at levity and crashed into his arms. Learco's fingers wrapped my shoulders, and I felt safe with the two of them here, despite the ravages left around me.

"Who would have done this?" I asked, still buried in the expanse of Cernun's pecs. Damn, he smelled good. My improvised scarf was wetting him and making his top cling to his abs. It was almost enough to distract me from the horror. "Do you think this is about Madison? About Angel's death?" But that didn't feel right. Hell, none of this did. "Or maybe Aiden's back in town?"

But firebombs weren't a witch's modus operandi. At least not this kind. No, this was a good ol' glass bottle, diesel fuel, and a rag. This was human through and through. Which, even though Aiden technically was, he liked to pretend otherwise. I didn't think he'd stoop to guerrilla warfare.

"I can promise you the Moral Authority will do whatever we can to find the perpetrator."

"And I'll help you rebuild," Cernun promised.

"I won't be much help in that arena," Learco smiled, "but I can pull the permits."

I really was one lucky witch to have these two amazing men in my life. Great sex aside, over the past three years, Cernun had proven himself not only to be a staple in my life, but a necessity. He was the first person I thought of in the mornings and the last person on my mind at night, and not only because there was merely an expanse of pillow and sheet between us. Sure, we'd had our issues, but squabbles were just a part of living. My mother used to tell me that friction was what made the elements work. That the rock butting heads with the water is what changed the flow to create the fertile valley. As a kid, I'd thought it was just another lesson about nature. Now, I saw that it truly was, in every sense of the word.

Too, despite first meeting only six months prior, Learco Clarke had become a mainstay almost immediately. Okay, at first, I hated everything I thought he stood for—with him working for the MAW and all—but my attraction had been there straight away. Though in fairness it took a run-in with a wannabe witch, a power-hungry sorceress, and the leader of the Dark Fae to unceremoniously bring us all together. Looking back, maybe that was all ceremony, serving only to speed up the inevitable. Cernun, Learco, and I fit into each other in ways I hadn't thought possible, both physically and emotionally. It made for some hot, satisfying nights. It made for some strong, steadfast days. Like the ones we were heading into.

I gave a cursory look at the damage and sighed. Still, I was glad it wasn't worse.

"*Idurosinsin ti iwon-ara.*"

I cocked my head at Learco's words as Cernun pulled a semi-charred board from a shelf and used it as a temporary patch on the broken window.

"Just a dimensional stability spell," Learco explained. "Everything looks intact, but I'd feel safer with a little bit of magical backup."

"Thanks," I smiled. "Ouch!"

My finger bled as it grazed a newly exposed nail from a countertop, and Learco quickly wrapped the remnants of t-shirt around it to stop the bleeding.

"I'll get in and do a thorough inspection in the morning," Cernun promised. His years of traveling in search of his birth parents had landed him on quite a few construction sites to help make ends meet. It was work he enjoyed—hands on and physical—and it kept his body strong. "It looks like the accelerant caused it to burn hot and fast, but not deep."

I nodded. The soot-covered remains of my livelihood blanched in the glow of the overhead lights.

"Damn," Cernun chuckled. "That was ripe for a dirty joke, and you missed it. Come on, let's head over to my place to be safe. We can help you get your mind off of things."

I felt strange leaving my shop and my home after it had just been attacked, but I doubted I'd get any sleep if I stayed. Plus, I still needed to have a conversation with Learco.

"I'll put up a protection ward," Learco offered. "And authorize it with the MAW to remain until our investigation is done. I can get casters here now and will have investigative agents onsite at first light."

"I'll meet them for the physical inspection," Cernun said.

My smile was weak, but it was there. I was happy the two of them were taking charge. Looking at the carnage made me feel, for lack of a better phrase, burnt out.

"That's the second dirty joke you missed," Cernun laughed. It did feel nice hearing that tingle in the air. Having its vibration seemed to temper the exhaust left by the fire.

"You guys go on ahead," Learco said. "I still have some work to do on the murder case. And I should inform the Moral Authority of this fire immediately. But I'll see you both tomorrow. I promise."

His lips felt softer than normal as they touched mine, and I savored the smoke-tinged salt of them. I would have to tell Learco the truth about my and Madison's endeavor sooner or later, just not tonight.

CHAPTER 4

The soft light of morning frolicked as it reached the bridge of my nose, stopping there to dance jubilantly before bringing its light to my eyes. Cernun's bedsheets were a soft, smoky gray and slipped like soapstone over my bare skin. His California King spread like a continent beneath me. It was glorious. Why didn't I spend more time at his place?

I dragged myself from the bed and slipped into a pair of gray sweatpants my lover had left draped across his reading chair, then padded my way to the kitchen. His fancy new espresso machine was powered on and hot, and a note he'd taped to it gave me step-by-step instructions on how to use it with little cartoon dicks drawn into the margins for good measure. The aroma of the fresh ground roast was sweet and earthy as the beans whittled down, and I tamped them into the portafilter with a little bit of force. His "thirty pounds is like five bricks" note meant nothing to me, but I assumed I had it right. After a few seconds, dual thick, golden-brown streams flowed over the ice in the glass I'd placed below. I preferred iced drinks even during the colder months. I waited his prescribed twenty-eight seconds and stopped the flow, then topped the drink with the sweet cream he kept on hand for when I stayed over. Cernun went with milk alternatives—usually oat, though I saw a container of hemp in there this time—but since I grew up on a farm, I still gravitated to traditional dairy.

Using the last of the carton, I tossed it into his recycling bin and told the digital assistant built into his new refrigerator to add more to the shopping list. If I was going to be staying here a while, we'd definitely need a restock. The screen thanked me by name, and I shook my head in awe at how closely the technological marvels of humanity mimicked magic. I found it amusing at how drawn to gadgets Cernun was. And now that we knew he was a Kyteler, and Learco had unlocked access to an ancient family trust Cernun was the heir apparent to, he could surround himself in those wonders.

A second note on the counter urged me "not to worry" and told me he'd "gone to meet Learco at HEX." He promised the two of them would handle the scene, and that they'd call me with any news. Damn, they were great guys. I was glad they were on the case. I was a bit too distraught to be of any use. I also didn't want to see my shop crawling with Moral Authority agents—that, on top of the fire damage, would be a spell too far. I hoped Verne and Stacey had gotten the messages I'd left for them last night and not shown up this morning. The last thing I wanted was to lose even more employees in the midst of this.

I stepped through the french doors onto the back deck as I sipped my drink. Even iced, the flavor was warming as the brisk morning air swept across my chest, perking my nipples and making me smile from the slight sting. Though he'd only had the Grant Park bungalow a little over a month now, Cernun had worked hard to ready the backyard for Spring. Already, winter jasmine, violas, and primrose shone their five petaled faces toward the slowly rising sun. A stone path swirled around cedar boxes waiting for their witch's crop. A few of them were greenhouse tented with early seeds already starting to germinate within. A fragrant juniper shaded a back corner of the lot for ferns and other lowlight plants, and a row of rich tea olives provided a nice buffer between his yard and the neighbor's. Come warmer weather, he had plans to prairie the small expanse of grass between his front porch and the sidewalk, but that was still in the hands of the historic neighborhood association. And as much as I would have preferred a wild mixture of creeping thyme, Black-eyed Susans, and Aster; the mental image of him shirtless and sweaty as he mowed the lawn was not so bad either. I asked permission from the tree before cutting a few small branches of cedar to twine together. I really needed the protective qualities of a witch's Winter bouquet to calm me. Plus, the fresh, piney scent would be great in the living room.

I tried my best to push the thoughts of last night's fire from my mind. If Cernun and Learco said they were on it, it was best to let them handle it. They were the two most proficient witches I knew, aside from my grandmother and maybe Uncle Gardner. Shit! I needed to call him. He'd want to know what happened to the store he'd built himself.

I stopped in the kitchen to make a second iced latte and arrange and tie the cedar branches into an attractive broom before I made my way back to my cell phone on the bedside table.

"By the Fae, boy! It's a hair past a freckle!" Uncle Gardner's voice was grumbly but strong as it sang through the line. "Those Atlanta nights must not be as hot as they used to be if you're calling me this early."

"Did I wake you?" I asked, knowing full well he'd been up for hours. He and his husband Bill loved to watch the sunrise from the Southernmost Point ever since they moved to Key West. *Most of the tourists ain't up yet,* he'd told me. *It's like we've got the whole of the ocean to ourselves.*

"Not at all, Darragh," he said. Hearing him say my name

soothed me somehow, despite what I knew was coming. "I just didn't sleep well last night. I was having a fright of a fitful dream."

He certainly was a powerful witch to have messages from the ether enter his dreams.

"Let me guess," I sighed mournfully. "Something to do with flames?"

"Faerie, fuck it, boy! It was real?"

"I'm afraid so," I said. My words caught in my throat, tripped over my tongue. "The shop was closed. It started a little after ten. Someone threw a brick and a Molotov cocktail through the window. Cernun and Learco are there now, discerning the damage and investigating the cause."

I heard Uncle Gardner's tongue click against the back of his teeth as he tried to find the appropriate reply. As hard as this was for me, I'd inherited the shop from him. HEX had been the center of his world for decades. He'd built it, and most of the display tables in it, from scratch back when witches still had to hide in the proverbial broom closet. Hearing that it had been destroyed under the watch of the witch he'd entrusted it had to be brutal. I know it was to be that witch.

"I—I'm sorry," I stuttered.

"Did you start the fire?"

"No…"

"Then it ain't your fault!"

His guffaw was jarring, but it did help to lighten the tension in my chest.

"Now you listen here, boy," he continued. "That place has burnt down more times than a clover has leaves. A spell goes wrong; some asswipe ashes their cigarette in a cauldron of fresh-dried honeysuckle. She's seen her fair share of fire. You just be glad nobody got hurt, you grab up your hammer, and you start building her again."

"Are you serious?" I asked.

No one, not even my mother, had ever told me about HEX catching fire before. And she loved telling me warning stories about her brother and the great, scary city of Atlanta.

"You think you and that hot, throbbing throuple you got there get into some wild times inside those walls," he laughed, "but I can promise you it ain't nothing compared to what she saw in the 70s and 80s. Back before I met Bill here and settled down, of course."

"Good morning, Darragh!"

Bill's voice was muffled as he yelled into the receiver from across the room.

"Morning, Uncle Bill," I called back.

I felt some relief that Uncle Gardner wasn't upset. Plus, hearing that it had happened before made me more determined than ever to re-open the doors.

"What worries me," Uncle Gardner said, suddenly serious, "are the human hands involved in this particular up in smoke. You don't think your fame from revealing magic to the world is finding its way toward infamy, do you?"

Fuck! I'd been so wrapped up in the damage done, I hadn't really stopped to even consider the intention behind it in the first place. If someone was targeting me and not just a magic shop, the destruction was far from over. I collapsed backward onto the bed and wished I could sink into the covers forever.

"You be alert up there, okay, boy," Uncle Gardner commanded. "And just give me a call if you need me to head that way. That new boy of yours might stop us from using our power directly on a human, but I know plenty of other ways to get back at those who need gettin'. And that's a promise."

I laughed as I pictured his 82-year-old frame brandishing fists and snark against those who needed "gettin'." While it was true we witches tended to enjoy longer lifespans—particularly now that we weren't getting flamed nearly as often—age had still taken hold of his long, slender limbs. Retirement, though, and the sweet humidity of the Florida Keys, had done wonders for his vitality. I could actually see him taking on an angry mob.

"Hopefully when you do come it'll just be for a visit and not to dole out justice," I smiled.

The historic sidewalks in old Grant Park were the perfect example of nature's dominance when mankind attempted to exert its control. Whole concrete slabs cracked and jutted around the roots of massive live oaks. Moss worked its way into the crevices between pavers to make them slick and ice-like with the morning dew. It took focus to prevent a flailing trip sending me face first onto the stone, but I was grateful for the distraction as I made my way through the neighborhood homes and to the titular park. Green space was just what I needed to regain my focus after yesterday's events. A reconnection to the soil, even if it was mostly dormant and in want for warmer weather, would do me good.

A few joggers and dog walkers passed me as I made my way past the Erskine Memorial Fountain and down into the park, but they paid me no mind. The hundred and thirty-one acres seemed both vast and small as it loomed before me. I could hear the morning keepers making their rounds in the adjacent zoo, and I smiled as I imagined them carting feed to the various encampments. I had never been one for non-native animals in cages, but I took heart in knowing the zoo itself had started from rescued circus animals. Plus, when I was fifteen and filled with rebellion, ranting about the shortened lifespan of animals in captivity, my father had simply smiled and pointed to the pigs and cattle we kept penned around the farm.

I walked north along the grass until I found a gentle clearing amongst the oaks, elms, and magnolias. I didn't mind that the grass was still damp from the crisp night air as I sat, cross-legged, and closed my eyes. I let my fingers weave through the blades at my sides and planted my palms firm against the soil. A soulful calm blanketed the area, wrapping my mind in the rising warmth of the sun. A few brave chipmunks risking the cold to replenish their Winter stores chittered beneath a nearby azalea in search of forgotten seeds or new grubs. Reaching further, beyond the confines of the park, I could feel the still-fresh wound from when I-20 severed Atlanta in two. Already its lanes were crammed with angry drivers headed to work, the rubber of their tires shielding them from the asphalt; the asphalt blocking them from the earth. I pushed past the interstate until I reached Oakland Cemetery's glorious ground. It was only a short jaunt away down Cherokee. Even in the winter, its gardens teemed with a heady mixture of life and death. I could feel the energy of the world moving in its cyclical form all around me. It was fractal; it was exponential; it was beautiful.

Fuck!

My eyes shot open as the static image of Angel's prone body filled my mind. It was her body, but it wasn't. The brutality of the way the forms of other creatures shaped her muscles and snapped her bones made her monstrous. She was lost behind the cat slit of her eyes.

I shook my head and began another attempt at connecting to the earth, but the vision continued to gnaw at me. Madison had been so adamant about their desire to regain the fabled shifting abilities of our kind, and here was their best friend, manifesting as if thirty failed transformation spells had fallen on her at once. I couldn't believe them capable of such horrific malice. I didn't want to believe it. But it was becoming difficult not to. And it didn't help that they appeared to be on the run and would not answer their phone.

I planted my hands back against the ground. I closed my eyes and inhaled deeply. I wished for some sort of guidance.

"How now, clever witch?"

My eyelids shot open, and I peered around. I was still in the Grant Park clearing, but a faint, shimmering light gave way to darkness just beyond the trees surrounding me. I stared as a tiny sprout pushed up through the dirt, unfurling its webbed leaves and culminating in a brilliant sparring of hay-yellow flowered tufts that, when combined, looked remarkably like a single eye trained on me. I had no doubt it was Silphium, the long extinct plant once favored by the Romans for its bevy of magical qualities. It had not grown in earthen soil in nearly two thousand years save for a brief moment last Summer when the folks at the Botanical Gardens had managed to revive it. But that was before Aiden had traded it to the Fomóraiġ in his attempt to siphon our powers for himself.

"Shit," I groaned, pushing down the beating fear that ramped its way up from my heart. "Balor."

In a flash, the warrior leader of the Dark Fae materialized before me. A single, oval eye stretched across his face, and his thin grin showcased the sharpness of his banshee-styled teeth. He could appear however he pleased, but with me, he seemed to like looking like a gruff and burly farmer in a pair of denim overalls, one strap unbuttoned to reveal a broad, exquisitely defined chest trilled through with red hair, bare feet, and a thick bulge despite the looseness of his garb. His curly red hair shone against his ivory skin and mimicked the ever-present flames in his iris. This time, a hearty red beard adorned his chin, full and rich and begging for a red robin to nest in its curls. Although he was able to control his appearance, he always retained his single eye as if he needed to find truth in the legends of his existence. As far as I was concerned, him being here was proof enough.

"Was it a wish I sensed just now?" he asked. His words slithered across his tongue as if the mere utterance of them was filled with venom and bile. "Say it louder for my feeble ears to hear."

"Not a chance," I bellowed before I could catch myself.

I scrambled to my feet, but it made little difference against his eight foot stature.

"Clever witch," Balor repeated and kissed the air between us. "Yet something does trouble you. And as you have been tasked with procuring our way back to your world, I can't very well have you distracted, now can I? I am, you see, beginning to grow oh so weary of the wait."

I heard the whispering giggle of the other Fomóraig, all hidden in the blackness beyond the grove, but listening intently all the same. Their voices clung to the stillness like a nonexistent breeze, undulating in the space between what was and what would be. An intoxicating mix of humored and unbothered, their whispers sounded like a song.

"A friend of mine was murdered, and my store was destroyed," I said, careful not to form any hint of asking with my words. Bargaining with the Dark Fae never led to a pleasant outcome, and I'd already been trapped there once before.

"Pity, pity," Balor scowled. "Had I been there—had I

been present in your world—I may have been able to stop both occurrences. Or, at the very least, stifled the perpetrators where they stood."

I couldn't help but scoff. The tales I'd heard of Fae-kind, especially of the Fomóraiġ, never ended sweetly. Growing up, I'd believed the tales to be simply parables, like those of the Bible or the German forests. But, after coming face to face with one of their ilk, I now believed them to be mitigated by the ticking of time.

Balor, sensing he would get no further covenant from me, smirked as he tried a different tact.

"Where do we stand on our previous deal?" he asked, trying nonchalant this time. "By my calculations, six mortal months have passed in your world. That's two and a half years left, Darragh Cullen, before I may claim your soul alongside those of Cernun Kyteler and Learco Clarke. Oh, what fine playthings three witches of your caliber will make. My daughter Ethniu has already begun to weave new outfits with which to dress you all. I particularly enjoy those which bind your arms yet leave your asses to the wind. I have a feeling you will find pleasure there too."

"We are working on it," I promised. And we were. Though we were also searching for loopholes in the deal. "A lot of magics were lost in the times since your banishment. It's going to take some time to figure out how to do this safely."

"Oh, clever witch. That's why I gave your coven three years. 'Twould be a shame for those as powerful as you three to not figure it out. Perhaps ever more fires would rage. Perchance more witches would die mid-shift."

"How did you—?"

"Eye and ears; eye and ears," Balor answered dismissively. "Plus, your mind has been a rage with images of both ever since you got here."

Shit! I focused on calming my brain, on keeping any looky-lous from intruding. Balor smirked at my sudden walls, the glint in his eye dancing as he watched me up and down and smacked his lips. I wasn't sure if my shields could truly keep him out of my head, but he wanted me to believe they would.

"I could give you answers," he grinned. "The whole who, what, where, why, and how of it all. Your little 'reporter's repertoire' so to speak. For a price."

As he spoke, Balor shifted his focus to a nearby magnolia. Its broad, waxy leaves seemed almost black against the emptiness beyond. His fingers tickled the air and a great white blossom sprung forward, yellowed, and dropped as he sniffed it. But his nonchalance was as put on as his farmer persona.

"No more deals," I said firmly. "At least not with me."

"Best you not forget the bargain we already have," he hissed.

He was on me in an instant, his great eye peering into mine, showing me the possibilities of a dark forever within their flames. But he didn't touch me. I couldn't feel his breath.

I realized our last encounter had occurred mid-spell when he'd been directly invoked. There, in that circle, he'd held power over our bodies or, at the very least, our spirits. He could touch us, interact with us. Hurt us. Now, he stood aloof. Our bargain must have connected us to allow for this moment, but unlike last time, he had no real power here. I was not in his realm, and he was not in mine. We were both merely interlopers, phantoms passing through the darkness of the in-between space, forgotten memories which blazed to the surface in moments of trauma.

He frowned at my realization, but I could tell it also excited him.

"Clever witch," he said. "Better than a dead one though."

A vision of Learco's crime scene photos flashed through my head once more, and Balor licked his teeth at my discomfort. I had to hand it to him: he definitely knew how to get beneath a witch's skin. It was what made him so dangerous. Well, that and his unbridled strength, massive, sharpened teeth, and intense connections to an otherworldly magic. I could not even fathom what would happen once he and his ilk were unleashed upon the real world.

I inhaled deeply to center my focus and push the images of horrific possibility from my mind. The scent of midwinter green brimming with the prospects of new birth filled my lungs. If I listened closely, behind the whispering cadence of the Fomóraiġ, I could hear the chirping rustle of the nearby chipmunks. I smiled. I was still in the park. And Balor was… wherever he was. I was on the more stable ground. At least I hoped I was.

"So why did you bring me here?" I asked. "Psychological warfare aside, was there something you needed?"

He squinted his eye at my attempt to turn the tables, pursing his lips as he began to pace a circle around me. He'd tried this the first time we met, like his gait was its own form of intimidation, like he wanted me to believe I was surrounded. But I was done playing his game.

I turned where I stood, doing my best attempt at unruffled while keeping my eyes trained on his.

"You simple, churlish farmer," Balor groaned. "All you earth witches, you're all the same. Thinking your plants and your soil and your air and your fire will save you somehow from what lies beneath your magics. Thinking you have some say in how your world works because you can push a breeze on a windy day or pull a wave from a tumultuous ocean."

He stopped his pacing and turned to smile at me. Deep rows of fangs glistened in the non-existent light.

"The Fomóraiġ—my kin and I—are the true power of your—and every—world. You would do wise to uphold my bargain in a timely manner, Darragh Cullen. While I am still of a mind to be gentle, I grow tired of waiting."

As he spoke, the ground at my feet rumbled. Thick vines ruptured the earth, entwining my legs and slithering like snakes up my torso. They bound my wrists to my side and pulled tight around my neck. A single tendril, capped in a thorn, hovered an inch from my left eye.

"Perhaps, were you more like me, you would see the situation better," Balor hissed.

My muscles pulsed against the vines as I struggled to pull breath into my chest. Any shift against my confines only served to pull them in tighter. The thorn filled my vision, dancing there like a charmed snake, ready to strike upon its master's will.

"It would serve you, witch, to serve me. Though I must say I find it quite enjoyable to break your will, we will both get further should you simply succumb."

A flick of his wrist tightened the vines further, pushing all the air from my chest. My body wanted to double over, crumple right there into nothingness, but the vines kept me upright. My breath came ragged as Balor's fingers danced in the air between us. The vines responded like puppet strings to pull me to and fro.

"Or should I twist you into shape? All the ways your bones could snap! All the forms your frame could hold! As long as you and your coven are beholden to my bargain, you are all at my will. You keep your shape by my good graces. Do not push me, clever witch. And do not think you are cleverer than I."

With that, the thorn jutted forward, barely missing my eye and scraping across my left cheek. My blood stung as it met the air and fell like tears down my face. The vines disappeared and I crumbled to a ball on the ground.

When I opened my eyes, Balor and the rest of the Fomóraig were gone. The darkness that surrounded the clearing had been replaced with Grant Park. A young mother—double stroller and leashed Lhasa apso at full and growling attention—watched me, frozen, from a nearby path.

I stared back at the ground, hands braced before me, as I struggled to catch my breath. A drop of red splattered from my check to my knuckles to pull me fully back into reality. Great. The last thing I needed, on top of everything else, were the fucking Dark Fae messing with my life right now.

I took a few deep breaths before I climbed to my feet. I smiled weakly at the young woman and gave a gentle wave to her dog before I turned, and I ran. I ran and I ran, as fast as I could, back to Cernun's place.

CHAPTER 5

I winced as Cernun's hand reached out to touch the cut on my cheek. It wasn't as bad as I thought it would be, but the fact that Balor's thorn had left a physical mark on me, one that carried over into the real world, worried me. A jagged line scraped from the top of my cheekbone to my temple, barely skirting the corner of my eye. I felt marked.

"Do you want a bandage?" he asked.

"I used some witch hazel I found in your medicine cabinet," I assured him. "And I figured I'd make a calendula poultice once I got over here to speed up the healing process."

I winced again as I remembered all the herbs downstairs in my shop were destroyed by the fire. Though it was possible I had some backup in my spelling case. I needed to do a better job of keeping that thing stocked. I'd just gotten so used to having everything I ever needed just down a few flights of steps.

It did feel good to be back home though, despite the chaos down at HEX. The smell of burnt wood permeated my space. It was a scent I actually found calming most times, if it hadn't meant my entire livelihood going up in smoke. I also sensed a mixture of angelica and rosemary in the air. I supposed Learco's agents had crafted a new protection spell for the place.

I fished the soft leather of my gladstone bag from the highest shelf in my closet and set it atop my bedspread. The case had been a gift from my father when I turned eighteen, and the luxuriously tanned hide had my initials—*D.C.*—emblazoned in gold.

"If you're gonna be traveling into the city on the regular," he'd said, "you're gonna need the tools of our trade close at hand."

Like a first aid kit for witches, he'd stocked the bag with tiny glass vials of dried herbs—unlabeled since "you should know what they are"—and quartz crystals of various shapes and color combinations. The compartment which held the spelling chalks was long since empty, but the hand-embroidered cleansing cloth was still folded neatly in its place. No calendula though. Damn it.

"The one thing I miss about the country," I complained, "is having a whole garden at my fingertips."

"I will have a garden at my house," Cernun taunted.

Although he hadn't directly asked, he'd made a few comments over the past month that insinuated he'd be open to us living together. But I couldn't give up living above HEX. Well, when HEX was functional, anyway. Nothing beat that commute, and I actually really loved my neighborhood.

"So, Balor was able to pull you into his realm unprovoked. Without you calling for him?"

I shrugged at Learco's questioning. He'd been watching Cernun's fawning from my upholstered reading chair with a concerned and calculating gaze. I could tell his mind had switched into Moral Authority mode as he tried to discern what that could mean for witch-kind.

"He all but confirmed that our bargain connects us to him," I said. "It wasn't my body, but I guess my spirit was fair game. But I think he could only pull me through because I was meditating in the park. Connected to the elements."

"Yes, but that's every time we spell," Learco sighed.

My mouth scrunched and my shoulders fell as I nodded. Even a simple, everyday incantation required an elemental connection. After learning it, that calling of the elements often became innate, our subconsciouses summoning the earth, air, water, fire, and spirit without thought. And the larger spells, those requiring a pentacle and a circle and an offering—that inviting of the elements would leave us sitting ducks for Balor. We needed to figure out how to get the Fomóraiġ off our backs if we expected a moment's peace ever again.

"You two should be careful as well," I said. "He may come after you just the same."

Learco tapped his fingers on the arms of the chair and pursed his lips.

"I suppose we'll see if the protection charms around the MAW headquarters are worth their salt against the Dark Fae," he said. "I've authorized agents to enact the same charms here in addition to the one they placed last night. They've sanctioned them since I do spend quite a bit of time in your apartment. I'll have them do the same for your home, Cernun."

Learco was sexy when he switched into business mode. A warrior witch with an eye toward compassion, I could see him check off items on the readiness lists he made in his head. The muscles in his neck tensed and caught the light seductively. His chapped lower lip pursed further out the harder he thought, and it was all I could do to not bend down to nibble on it.

Damn. I was still riled up from the morning. The danger and excitement from my encounter with Balor had left me pent up and horny. Cernun, always the first to sense my moods, bounced his eyebrows at me from his perch on the bed. Learco caught the gleam in my eye.

"Dammit, Darragh," Learco grinned. "Do you ever think of anything else?"

I recognized the warm, vibrant pulse of Cernun's aura immediately as it wrapped to hold my body, drawing me closer to him. It was an exquisite feeling, succumbing to another witch's aura—for both the aur-er and the aur-ee—and I couldn't let him have all the fun. I sent my own spirit out to meet his, and he gasped as I tapped the nape of his neck.

Learco, still sitting in his chair by the window, moaned as we washed over him, grasping the upholstered arms and spreading his legs wide as he planted his boots on the floor. He looked so decadent, so powerful as he bit his lip and tilted his head back into the path of the afternoon sun.

Cernun lifted his head from my neck, and the sudden absence of his tongue made me shudder.

"You coming?" he asked Learco.

His tongue swam across his lips as a wide smirk landed on his face. A mischievous glint sparked from his eye.

"I think I'd rather watch," he said.

His aura vibrated in a quicker rhythm than Cernun's, and I stretched as it trilled across my skin. Holding one another, we watched as Learco slowly unbuttoned his bespoke gray shirt, fanning it out to reveal his tight, toned pecs and well-defined abdomen. The way the light skipped across his dark, flushed skin was intoxicating, and I turned to press my lips to Cernun's.

He tasted warm and rich, like cayenne and hot chocolate, and I nearly lost myself early as our mouths opened, our air mixed, and we breathed one another in. I loved to kiss that man. His lips were soft, but strong, and he knew just when and how to apply pressure, to work his tongue against mine. He moved from my lips to my neck, licking that space behind my ear right where my jawbone met up that he knew would drive me crazy. I growled as I clawed at the fabric covering his skin, willing it to leave his body.

"Mmmhmm," Learco moaned as I freed Cernun's torso from

his shirt.

I took a moment to admire the fine, black chest hair and the bold, colorful tattoos that stretched across his body. My fist punched his pec, then scratched from his collarbone to the hem of his jeans. He huffed as he pulled the t-shirt I'd borrowed from his closet over my head and tossed it to the floor. It was a little big on me, but I liked that it smelled like him. The scent following me around all day was probably part of why I was so turned on.

My head fell back, mouth wide, as his tongue found my nipple. He teased it with his teeth. My aura throbbed as it wound between his and Learco's, all three of us using our spirits to heighten the intensity for one another. Fuck, they felt good. This was exactly what I needed after the last two days.

Cernun's hands held my hips as his tongue slipped down my stomach to the edge of the gray sweatpants he'd laid out for me this morning. The loose, terrycloth fabric left nothing to the imagination, and he moaned as his lips traced the outline of my cock. It jumped to meet him, begging for air, begging to be covered once more.

Growling, Cernun slipped the elastic band to my thighs and smiled as I bounced against his face. His thick hand wrapped the base of my shaft, and he teased the tip with his tongue.

"You sure you don't want some of this?" he asked Learco, offering my dick to him with a wicked gleam in his eyes.

"Trust me," Learco replied. "The view from here is quite glorious."

And with that, Cernun swallowed me. I gasped as I entered his throat, then moaned at the sudden heat and cool as he pulled back. His coal black hair twined around my fingers as he sucked me in again. And again. I bit my lip and moaned loudly.

"This isn't fair at all," I whispered. "You're still wearing pants."

His mouth refused to release my cock as he fumbled with his button and pushed his jeans down to his ankles. As he sucked me, my hands massaged down the broad muscles of his back to cup his beautiful ass, choking him a bit as our bodies stretched for the position. Breathing deeply, he rose back, forcing me upright again, and grinned as he wiped the remnants of saliva from his lips. My eyes fell down his body to where this thick, firm member stood at attention between us.

His eyebrows bounced as he clutched my arms and laid me down against the mattress. As our lips met, our legs squirmed free of the last of our clothing, and our bodies writhed together in unison. The weight of him against me warmed me to my core. Our auras—the three of them—made it feel like I was floating on air. I relished the sensation as they cascaded around me like currents, like flames, like fawning hands holding me up to the sun.

I smiled seductively at Learco as his hand stretched the skin across his chest. The bulge in his tight wool trousers told me he was aroused, and the restraint he demonstrated in not freeing himself was almost as hot as having his body here in bed with us.

Cernun's legs straddled my torso, and I took the opportunity to pull him into my mouth. His thigh muscles tensed as he grasped the headboard and worked his hips, a little too forcefully at first, but hot all the same. I grasped his sides and helped guide him into a steadily quickening motion, almost a circle swaying back and forth, and let my tongue work its own form of magic. I moaned as he came, swallowing down his sweet, sticky ejaculate as his body quivered above me. He trembled as he pulled away. The sudden loss of his cock was quickly replaced by his tongue as he bent down to kiss me.

"Fuck!" Learco growled from across the room. His tongue worked his lips as if he could taste us through our auras.

As our lips parted, Cernun laughed and stared deeply into

my eyes before spinning on the mattress and planting himself on all fours. Both our gazes locked on Learco as I saddled up behind him. It was hot as hell, performing for our lover, even as the strumming vibration of his aura let us know he was playing with us too. I could feel him, tapping and teasing from across the room as his hands sought out the pleasures of his skin. The entirety of Cernun's body tensed then relaxed as I entered him. His aura snaked around me to urge me onward. Slow, at first, and steady as we found our connection. Then faster as our two bodies and three auras quickened their vibration to climax.

We collapsed into a pile of sweat and twisted limbs on the mattress. Our auras retracted slowly back into ourselves, none of us wanting to give up the sensation of the late afternoon tryst. I sighed as my back found the crook of Cernun's body and his breath hummed against me.

Learco grinned widely as he stood and crossed the room to the foot of the bed. Gently, he bent to kiss us each on the forehead—first Cernun and then me—and sighed as he stood upright to re-button his shirt. His erection was still firm, but diminishing, as he tucked the tails back behind his belt.

"Thank you for that much needed escape," he whispered. "I hate that I have to go back to work."

"You gotta catch the bad guy," I said, then shuddered as my thoughts turned to Madison.

I knew it wasn't them. There was no way it could be. But Learco had a job to do, and if finding Madison brought the MAW closer to capturing Angel's actual killer, so be it.

"I do," he sighed. "You guys staying here or heading back to Grant Park?"

"I've got a meeting with some of my old construction contacts," Cernun said, rising and leaving my back cold and longing in his sudden absence. "But you should gather some things and head back over to my place," he said to me. "Even though I trust the bolstering and protection spells the MAW put up, it's going to be pretty loud here once work gets underway. Plus, I think there's some calendula in my pantry. And we can both join you there later."

I groaned, stretching across my mattress and letting the familiar warmth of the Winter sun bathe me from the window. I really didn't want to leave my place. It was home, and it was mine. I felt whole when I was here; focused. Of course, it would be hard to feel centered with hammers banging away downstairs. I twisted my lips but nodded.

"Guess I'm on my own for dinner then," I moaned, still not willing to rise from the bed.

"Oh, you can handle that," Learco joked. "You're a big boy."

"Yes, he is," Cernun smiled, and I blushed as I buried my face in the covers.

"What the hell happened?" Paul asked as I pulled up a stool to the bar at Aunt Paulina's. I preferred my back corner booth, but I felt odd taking up a whole table as one person.

"Thorn," I said, feigning a wince as I touched my cheek.

"That's just a scratch, kid," he bellowed. "What the hell happened to HEX?"

I grimaced as I studied the troubled expression on his painted face. His choice of foundation, always a shade lighter than his actual complexion, made the worry lines surrounding his crimson lips all the more evident. The cyan on his eyelids weighed heavy on his concerned eyes.

"I didn't even see a firetruck," he said.

My sigh was heavy as I squirmed atop the vinyl of the barstool. Every time I had to recount the story was like reliving the flames.

"Molotov cocktail," I said. "The Moral Authority is handling it."

Paul scoffed as he began pouring sugar, bitters, and whisky into a tumbler to mix my go-to drink. A woody, sweet aroma filled the air as he added ice and stirred briskly.

"Fucking MAW," he said, aping a phrase Madison was all too keen to use, even in Learco's presence. I guessed they had spent more time hanging out at Aunt Paulina's since I'd hired them than I'd assumed. It made sense if they were attempting to court his niece. "Sounds to me like it's human hands what done the deed, should be human hands helping to clean it up. Even if it happened in your little magic shop."

"The MAW's shit sometimes," I replied, "but they also get shit done."

"And it helps when the head honcho is dynamite in the sack." He glared accusingly as he spoke, but I could hear the joke in his words. "At least, that's my assumption from watching you three carry on in that booth of yours."

He strained my cocktail into a rocks glass and slid it across the bar to rest in front of me. The swirl of the amber liquid around the single large ice cube called my name in eager gasps.

"I been watching those agents in their sleek black suits milling around your place like ants at a picnic. I tell you, whatever spells they got up those tailored sleeves of theirs done scrambled my security cameras since right 'round midnight last night. There ain't nothing but fuzz down that whole side of the street. You having your usual?"

An early dinner of a perfectly cooked burger and Aunt Paulina's famous crispy fries were just what I needed to recharge after my afternoon delight, but the thought of Paul's security cameras piqued my interest even more. As sure as I was that Learco had his agents running rituals and conducting black-ops surveillance to find the perpetrators, sometimes, when it came to the what's what of mortal comings and goings, good old fashioned human technology couldn't be beat.

"You say the cameras went down after midnight?"

"Sure as a whore sweats in church," he laughed, rinsing his bar tools and setting them up for the next order to come through.

"So, do you have a tape of what happened before that?" I asked hopefully.

Paul laughed and swatted his bar towel at the counter between us.

"I thought the Moral Authority of Witches was on it," he mocked.

"Fucking MAW," I shrugged.

"Fucking MAW," he mimicked. "Yeah, there should be some footage of what went down. HEX is a bit of a ways off, so I can't promise it'll be clear, but you're welcomed to have at it."

I smiled and grabbed my drink from the bar. The first luxurious sip swam across my tastebuds. If Learco was focused on catching Angel's killer while Cernun put his efforts into rebuilding HEX, the least I could do was investigate who started the fire in the first place. And now I had an actual lead.

"Katrina's using the office to study up on drink recipes, but I'm sure she wouldn't mind the company," Paul said, pointing to the swinging door that separated the bar from the kitchen. "And I'll send your meal on back there."

Paul's office was situated between the mop sink and the walk-in cooler at the back of his small but efficient kitchen. The cooks looked up from their work but paid me little mind as I passed through and tapped at the painted black door. A colorful sign—

glitter and puff paint and makeup—proclaimed the space as "Aunt Paul's Office." It was faded with age and cooking grease, but I could still make out the lipstick kiss by his name.

"I ain't ready," Katrina chimed through the wood. "I got the French 75 down pat, but the Negroni's still confusing me."

"Think of it like a gin Old Fashioned," I smiled, slowly swinging open the door with a gentle wave at Paul's niece. "You got your sweet vermouth for the sugar, and your Campari for the bitters, then you round it all out with the gin. Or maybe it's closer to a Manhattan. At any rate, most classic cocktails are about balancing that bitter with that sweet to compliment the spirit."

"Oh, hey, Darragh," Katrina grinned, shrugging as she gathered the drink guides spread across the desk. "I thought you were Uncle Paul checking up on me again. What can I do you for?"

"Paul's letting me check out his security footage so I can see if it caught the assholes who firebombed my shop."

"Oh, shit! That's right. I saw the carnage when I came into work this morning." Katrina frowned apologetically as she spoke and piled her papers on the edge of the desk. "Sorry that shit happened to you. I'm guessing everybody was alright?"

She didn't flat out ask about Madison, but I assumed her question was about them. I thought it best to avoid talking about the murder inquiry they were caught up in.

"Yeah," I sighed. "It happened after close, so no employees harmed. Lost about ninety percent of my stock though. And the sales floor's gonna need to be rebuilt."

"Fuck." Katrina shook her head. "Glad you're all okay though. Sucks it happened during the V-Day sales rush though. Come on in. I'll get the footage cued up for you. Uncle Paul's machine is kind of ancient, but it gets the job done."

The office was smaller and messier than I'd imagined it would be. Stacks of papers jutted their corners from file folders stacked in bins atop file cabinets. Half filled out schedules, written in Paul's erratic script, lay in heaps at the edge of the desk. Too short cables stretched the gap between a dot matrix printer and the behemoth of a computer Paul had catty-corner on his desk, blocking the walkway to one side.

"Do they even still make ink for that thing?" I asked, and Katrina rolled her eyes.

Uncle Gardner had a similar reticence to updating HEX to modern tech. Sure, I'd gotten a snazzy new point of sale system, but I still did all of the paperwork by hand in honor of him.

"Uncle Paul's got a case of ribbons for it I think he bought when I was knee high to a toadstool," she laughed. "Gonna be the first thing I upgrade when he finally hands the reins of this place over to me. Not that I want him gone. I just want him to enjoy his retirement while he's still got some kick in him. What time did the fire start?"

"A little after 10 last night," I said, picking up a hinged dual photo frame from the desk to study while Katrina brought up the footage.

One picture featured a much younger Paul, face painted to the gods, with his arms wrapped around Uncle Bill and Uncle Gardner, standing in front of the Ansley Mall Mini-Cinema. Though the theater was long gone, I knew the story of the police raids fifteen minutes into Andy Warhol's *Lonesome Cowboy* screening, and the "Stonewall of the South" which followed. I'd had no idea my uncles and Paul had been part of that revolution. But it made sense. Uncle Gardner still had the paper grocery bag he'd worn over his face during Atlanta's first Pride celebration a few years later. He kept it framed behind glass in the guest room of his new condo.

The second photo featured a decidedly male-presenting Paul,

save for a bit of eyeliner, standing next to a woman who could have been his twin. An infant in arms, Katrina beamed gleefully at the camera. They were standing on the sidewalk in front of Aunt Paulina's. The sign out front looked decidedly new.

"Twenty-some years goes by fast, huh?" Katrina asked when she saw me eyeing the picture.

"Too fast," I agreed as I placed the frame back on the desk.

She clicked a few more keys and pressed enter, then sat in Paul's chair and motioned for me to sit in one of the dining chairs placed opposite the desk.

"Part of being ancient means it's hella slow," she sighed.

"You talking about me?" Paul laughed, popping in with a beautifully plated medium rare burger and still steaming french frics.

"I'm talking about this arcane brick you call a computer," she laughed back.

"She serves me fine," Paul insisted. "You just gotta treat her like a lady."

"We talking about you or the computer?" Katrina snapped.

I enjoyed their playful banter. It showcased just how close the two of them actually were. It reminded me of my own relationship with my uncle. I thought of him wistfully, and then shook my head as an image of his destroyed legacy across the street filtered through.

"You got them drinks memorized?" he asked, switching back into boss mode.

"Getting there," she insisted. "A Negroni is like a gin Manhattan with some Campari thrown in for balance."

She gave me a sly wink as Paul handed me my dinner and pulled a couple napkins from his apron pocket.

"Great!" he smiled. "Now what's in a Sidecar?"

Katrina's smile faltered, and she pursed her lips.

"Get back around here and study up," he said. "Let Darragh see what he can make out on the footage. Guess it's still me back behind the bar."

Paul pulled the door closed, and I lifted the plate above my head as Katrina and I shimmied by each other to trade sides of the desk. I sat the burger down and eyed the ticking screen as the video buffered. I took a hefty bite and let the warmth of the food wash through me.

Katrina pretended to study her recipe charts, but a new and sudden worry clouded her face.

"You—uh—" she stuttered, "you don't really think Madison could have killed their friend, do you?"

The question was abrupt and frightened and seemed to shock us both.

"How did you—?" I started, then chose to answer: "No, of course not."

"MAW agents were in earlier asking questions," she explained. "They aren't exactly covert in their interrogations. I think they think non-witches are below them. That or just dumb. Fucking MAW."

She seemed satisfied with my answer but still on edge. I couldn't blame her though. Even if she didn't know the gruesome details of Angel's death, she knew a young woman had been killed all the same. What struck me more was first Paul's and now her mimicking of Madison's favorite phrase.

"You don't know where Madison is, do you?" I asked.

Katrina gulped down her answer as she looked me in the eye. I held up my hand to stop her voice. It was better if I didn't know. That'd be one less thing I had to hide from Learco.

"Nevermind," I said, and relief crept across her face. "I think the footage is ready."

The video was grainy and dark with the crisp Atlanta night,

but I could still make out the edges of the building and brief blurs of motion beneath the streetlights. A group of four or five figures congregated near my storefront. Their frames merged together, and their features were non-discernible at the security camera's resolution. I wished real life was the way they showed it in movies, where I could press "enhance" and suddenly the entirety of events would come clear on the screen. Still, the ignition of a gas-soaked rag gave them away as I saw the sparks that consumed my shop in fire spring to life.

In a flurry of motion made jagged by the camera's frame rate, the hooligans tossed first a brick and then their homemade bomb through my window. The flames spread almost instantly, urged on by the accelerant in their now broken bottle. But even with the added light, I couldn't make out a single feature.

Damn it!

The group started to disperse quickly, and I hadn't garnered a single thing from the footage. I sighed. I'd known it was a long shot anyway, but I'd allowed myself to get my hopes up. I replayed the attack, but it was no clearer. Slumping back in the chair, I relived the anxious horror as the fire flared on the screen. I couldn't bear to go through it again.

As I reached to turn it off, I focused on the aftermath. Two silhouettes trounced off screen in the opposite direction. But two others, they were running toward the camera!

It was dark and blurry, and they kept their heads down, but the spacebar managed to stop the footage right as one of the criminals passed beneath the camera. I clicked through the frames one at a time, trying to discern the features of her blurred face as she ran. I didn't recognize her, but I'd managed to catch the only telltale sign I needed: a back patch haphazardly stitched to her denim jacket.

Fuck! Cernun was not going to be happy about this.

I pulled out my cell phone and snapped a photo of the screen. There, in the lower left corner, the letters were perfectly captured: DMFM. I rewound the tape a few frames and took a few more pictures.

"What does that mean?" Katrina asked, her brow furrowed as she studied both the patch and my anxious expression.

"They're with Defend Mankind From Magic," I said. "The hate group that's out to eradicate all witches. The hate group founded by Cernun's adoptive parents."

CHAPTER 6

It was pushing midnight when Cernun got home from his dinner with the boys, a little tipsy and grinning widely as he tumbled through the door. His smile stretched even further when he saw Learco and me sitting in his living room. My phone—and the photo on it—beamed like a warning beacon from the coffee table between us.

"I'm so glad you're up!" he bellowed heartily. "It took some doing, and maybe a couple lap dances at Tattletales, but I got the fellas from that Morningside job I did last April to agree to do the work for cost plus five!"

He was so proud of himself—and I was happy too! Though I was certain we could rebuild HEX with our own hands, having a crew meant I could reopen the doors much faster. It made what I had to show him even harder.

Cernun's childhood had started out as a somewhat rocky one, but once he hit puberty and his innate magic began to manifest, his intensely religious adoptive parents saw the devil in him. He'd grown up in Albuquerque, New Mexico as a son and a brother. Mavis and Todd Marshall had adopted him in their early twenties, back when they thought they couldn't produce any children of their own. But when Brian and Jason were born, Cernun became more of a Cinderella than a first-born. His brothers bullied him; his parents ignored him through prayer. And when his "surly, queer, teenage" self—his words, not mine—tossed his advancing brother to the wall with just a thought, Cernun ran away and changed his name. He'd been on a search for understanding, and for his biological parents, ever since. His chosen surname of Murphy had become Kyteler once his lineage was discovered, but he was still no closer to finding any other of his biological kin.

What was worse for him though, despite the pain which ravaged his eyes every time he thought back to those years, was thinking about what his parents and his siblings had become after he left. Mavis and Todd, bolstered by their beliefs and the cast on Brian's arm, began to organize community meetings in their garage—at least that's what the news articles said. They preached of magic as a sign of Satan's impending arrival and found others with similar stories of manifest powers the MAW hadn't covered up or even detected. Small things like Old Miss Williams whose flowerbeds thrived even in the desert heat. Or Mister Jordan who won at least twenty dollars on every scratch-off he played at the corner store. Most of it was bullshit, but enough voices raised in anger or jealousy or fear can convince a herd of almost anything. And thus, Defend Mankind From Magic was formed.

It was a fringe group, really, derided by most and dismissed by others, but nearly four years ago—when my very public spell to save Cernun from an out-of-control vehicle exposed magic to the world—the DMFM exploded across the States with Todd and Mavis as its founders and Cernun's brothers as its generals. The MAW classified the organization as a hate group, and some states had followed suit, but they were largely ignored by the federal government. Witch dealings were the Moral Authority's prerogative as far as they were concerned.

And the Moral Authority of Witches told me I had to tell

Cernun the truth, or at least Learco had. He eyed me expectantly from the armchair as I fidgeted on the couch.

"They're finishing up a job in Castleberry," Cernun continued. He'd kicked his boots off into a pile by the front door and danced ecstatically in front of us as he spoke. "Then, they're all ours. Johnny even said he could probably spare a few guys as soon as Thursday to get us started if you think the MAW can pull the permits in time."

"Consider it done," Learco smiled. It was obvious that neither of us wanted to rain on his parade.

"Come on, guys! Why aren't you celebrating with me?"

Cernun danced to an unheard beat in his head, swishing around the living room like a freshly blown dandelion seed. Maybe he was drunker than I thought. He wasn't as used to hanging with the construction guys as he'd once been.

I finally found my voice.

"I want to celebrate. I do," I said, my best attempt at casual doing little to hide the quiver in my words, "but—. Babe, why don't you sit down for a minute."

Cernun's expression of mirth quickly fell to one of concern as he watched my hand pat the couch cushion beside me. Sighing, he skirted around the coffee table and plopped down on the sofa. He stretched his strong, muscled arms across the seat back and stared at me expectantly.

"We—," I started, then steeled myself to continue. "We know who started the fire."

"Fuckin' Fae!" he bellowed, slapping his knee as the joy returned to his face. "That's amazing! Why didn't you lead with that."

"Because…" I sighed, fetching my phone from the table and pulling up the photo I'd memorized every pixel of throughout the last few hours.

I handed the screen to Cernun, and he squinted to make out what I now saw so clearly. His face fell, and his foot began to rapidly tap at the floor. He swallowed hard as he studied the image.

"Well, that'll sober you up right quick," he sighed. "What does—? How did you—?"

"The security cameras at Aunt Paulina's aren't the best," I explained, "but the back patch is pretty clear."

Cernun's face was a worried jumble of emotion. Fear, anxiety, and every troubled bit of his childhood played out in nervous tics of expression. I wrapped a hand around his thigh and inched a little closer to him on the couch.

"Does this mean my parents are in town?"

Cernun rarely referred to the Marshalls as his parents, except when he was too upset to voice their names. The question was directed to Learco. Though they denied it, we all knew the MAW kept tabs on those suspected to be in—or proudly a part of—the DMFM.

"Mavis and Todd are still in Albuquerque as far as we know," Learco stated matter-of-factly, like he was switching into briefing mode at his office. Maybe it was for the best. It could calm the cloud of tensions floating around the living room. "It is possible that one or both of your brothers have come to Atlanta by way of Jacksonville though. Both spoke at a rally there last weekend. I'm still waiting for confirmation."

"They're here," Cernun grumbled. "Which means it wasn't just some random punks or an attack on a magic shop. It was an attack on me. Fae, dammit!"

I snatched my phone back from his hands before he threw it across the room. He slammed his heels to the floor and stood, marching across the room to his bar cabinet, and reaching to the back for a bottle of the good stuff. He poured himself a hefty splash and angled the bottle toward me and Learco. Learco declined, but I held up two fingers to signify the pour I needed to take the edge off.

"I'm sorry, babe," he moaned as he handed me my glass. "I never wanted you to get caught up in the crazy of the folks who raised me."

"This is not your fault," I insisted. "Plus, I'm in it for the long haul. This was an attack on us. Plain and simple. And now that we know who it's from, we can prepare ourselves for any future developments."

Cernun's weak smile told me he believed me, but he wasn't convinced. He paced the room as he sipped on his drink, playing out a thousand what was and what ifs in his mind.

"How is the fucking DMFM still a thing?" he asked, growling his words as they swam around his whisky. "Why hasn't the fucking MAW gotten rid of them by now?"

It sounded accusatory, but Learco knew the anger was not directed at him. A stalwart of "by the book," Learco knew the book sometimes needed to be re-written. But he also knew the danger they placed the world in when factions within the Moral Authority decided to go off-book. It was a no-win situation, but one he hoped to change. From the inside.

"Even with our members at the capitol and in congress," he sighed, "we've made little headway on getting the government to actually classify the organization as a hate group. And with our rule of 'no magic may be performed on a mortal,' there's little we can do but watch."

"You mean your wands are handcuffed behind your back 'cause you don't want to upset the status quo," Cernun growled and Learco winced.

He was processing a lot of anger right now, and we both were willing to let him get it out.

"You know there's actual Defend Mankind assholes in that very congress now too, right?" he continued. "Preaching shit about being Constitutional Loyalists and claiming the 'man' mentioned there right at the beginning doesn't include women or witches."

"Even though we all know Benny Franklin was a witch," I smiled, hoping to break the tension a bit, but Cernun simply scoffed.

"Point is," he said, "they're gaining ground, and we are losing it. And the MAW ties up our hands and our spells, and then holds theirs up screaming 'I'm doing all I can.' It's bullshit, is what it is."

Learco chose his words carefully. I had to hand it to him for not getting upset. I supposed he'd had lots of practice though. Most witches outside of the MAW weren't very fond of those within it.

"The rules of the Moral Authority of Witches have kept our kind safe for millennia. They are there for a reason. And they may change when necessary."

"Well, I'd say it's pretty fucking necessary," Cernun snapped back.

"And perhaps this incident will allow me to do some of that work to change them," Learco said.

Cernun quit his pacing and looked sorrowfully at Learco. He took a seat and dropped his head to his knees.

"I'm sorry," he said. "I wasn't trying to attack you."

"I know that," Learco confirmed. There was a gentleness to his firmness that I admired. I was sure it came in handy in his position. "So now, we're faced with our real dilemma. What do we do with this new tidbit of information?"

"You haven't already informed the MAW?" I asked, shocked our structured and tucked-in boyfriend hadn't phoned it in immediately.

"They are on alert for DMFM members," he explained.

"The agents not dedicated to finding... Angel's killer, that is. I'm assuming they sense a connection to the fire. They are smart witches. But this is a family matter. And I consider us family."

I didn't even have a moment to appreciate his leaving Madison's name out of it before I was blindsided by his statement. We were all very close. Our sex, our attraction, and our run-in with the Dark Fae had seen to that. But this was a level I hadn't realized he was ready for yet. I expected him to blush, but Learco was as matter of fact as always.

"Did you just—?"

"I did," Learco smiled. "But we can discuss that later. And vigorously. Now, though, we have to figure out this."

Cernun and I shared a wicked smile before we fell back into the somber station of the night. Learco was right. As big of a moment as this was, we had all the time in the world to figure out what this meant for us. Or at least the two years and six months before the Fomóraiġ pulled our souls to their ether.

"Once I phone this in, because I was there in the building, this will be classified as an attack on the Moral Authority. And our agents... deal with those things... differently."

"Even if Jason and Brian didn't green light the hit," Cernun sighed, "the DMFM is still behind it. They destroyed HEX. And we could have been seriously injured. They deserve to get what's coming to them."

"Yes, but they are still your brothers."

Cernun considered Learco's words carefully, taking in what he was offering alonside the weight of what his next utterance could mean.

"I haven't seen them since I was fourteen years old. They aren't my kin. They've spent the last twenty some odd years proving as much."

I frowned as I reached to grab Cernun's hand. Though his

words were bolstered by anger and alcohol, we could all sense the pain in his statement. Even though he was hurt, he'd never really prescribed to the "us versus them" thing before. And he certainly didn't want to start now, no matter how mad he was. I raised my eyebrows in wary question to Learco. He shifted uncomfortably in his chair for a moment, then rose to pour himself a drink from Cernun's bar.

"This doesn't leave this room," he said, still facing away from us as if embarrassed by what he had to say. "The MAW's 'no magic on mortals' mandate becomes a little… loose when there's been a physical attack on our kind."

"That doesn't surprise me in the least," I laughed. It felt good to break the tension.

Learco winced as he turned back around to face us, clearly uncomfortable with the duplicitous nature of his organization. He fortified himself with a quick sip from his glass. He knew our opinions on the MAW—Cernun and I hadn't been exactly shy about them—but he also believed in the heart of what the organization stood for. I had to admit I admired that about him. Still, acknowledging their more under-the-table dealings was difficult for him.

"What I mean is, once Defend Mankind From Magic can be directly connected to the attack, it will be a very… unpleasant experience for all traceable members in the city. Brian and Jason included, if they are here."

Cernun's face fell as he stared at my cellphone on the coffee table. That image along with the rest of Paul's security footage would be proof positive as far as the inner workings of the Moral Authority was concerned. Even if his brothers were estranged, informing the MAW felt a lot like condemning them. His eyes filled with question as he looked at me.

"It's your shop," he said. "The store your uncle built. That's what they destroyed. It's up to you."

I shook my head.

"No. They're your brothers. In some sense of the word, anyway. HEX can be rebuilt. And you're helping with that. This decision is yours. And I'll support you in whatever you decide."

"As will I," Learco chimed.

I hated to put the ball back in Cernun's court, but it really was his decision to make. Sure, I was angry at the DMFM, but in the end it was just some herbs and some wood. The stock could be regrown; the shop could be cleansed. But this could have repercussions Cernun wasn't ready for.

He nodded in understanding.

"Can I have the night to think about it?" he asked.

"Of course!" Learco said, taking his seat once more and placing his drink next to ours on the coffee table.

I reached out to squeeze his hand. I knew it was difficult for him to choose his care for us over his obligations to his job. It did not go unnoticed. He quivered a bit at my touch but smiled as his emotions won out against his rational side. Or maybe, in this instance, they were one and the same.

"In the meantime," he said, "it's nearing 3AM. I brought the supplies necessary for the protection spell on your property. I figured I could teach it to you; that we could perform it together."

"Let's do it!" Cernun smiled. "I've been hoping I'd get to show this off!".

Every witch worth their weight in salt knew how to structure a strong protection spell. Our parents spent our youths pointing out which garden plants were best for which type of safeguard, and the incantations were some of the first words we learned when we came into our power during puberty. But those spells, as majestic as they were, were weak compared to the magics the MAW had erased from our Books of Shadows and kept hidden from the masses for so long.

I shivered when I thought about the magical abilities—our birthrights, really—the Moral Authority had kept shielded from us all. Like the protection spell Learco was preparing, or Madison's shapeshifting desire. There was so much of our heritage lost or forgotten. Had our broomsticks really once flown through the full mooned sky? Had our ancestors really communed with black cats as familiars in order to increase their hold on their powers? Hell, now that we'd discovered that the Fae were real—the Dark ones anyway—the all the old wives' tales seemed steeped in probability. But there was shit in those stories even darker than the Fomóraiġ.

Perhaps not everything the MAW was hiding from us needed to be let out.

Cernun had turned his spare room into an exquisite spelling quarters. Beautiful, hand-carved tables and cabinets lined the far wall with jars of herbs and stones filling their nooks with promise. The wood-mounted staghorn fern I'd given him for his birthday a few years back was displayed prominently on the wall. Its long, gray-green antlers rose in triumph from its brown shield fronds. A gorgeous pentagram was branded into the wooden floor at the center of the room. I could tell at a glance that it was six foot four inches in diameter—Cernun's precise height—which attuned the circle to the witch and made the spells performed there more powerful. He grinned as he saw me appreciating the dark hue of the charr.

"It's not exactly the wood inlay of the one your uncle did in your living room," he said, "but I think it kind of fits me."

"It's perfect," I agreed, and wrapped my arms around his shoulders.

Four years ago, this man was always on the move, traveling from city to city, never putting down roots, as he ran from his adoptive family in search of his biological one. Now, he was building a home—and one he obviously intended to stay in for some time. I was proud of him, and happy to have played some small part in it.

"The herbs and stones are all from HEX," he smiled, then quickly added, "Don't worry. I had Madison ring me up for every last ounce of them, much to their chagrin at charging me. But I wanted this place to be a surprise for you."

"It's beautiful," I replied. "But what's the use in fucking the owner if you don't at least go for the industry discount?"

Learco laughed as he finished pulling his things from his satchel and laying them out in a line on the ash wood spelling table.

"That's everything," he said. "We just need a handful of soil from each of the property corners. And a drop of blood from the owner."

He fumbled over the last words, rushing them out in a slur of unwanted syllables.

"This is blood magic?" I asked, and Learco winced.

"Technically," he said. "But it's not at all like the ritual Aiden and his father tried to perform. This one is clean. The blood and dirt just seal the spell to the owner and the land."

I wasn't so sure how to respond. Blood spells, like ritual sacrifice, had long been a part of our histories. But those spells tended to be filled with some unexpected, and often unfortunate, outcomes.

"How did you spell HEX then?" I asked. "You never asked me for my blood."

Learco blushed. His eyes swam the toes of his shoes.

"Remember when you cut your finger on that nail?" he asked. "The blood from my t-shirt was enough. It really only takes a drop. I was going to ask you, but you just had so much on your mind."

I frowned, but I understood. And at least I knew the protection spell around my shop and my home were tied to me.

"I mean," I said, "I just kind of want to know if my blood is being used for magic."

"I know. I'm sorry."

"Hey," I sighed, letting him off the hook. "You were doing what you had to do to protect me."

I was still wary of the spell, but I didn't want Learco to think I was holding it against him. Besides, I did not have much room to talk when it came to withholding information.

"Now that that's settled," Cernun smiled, "I'll go collect the dirt. A handful from each corner, right? Kept separate or combined."

"All together is good," Learco nodded and twisted his face in apology to me once more as Cernun left the room.

"It's really fine," I assured him, crossing the space to wrap my arms around his shoulders and kiss him.

He relaxed immediately into my arms, and I relished in the weight of his body. His lips always tasted of cinnamon to me, and I often wondered if he had a secret stash of snickerdoodles that he carried around with him. I really needed to tell him the truth about the spells I was researching for Madison. Even if it didn't look great for me. Or for them. I promised myself I would come clean to him after the ritual. I didn't want to cloud his head with distractions beforehand. At least that's what I told myself.

"Okay," he sighed, and kissed me once more before switching back into instructor-mode. "While Cernun grabs the soil, we can place the offerings to the elements around the circle."

That I could handle. I'd called a circle or two in my day. Unless this blood ritual required items funkier than the usual.

"Don't worry," he said, sensing my hesitation. "It's exactly what you're used to."

Cernun's tiny cast-iron offering cauldrons looked brand new, and I supposed he'd purchased them at HEX as well. Since I wasn't sure if he had already done so, I laid them out on the table for Learco to perform a quick incantation to cleanse the surfaces before I placed the five of them at each corner of the pentagram. It was always good to clean one's equipment before a new spell anyway. And I think it helped to bring Learco's guilty thoughts back to the task at hand. Though, in all honesty, mine were doubled.

As he reviewed his notes, I placed our herbal offerings in their corresponding cauldrons. First, a batch of dried periwinkle filled the Water point cauldron. Its forces of power and protection would summon the element and guide it toward our purpose. Then Nettle at the Fire point for its enrichment and protective properties. Verbena's protective and purification properties at Earth would fill the room with a bright, lemony smell, while Dandelion at Air would aide in the manifestation of our goals. At the apex of the pentagram, I placed cedar taken directly from Cernun's yard. Not only would it smell amazing as it burned in offering, the direct connection of place would amplify the protective powers of the spell as a whole. Using one of the branches I'd cut earlier for the witch's bouquet in the living room meant it had dried enough to ignite.

Cernun's frame filled the doorway just as I finished placing our offerings, his muddy hands abundant with a ball of fresh soil. Learco instructed him to spread it through the center of the pentagram, promising he'd be the one to sweep it up when all was done, and smiled sheepishly at me as Cernun excused himself to wash his hands clean for the ritual.

We placed our watches and cellphones—anything which could serve as a distraction or whose signal could break our concentration—outside of the door and took our places equidistance around the pentacle.

"We should be mindful as we do this," I reminded all three of us as we settled into seated, cross-legged positions at our posts. "Balor may be able to pull us through to his realm when we spell. Though hopefully, with all three of us working, we will be okay."

"Let's hope you're right," Cernun sighed. "At least we are all here together this time."

Learco swallowed hard and stretched his back as he readied himself for the magic to unfold.

"This is really very simple," he said. "We call on the elements to set our circle. Then, I say a brief incantation of intent. And finally, Cernun, you prick your finger to add a single drop of owner's blood to the mound of soil in order to seal the protective border."

"Simple enough," I nodded, though I was still unsure about the use of blood, even a small amount, in the spell. I'd always been taught our power ran through our blood, and, once freed, it was impossible to know how the elements would react without our minds, our spirits to tame them. But I trusted Learco. And I knew he would not willingly place us in danger.

"Oh! That reminds me!"

Learco hopped suddenly to his feet and padded over to his leather satchel. He fished around inside for a moment before producing a wondrous athame. Its obsidian black blade shone brightly in the overhead light, and a solitary emerald adorned its leather-bound hilt. It was a truly magnificent knife.

"I pulled this from the archives at the MAW headquarters,"

he explained. "It once belonged to Alistair Kyteler and was left behind when the surname moved into hiding long after your ancestor Alice fled her captors. Thus, Cernun, even by MAW edict, it now belongs to you."

He presented the blade lengthwise to Cernun's eager, outstretched hands.

"I figured you could use it for the finger prick at the end of the ritual," he continued.

"Th-thank you!" Cernun stuttered.

His face beamed. The money from the Kyteler trust aside, this was the first physical object of his ancestors he had ever owned. Historical tools meant a lot to a witch. They strengthened our connection to our past and to our power. Plus, Cernun really had a fascination with antiquities.

Learco returned to his seated position and stretched once more. I loved the way the light sparked off his collarbone as he writhed.

"Let's begin," he said. "I will call the elements of Water and Earth. Cernun, you call upon Fire and Air. And finally, Darragh, use your energy to summon Spirit to round out and seal our circle."

I nodded and closed my eyes as my lovers called the corners. With each new summoning, a tiny flame burst to burn our respective offerings, filling the room with the earthen, musky scent of dried herbs. I tried to feel the energy flowing through the room, but something was wrong.

Something was missing.

I shook it away. It had been a long couple of days. Of course, I'd be a bit off my game. And my reticence for the blood of it all was probably getting to me. I'd be fine when it came around to me.

"Eternal Spirit," I said, forcing my voice to sound stronger, more solid than my vocal cords were willing. "We invoke thee. Take this, our offering, and connect us in power as we connect you through the nature of the world."

I waited for the spark of flame to ignite the cedar and fill the room with its clean, vibrant aroma. But… nothing happened.

"Eternal Spirit," I tried again, more forceful with my calling this time.

Still, nothing happened. No spark of fire called forth the binding element. I couldn't even feel the start of the circle my boyfriends had brought forth.

Then, suddenly, a sharp pain erupted across my cheek. I could feel the blood flowing toward my chin even without seeing it.

I swooned.

The room went dark.

CHAPTER 7

Clouds swirled around me. At least, I thought they were clouds. It was hard to make out anything through the darkness. Whatever they were, I could feel them—empty but weighted, solid yet ethereal—as they slipped past my body and disappeared into the nothingness. Lightning—or something like it—flashed in the distance, sending a hazy red and yellow light to flicker through my surroundings. Like a storm on the horizon of eternity.

With the introduction of light, the ground beneath me shifted and I pulled my legs close together to keep from plummeting from the very high, very precarious precipice I found myself atop. A wind picked up, pushing through the ether like a cyclone. Gaining traction, the clouds shifted and spun. Except, they weren't clouds.

The lightning gave me brief glimpses of features: a torso twisting on the air; an arm pulled quickly into blackness; faces I felt I should have recognized but just couldn't place. These were people! Or memories. Or spirits. I wasn't sure. I wasn't certain of anything.

Whatever they were, they rode the air around me, increasing in speed until each gentle swipe became a battering ram against my shoulder, against my thigh, spinning me, sending me closer to the edge of the cliff. I tried to find my voice, but my throat was closed. Cut off from me as if it had never really been mine to begin with. As if my words had never been a part of me.

I had a voice, didn't I? I had had a voice. But that was something of another time—of a place where time actually meant something. Here was fragmented. Now collided with Then in a kaleidoscope of fractals.

Angel appeared before me. Her long blonde hair whipped in a tornado around her face, striking her gentle features, her slumbering eyes, like whips urging the animal forward. She looked almost peaceful as she floated there before me. At first.

Suddenly, her limbs twisted into awkward, painful positions. Her face grew gaunt and pale as her clothing vanished from her body. Skin ripped and bones broke, forcing their way through muscle to meet the air as if they had always been there. As if there was where they belonged. Whole patches of her body churned as witch skin became the keeled scales of a reptile, the calicoed fur of a feline. Her mouth stretched as her teeth grew shark-like and hungry.

"You didn't save me!"

Her words bellowed from the ether, carried on the storm that whisked around us. I tried to respond—to apologize—yet no words came as her visage floated off to join the great surge of churning spirits around me.

A familiar electric blue shot through the sky to form Madison's locs. The worry on their face was palpable as it shifted into being before me. Vacant eyes searched right through my own, looking for something I wasn't. Something I could never be.

"You were supposed to help me, weren't you?" they asked. "Now look what's happened. The beast is nearing. The wild things are upon us!"

My hands glowed, wet and maroon, as I reached out toward my friend, even as they vanished. It was true! I had blood on my hands. And nothing I could do would wash them clean.

My legs collapsed beneath me, and I fell to the ground with a thud. The clay shifted as the precipice grew more narrow, great clumps of it descending into nothingness, closing in on me from all sides. Below me was only more black, more darkness, more despair. Lightning flashed like fires around me, turning the spirits of the air into flames. They turned to watch me fall, all of them separate, all of them one single iris.

I steadied my breath as the rocks fell away.

"There he is. Here. Drink some water, babe."

The smell of calendula and rosemary were strong, and I could feel the drying poultice still planted on my face. My head swirled as I tried to sit up, and Cernun guided me gently back down to the pillow. I was in his bed. How had I gotten to the bedroom? The last thing I remembered was… I wasn't sure what I remembered.

"What the hell happened?" I asked, my voice shaky and scratchy as if I'd been asleep for days.

"We don't know," Cernun admitted. "When you tried to conjure, the cut on your face ripped open, and you passed out. We think Balor may have marked you somehow. Learco headed to the MAW's archive room to see if he can find anything like this happening before."

Balor? Conjuring? Yes! We were performing a protection spell on Cernun's home. I was calling forth Spirit to set the circle in our ritual when it felt like my face caught fire, as if all of my magical energy were being syphoned through the scratch on my cheekbone. I must have passed out from the pain. All I could remember after attempting my summoning of Spirit was darkness.

"Did you—did you finish the ritual?"

Cernun chuckled as he offered me the glass of water once more.

"Always looking out instead of in," he smiled. "You seriously just went dark, babe. The house is fine. We can do the spell tomorrow night. We were more worried about you."

The water felt rough as it fought its way down my throat, and I winced as it hit my stomach. I felt empty and cold as the liquid sloshed within my gut, desperate to fill the space of what was missing. A faint, tingling sensation buzzed beneath my thoughts. How long had I been out?

"We need to do it tonight," I insisted. "If your brothers are in town, your new house is as much a target as HEX was. We need to make this happen now."

"You need to rest," Cernun scolded, taking the glass from my hands and rubbing gently on my thigh.

"I'm fine," I swore. "It's just been a long few days. See?"

I swirled my hands in a grandiose circle, intent on producing the subtle light formed when elements danced like fireworks at my fingertips.

Nothing.

I tried again, placing a bit more thought into it this time. There it was. That familiar vibration. I just needed to guide my focus to….

"Fuck!" I cried, collapsing back to the mattress. My cheek began to burn beneath the salve Cernun had applied there. "I can't conjure. I don't… I don't feel my power."

But that wasn't true. My magic was there, waiting inside of me. I just couldn't seem to reach it. It clawed from within, raking my heart, my thoughts, until I wasn't even sure if they were mine anymore.

Cernun bit his lip and moved his hand to massage my shoulder. He attempted his best reassuring face, but his eyes betrayed his worry.

"We think it has something to do with that thorn that scratched you. Like, Balor marked you or something. Do you remember what vine it was? It could help us figure out a counter-spell."

My mind spasmed as I tried to remember… anything. Flashes of red and yellow swirled where my thoughts should have been. I tried to breathe, but the air caught in my throat. I let go of the threads of the magic I was trying to grab and felt the absence, calm and empty, pulse through me.

Cernun's hands wrapped my shoulders, and I let his strength enter and calm me. My breath slowed and began to flow once more. That man! He could always comfort me so quickly. Even when my world was falling apart. I sank back into the pillows and covered my eyes with my hand.

"We're going to figure this out," he assured me as he pulled the covers up around my chest. But he didn't sound convinced. Or maybe it was me who wasn't. "For now, though, just try to get some sleep."

"What time is it anyway?" I asked.

The soft haze of night swam through Cernun's bedroom windows. Everything seemed so calm there, tucked into the tree lined streets of the Grant Park neighborhood. The lush foliage, even in the Winter, was a blanket on the world. The night was darker. The circadian rhythms of the streets hummed a soulful lullaby.

"Half past four. Get some rest. I'll be in soon to check on you," he promised, and I listened as he turned the lights out and the door clicked closed.

Cernun's bed was so comfortable. The vastness of the California King offered unexplored worlds beneath me. The rustle of my skin on the sheets was a lullaby of melodic white noise. Maybe I could sleep. Maybe everything would be better once I awoke.

I listened to Cernun's muffled voice from the hallway.

"Yeah. He woke up, but I've put him back to bed," he said. "He can't remember. Have you had any luck in the archive room? … Well, it's nearing five already. You should get some sleep, and we can start fresh tomorrow. I know your place is closer to you, but you're welcome to head back here if you want… No, I get that. I'll look after him. And we'll both see you tomorrow… You, too. Goodnight, babe."

Damn. Learco hadn't had any luck in the archive room. I guessed that was to be expected. The place was vast and unorganized, even if it held multitudes of magics lost to the annals of history. It would take some effort to sort through it. I hoped we'd have the time. And that it would move fast. I did not want to live without my power.

I felt Cernun's weight as he pulled himself into bed, and I snuggled myself into the concave of his body. His breath was warm against the back of my neck. His arm wrapped me, and his muscles relaxed. My eyes closed. I slept a dreamless sleep.

The new light of morning—or, more accurately, midday—gave a funambulist's leap through the window, summersaulting through the room like possibility was really there for it to promise. At least the natural world still had some glimmer of hope in it.

My body did not. My arms were worn and heavy as I stretched the rest of myself awake. Every cell in my body felt off, as if something had forced them just slightly out of place, out of congruence with reality. I balanced on the tip of a pin. I scratched against myself.

Cernun smiled at me from the stove when I entered the kitchen. The sizzle of bacon in the pan aroused my senses, and I eyed the waiting slices of bread, lettuce, tomato, and mayonnaise resting on the marble countertop.

"How're you feeling?" he asked.

"Coffee," I moaned.

Cernun laughed at my reply and nodded toward his espresso machine. A freshly tamped puck waited in the portafilter.

"It's good to know you're still you," he joked.

That's debatable, I wanted to say. Instead, I gave what a hoped to be a genuine smile.

I locked the brewing handle into place, and breathed deeply to welcome the aroma the water would awaken as it pushed through the grounds. An iced latte was just what I needed to jolt myself back into place. Coffee would make everything better.

I pressed the button to start the brew and yelped as hot water spewed out in all directions from the filter. Without a word, Cernun shifted his frying pan from the burner and stepped quickly to my side, stopping the pull and dumping the filter in one swift and practiced motion.

"Let me get that for you. You just have a seat at the table."

Cernun really was a jack-of-all-trades. His flights from city to city from the time he was fourteen until now had landed him jobs in construction, as a barista, in kitchens or slinging drinks, or digging holes for landscapers. The only jobs he couldn't stand were those that placed him in a cubicle and worshipping a screen. I slipped into a dining chair and watched him work.

"Learco swung by earlier," he said, "but we didn't want to wake you. He found some references to a bramble spell used by the

Greek nymph Smilax in her courting of Crocus. She attempted to claim the young mortal as her lover by marking his brow with a thorn. Instead, it was sort of like *Sleeping Beauty.* He fell into a deep sleep, and the gods turned Smilax into her namesake vine as punishment. Crocus, condemned to eternal sleep, was transformed into the first flower of Spring."

"Great," I groaned as Cernun slid my iced latte and a cut-in-half BLT in front of me. "At least when all this is over, I can be a pretty purple flower. You can plant me in your new garden."

Cernun's mouth twisted as he sat across from me and took a bite of his sandwich.

"You know those are just myths," he said.

"Are they? A year ago if you'd asked me if Balor and the rest of the Fomóraiġ were real, I'd have laughed in your face. Who's to say the tales of the Titans and the Olympians aren't real too? Fuck, they could be the same entities. Balor isn't too far off from the Cyclops, is he?"

"What I mean is: the myths aren't direct correlations to reality. They're parables. They're meant to teach us something. And often the secrets of the spell are hidden inside of them."

His voice was slow and measured, even as my obvious anxiety filled his breakfast nook. It was kind of comforting, our abilities to shift for one another—to be the calm when the other needed to be the storm. Even if the intense sexual desire wasn't there, that alone would make us work.

I nodded, and sighed, and took a bite of my lunch. Damn, it was good. I took a few more bites before I tried to speak again.

"I'm sorry," I said. "I don't mean to be an asshole."

"But you're just so good at it," he smirked, and I actually laughed at his joke.

It felt great to laugh. It had been one thing after another for days on end now. I hoped the worst was behind us, but—even without my connection to my power—something told me it was just beginning. I shivered to shake off the feeling of dread as I finished the last bite of my sandwich and swallowed it down with a hefty swig of espresso-sweetened milk.

"I've got a meeting scheduled with Johnny at the shop in about an hour so he can get a lay of the land before we start the remodel," Cernun smiled as he grabbed our empty plates and raked the crumbs into his sink. "But I can cancel it if you'd rather me stay here with you."

"I'd always rather you stay here with me," I cooed, kissing the air in his direction. "But go. The sooner we can get HEX rebuilt, the sooner things can start to get back to normal. Even if now I'm just some non-powered wannabe selling tricks to magicians."

Dishwasher loaded, Cernun crossed the room again to kiss my forehead.

"We're going to get your magic back," he promised, but I wasn't so sure.

I took my time in the shower, hoping the cascade of fresh water would cleanse me. The heat and the steam reminded me of something I couldn't quite place, but I shook it off as the musky, piney scent of Cernun's soap washed down my body.

Maybe it wouldn't be so bad being powerless. It wasn't like I hadn't considered it before. Back then though, when I was all but certain the MAW was looking to strip me of my magic—or worse yet, flame me at the stake, it had all been hypothetical. This was real. And feeling my power still locked away inside of me made it almost unbearable. Like the thing I needed most in the world was right where I left it and exactly three inches out of reach.

I wrapped my waist in a towel and used my hand to wipe the condensation from the bathroom mirror. My eyes, the rich green of holly leaves, were stung through with brown as if the edges of the plant were wilting, were dying. The sharpness of my nose seemed weaker somehow, and my lips quivered with a lost language. I looked ragged and wild, like a distant memory of myself. Hazy. But I told myself it was probably just the steam.

I dressed slowly, unsure of what to do with myself. Unsure of my worth without my shop. Without my magic. Deep down, I knew my power was not what defined me, but not having access to it sure hurt a hell of a lot. Mentally as well as physically. I could get used to it though.What would it take to become accustomed to the prickling feeling of my body fazing just outside of where it belonged?

Cernun had left a fresh latte for me in the fridge before he headed off in a Broomer to meet Johnny at HEX. "Just add ice," his note read inside of a heart. I was glad he was so on top of handling the reconstruction efforts at my store. I imagined, now that he knew his adoptive family—directly or indirectly—were responsible, he'd be doubly so. Even though we all knew it wasn't his fault, the actions of the Marshalls still stung him deeply.

It was warm for a February afternoon in Atlanta: pushing sixty, but with a steady breeze to remind us all that Winter still had her hold on the city. Although it was still early, the sun was deep into his march toward the horizon, ceding the season to his sister, moon's reign. I stepped from the deck timidly, saddened when my usual earth-connection failed to resound through my body. Even if I could no longer feel the energy of the natural world course its way through my body, at least I still knew it was there. That's what I told myself anyway. That was something Balor could never take away from me.

I walked the garden slowly, letting my fingertips trace along the wood of Cernun's finely constructed raised beds. There were six of them in total, each brimming with soil and mulch, using the cold calm of the season to ready themselves for the advent of new life. A removable greenhouse constructed of iron and glass was mounted atop two of them to get an early start on the seeded herbs we would transplant around the property come Spring.

Cernun had done a fine job in preparing his own witch's garden in the short time he'd owned the house, even under the confines of the dormant season. It was a truly beautiful space, even if I couldn't feel the magic it contained.

The chill in the air was at the perfect state to carry the aroma of the rich minerality of the soil, and I breathed it in heartily, hoping it would spark something from within me. I caught sight of the disheveled dirt at the back two corners of the lot where Cernun had retrieved the necessary spell ingredients from the night before. I could, at the very least, smooth the soil. I wasn't completely worthless.

I dropped to my knees and used my bare hands to spread the topsoil into place. Still nothing. I tried to feel the life it held, the many incarnations it had lived and died and promised, but it just would not come.

"This soil contains all that ever was and all that will ever be," I heard my mother's voice say.

I was eight, maybe nine years old, covered in the dust and abundance of youth, and sat cross-legged in her garden between the spiny branches of rosemary and the feathered stems of wormwood. Mom was smiling at me as her fingers worked the stalks of her yarrow, snipping at the yellow flowers to be dried and used in her later spell-work. My father was nearby, singing what sounded like a sailor's song as he slopped the pigs in their pen.

"Reach your fingers in and you can feel it," she said. "Life and death and everything in between. It's all a part of the cycle. We grow from this soil, and when we have served our purpose, we return to it once more."

I plunged my fingers into the black and closed my eyes. The land vibrated. Grubs, new to life and only just beginning their journey, squirmed within the darkest recesses of the ground. My father's measured footsteps pounded as he tossed potatoes and apples, fresh barley, and the remnants of last night's dinner into the trough. A stiff Summer breeze whipped at the pecan tree all the way across our property, and I felt the tug of its roots as its trunk stayed steadfast against the wind.

"I can feel it, Momma," I said, beaming up at her and reflecting the sun like I was a dandelion on her chin.

"Yes, you can, sweet child."

She knelt beside me and touched my cheek. Using her apron to wipe the grime away from my hands, she kissed my forehead and smiled.

"The earth is always with us," she said. "Always. And not just because we are witches. That magic you feel, don't you ever let it go."

I was eight, maybe nine years old. I felt it surge within me.

"In a couple of years," she continued, "when you come into your power, that connection you've got will be magnified to levels you won't always understand. But what I'm asking you now, Darragh, is to remember this moment. Remember this connection. And know that this is the base of who you are. All of us—witch and non-witch alike—are connected through the soil. Don't ever forget that."

"I won't forget, Momma," I smiled.

"Use your hands, Darragh. Not your power."

I was fourteen now, and my father had me working the

manual tiller to ready a small patch of land for the planting. We had a tractor. We had our magic. It could all be done—the whole farm—in a few hours time if we wanted, but he insisted the newly-formed callouses on my palms were part of the necessity.

"Why don't you just tie me to a yoke and turn me into a mule?" I smirked.

"Joke all you want," he smiled, "but there's valuable lessons here in this soil."

I stretched my lanky limbs, still sore from the sudden growth spurts of puberty, and firmed up my grip on the wooden handles. In all honesty, it was only twenty square feet of earth, adjacent to Mom's garden, and—when I was done—it would be mine.

"Rebellious" teenager that I was, I'd already picked out seeds of Belladonna and Hemlock to sow in my first witch's garden.

"There are other, more practical plants in the nightshade family," my father told me as I poured over books to choose my perfect planting. "Those eggplants you like breaded and fried up in bacon grease, for one. Hell, even this potato." He tossed the spud into the air then caught it with a wry smile. "But the flowers on those are real nice," he smirked.

He watched me from the perimeter of my clearing, whistling a sea chantey as he absently whittled the chunk of pecan wood in his hands.

I pushed the till a few feet further. Its sharp metal spokes churned the earth and kicked up the sweet, stinging scent of life and decay at my feet. The rotaries seized as they found a rock, and I dropped to my knees to fish it from the spokes.

"Got another one for the pile!" I called, and my father instructed me to stack it at the edge of my workspace alongside the others I'd found.

"We'll use these to build your border," he said. "The wall to your secret garden. The earth is going to give us everything we need for your planting. It's all right here. Waiting."

Despite the late Winter chill, sweat streamed down my face as I moved the stone to stack it with the others at my father's feet. My hands were brown from the work and felt as if they were ready to bleed. I squinted up at him through my mop of curly, auburn hair.

"You building your garden, connecting with the elements," he said, "it's a journey. It's about how you get there, not about where you're going. That's what I need you to understand. That connection—the hand to the soil to the hand to the seed—it makes the crop stronger, sweeter, stalwart and true."

At the time, I almost thought he was just reciting lyrics to one of his go-to Irish folk songs, but his words seemed pregnant with purpose, with the lessons of generations come and gone. I nodded as if I understood and returned to my duty. Even then, I figured it would make sense someday.

Always wiser than I gave them credit for, my parents were. I smiled at the memories as I patted down the final patch of soil in Cernun's yard. I'd finished in the back and rounded to the front lawn, waving my dirt-covered fingers at the neighbors who timidly smiled back before letting me go on my way.

My parents were right. I could still be connected to the elements, even if I'd lost touch with my magic. I was more than the power that waited inside of me. And I could figure out how to get it back. It was just going to take some time.

I turned to face the house, its windows beaming life and comfort in a way I'd never noticed before.

Maybe I could move here, I thought. *What kind of self-respecting witch runs a magic shop with no magic?* At least at Cernun's place I could wake up every day in his bed, get my palms dirty in the garden. Bring forth a different kind of power from the earth. Maybe it wouldn't be so bad to give up the life I had built if it was being stripped from me anyway. I thought I could talk myself into it, couldn't I?

Even my *woe is me* pout knew that was a lie.

I wiped my soiled hands on my jeans and started toward the front porch just as a Broomer pulled up to the curb. Katrina tumbled from the back seat, barely remembering to shut the door, with a crazed, frantic look in her eye.

"Darragh!" she yelled.

Her country lilt sounded strong on my name, pulling out more sounds than even the unpronounced letters accounted for. My head cocked in question as she traipsed across the lawn.

"It's Madison," she said, out of breath and anxious. "They're missing!"

I shook my head quickly as I snapped back into the present. I'd been so wrapped up in my own shit, I'd forgotten that Madison was the one in real trouble here. And if their disappearance was connected with Angel's death, I worried we wouldn't have much time.

Katrina panted as she stopped her macrh toward me and filled her lungs.

"They were hiding out with me," she admitted. "And now they're gone. I think they may be in danger!"

CHAPTER 8

"Slow down. Let's start again," Learco instructed, and Katrina flushed as she tried to catch her breath.

We'd taken a Broomer and called Learco to meet us at Aunt Paulina's as it was "neutral territory." Cernun, who'd told Katrina where to find me, was already waiting in our booth when we arrived. His pained expression as we entered told me she'd unloaded on him before she found me. Paul hovered nearby to watch over things, and Katrina looked to me for encouragement before she continued speaking. I'd had to assure her multiple times as we waited for Learco that he could be trusted, even if he was the head of the Southeastern Division of the organization currently on the hunt for our friend.

"Madison's been staying with me since Monday night," she admitted. "After they left here, when you gave them the rest of the night off after you couldn't find whatever spell you were hunting for in the MAW archives or whatever, they tried going home…"

Learco tilted his chin and raised his eyebrows in question as Katrina spoke. Shit. I still hadn't told him the truth about what I'd been up to with Madison, about why I'd truly been at the MAW headquarters that day. I guessed it was about to come out now. I frowned and hoped my eyes promised him an explanation soon.

"They got about a block from their dorm when they noticed the agents and the jet-black sedans swarming the area. Y'all really ain't trying for subtle, are you? Anyway. They snuck back here and rang the delivery doorbell in the back alley behind the restaurant so they wouldn't be seen. And they've been with me ever since."

Nothing like a trauma bond to bring two souls together, I thought. It also explained why Katrina and her uncle had been spouting Madison's catch phrase nonstop. I just hoped the trauma bond wasn't what kept Learco with me and Cernun.

I nodded at Learco's *we'll talk about this later* glare and tapped the rim of my Old Fashioned glass.

"Did they tell you anything about Angel?" Learco asked.

"No," Katrina insisted. "We didn't even know she had died until we saw it on the news this afternoon."

The charmed amulet of white alabaster Learco had slyly snuck onto the table retained its dim clear glow, telling us all that Katrina was telling the truth. Or, at the very least, the truth as she believed it to be. I bit my lip at Learco's wince.

"Angel's murder was on the news?" Cernun asked, eyes wide as he looked to Learco in question. It wasn't like the MAW to let things slip through the cracks. Especially something so big.

"She was murdered?" Katrina cried. "Oh shit, oh shit, oh shit."

Her worry was obviously placed on Madison. I watched her features dance as she imagined the impact on her would-be lover. I recognized the cyclone of emotion, having seen it in my own mirror too many times before. Those moments when love was young and the object of my affection had reared his face in every interaction, becoming wholly a part of every thought that crossed my mind. Seeing her so distraught was painful, though it was also kind of endearing.

"The Stewarts have been unhappy with the progress the

Moral Authority has made in apprehending their daughter's murderer," Learco sighed. "Their going to the media was meant to be a motivational tactic to light a fire under our stakes."

"In house maneuvers, I see."

I wanted to laugh at Cernun's attempt at a joke. For the past few hundred years, the MAW had been responsible for just as many witches flamed at the stake as the humans were. Hell, maybe even more since the humans often got it wrong. But it was not the time for laughter.

"Wait!" Katrina nearly yelled as her shock wore off and understanding took hold. "You think Madison murdered Angel?"

"There is evidence..." Learco started before Katrina interrupted him.

"Not a snowball's chance in hell," she bellowed. "Angel was their best friend. Fuck, they even told me they were in love with her for a while. Unrequited. But that wouldn't be a reason for them to go all stabby."

I sipped my cocktail and swallowed hard. At least the news hadn't revealed the true nature of Angel's death. That was a small blessing if nothing else. A magically manipulated body would stoke divisions that had been simmering to a boil. The pitchforks and torches would already be raised toward the skies if they had.

"Besides, how do I know this ain't just the fucking MAW experimenting with magics on your own kind?"

My mouth gaped at Katrina's suggestion. A spell this powerful would require access to the ancient archives. And we'd all witnessed firsthand in Samara Byrne what happened when a MAW agent went rogue. Learco, however, did not seem convinced. His face was as non-reactive as the white alabaster stone as he continued his questioning of the witness.

"This is not a question of what ifs. This is about Madison," he told her. "Did they mention anywhere they may try to go?"

Katrina clammed up as she rocked in her seat. The ball of nervous tension inside of her looked ready to explode. I reached my hand across the table to comfort her, but she refused to take it.

"You don't have to believe me," Learco continued, "but I am on your side. And Madison's. If they mentioned anywhere they may try to hide, it could really be helpful in clearing their name."

Her head slumped as she buried her chin in her chest. Paul took a few strides toward our table, armed and ready to comfort his niece, but I help up my hand to stop him.

"Katrina," I called, attempting to keep my voice calm and steady even though I was bustling with the same nervous energy as she was. "The MAW may have its… issues. But Learco is one of the most honest and true people I know. If he says he wants to help Madison, I believe him."

"Is that why you couldn't tell him you were searching for the shifting spell?" she snarked.

My body froze. Somewhere a heart beat so loudly it drowned out the punk anthem sounding from the nearby jukebox. It took me a moment to realize it was coming from my chest. Learco's jaw dropped, and Cernun clamped his hand on my thigh.

"You and Madison were researching witch shifts?" Learco asked.

His voice was calm and collected. Practiced and inquisitive. I was no longer his partner but his suspect as I slumped into my seat across from his interrogation. My face fell, and I bit my lips.

"Looks like y'all have your own shit to sort," Katrina said as she scooted over, forcing Learco to stand to let her out of the booth.

"Find Madison," she said to me as she stood and stormed off to the kitchen. I watched the door swing in her wake, a pendulum ready to slice me in two.

Learco remained standing, his eyes jostling as his mind

raced at the revelation. Cernun's eyes pleaded with mine to say something—anything—that would make the situation better. But no words would come. Guilt and shame lambasted my core, nearly making the agitation I felt at being cut off from my magic child's play.

The lie by omission had been bad enough at the start, but now that a witch was dead through a shift curse, and I still hadn't come clean, it was so much worse.

"Your drinks are on me," Paul said as he grabbed our half-finished imbibes from the table and nodded toward the door. "You're always welcome here, but I think the conversation y'all need to have is best hashed out across the street."

HEX already looked so much better than it did just a day before. Cernun had spent most of the afternoon clearing the charred wood and soot from the sales floor and fanning the smell of burning out the front door. He'd even had someone out already to replace the store front window where the brick had burst through. From the outside, no one would ever even know there'd been an attack. I hoped he understood why I wasn't smiling when I saw it. But he wasn't smiling either. Learco's practiced gate practically seethed with rage as he marched two steps in front of us toward the stairs to my apartment.

"How could you not tell me?" he bellowed as soon as Cernun closed the door.

Any joy I could have felt by being home was quickly swallowed up by my shame.

"I wanted to," I pleaded. "Really, I did. But with your job, with your position, I didn't want to force you to have to choose between the MAW and me."

Learco shook his head and tapped his fingers hard against the kitchen island. I could see the anger dance behind his eyelids. I could feel the hurt seeping from his every pore.

"So you don't trust me," he spat.

"No. That's not it at all."

"That's exactly what it is. You thought I would choose my job over you, so you took the path of least resistance. You didn't trust me enough to understand where you were coming from. Or to meet you there."

My face went numb. Every inch of my body wanted to turn and run away. But I needed to face this. The repercussions of my actions were coming due.

"I wanted to tell you," I argued, as if that could make it better.

"He really did," Cernun chimed.

"So you knew about this too?" Learco growled, turning his attention to Cernun before I stepped into his eye line.

"This is not about him," I said. "This is my fault."

"Yes," Learco glared. "This is your fault. You went behind my back to search spells long deemed illegal by the Moral Authority of Witches. You hid not only your intentions from me, Darragh, but also those of Madison Ridge. And now, two young witches are dead; their bodies both mutilated and riddled through with transmogrifications as if they were livestock. Test animals in a lab."

My breath caught in my throat.

"Two?" I stuttered. "Is Madison dead?"

"No."

The anger is Learco's voice faltered as he saw the worry wash over me. He took a deep breath to calm him emotions, and when he spoke again the cold artificiality of his job had taken hold.

"I'm choosing to trust you with this, even though you could not extend me the same courtesy. The reason I was late in meeting you and Katrina across the street is that I was across town at a new crime scene. This was a male, late twenties. We have a name from the rental agreement of the home but have not and may not be able to make a positive ID based off the mutilation of the body. Dental records are useless unless he's always sported fangs; and the antlers now protruding from his skull may prove problematic when it comes to a facial reconstruction."

I allowed myself to sit on one of the barstools at the kitchen island as Learco spoke. I couldn't believe another young witch was dead through such horrific means. I did not want to accept the eerie similarities between their deaths and the spells Madison had been searching for. With my help. I did not want to believe my lie could have paved the path for another death.

"Madison's disappearance from Katrina's right before another killing took place does not look good, does it?" I gulped, forcing myself to say it out loud. Even if that made it real.

"No, it does not."

Learco's stern demeanor wavered slightly as he saw my pain, but he pushed back his shoulders and regained his composure. He stared directly at me for an oh-so-eternal and way-too-brief moment, then looked to Cernun and closed his eyes.

"If you will both excuse me," he said, "I have an investigation to continue. Darragh, I truly believe you did not know of Madison's whereabouts until tonight, but if that was another lie, please tell me now."

I felt the tears welling in my eyes as they pleaded with his for forgiveness. I shook my head, slowly, side to side, as my heart continued its symphony inside my chest. I wanted to speak, but no words seemed adequate. I'd forgotten them all anyway. The only one I knew was his goodbye.

"Very well then," he said.

He opened the door and stepped out onto the vestibule at the top of the stairs. He paused, hands clenched at his sides as if he too was searching for the right words and thinking better of them in the instant they appeared.

I scrambled to my feet and rushed toward the door.

"Learco!" I was crying now. I could not stop the tears. "Please don't leave here mad. We need to talk this out."

He turned slowly, the quiver in his lower lip betraying the stoic stone of his face.

"I'm not angry. I'm hurt," he said, and he closed the door.

Cernun kissed my forehead as I wept into his shoulder. One of his arms wrapped my shoulders to hold me close while the other massaged my thigh from our perch on my sofa. I oscillated through tears and ragged breath as I fought to make sense of the evening, of everything else the past few days had brought. It was a shitshow, and I seemed to be snuggled tightly into the core of it.

"I really fucked up, didn't I?" I sobbed.

"We both did," he whispered before squeezing me tighter and adding, "Learco just needs some time to cool down. And we have to be strong enough to give it to him."

"You can say 'I told you so.'"

He had urged me from the beginning to be honest with Learco about my search for the ancient spells on my trips to visit the Moral Authority headquarters. I should have listened to him. Even back then I knew that. But I appreciated that he'd allowed me to choose my own path, even if that had landed me here.

"I'm not going to say I told you so," he smiled weakly, and the sympathy felt nice. "But it's good that you already know it's true."

My tear ducts spent, my eyes were sore and dry as I peered around my apartment. It felt good to be back in my own space with my own things. I needed that bit of normalcy even as the rest of the world exploded. I caught my reflection in the television, and, even in the soft black haze that stared back at me, I knew I looked a mess.

Cernun had been right all along, so perhaps he was right about this too: I just needed to give Learco some time. Me attempting to force an understanding would only make things worse. On the plus side, I barely felt the sting from the absence of my power anymore. Of course, it was replaced by the pang of something much worse.

"We can stay here tonight if you want to," Cernun said, releasing me from his grip and standing to clear our rocks glasses from the coffee table. "But Johnny's sending a couple guys over tomorrow, and you know construction folk like to start early. You'd be able to sleep in at my place."

"This is all a ploy," I said. "I think you just like having me there."

"Guilty. But with these guys, we should be able to get the walls and the foundation work checked off in a couple days. Then it's just display tables and stock, so you'd be able to move back in on your own and leave me all alone in my great big house across town."

I started to laugh at his obvious guilt trip, but I stopped myself. Damn, it felt good to smile. But it also felt like a betrayal to Learco. Even if it wasn't, I didn't need another jockey riding my conscience. How could I have been so stupid?

I washed my face in the bathroom mirror while Cernun called a Broomer to take us to his place. The last of the calendula flaked off onto my towel, and I leaned in close to study my cheek. Cernun's poultice had worked wonders. The last of the scratch was gone, and only a thin white line remained in its place. I hoped it wouldn't scar, but even if it did, at least all the markings of the last few days would not be strictly internal. I obviously needed some physical reminders to keep me from repeating my mistakes. My breath fogged the mirror with my heavy sigh, and I left to join Cernun to wait for our car on the sidewalk.

The darkness brought with it a colder wind, and I snuggled close to my boyfriend to keep warm. In my haste to bring Katrina back to tell her story, I hadn't even thought to grab a heavier jacket, and it was too late to go back upstairs to grab one. Any other time a simple incantation, a quick mental spark, would have sent warmth cascading over my body. But now the night was frigid and empty. My lack of connection to my power even made the shadowy recesses between the streetlamps seem darker.

"Hello, Mitchell."

A finely dressed man in a sleek brown two piece and a wool overcoat stepped into the light in front of my shop and smiled thinly. A lapel pin in blocked, serif letters identified him as a member of the DMFM. It was a completely different font than the more punk-rock inspired back patch we'd seen in the surveillance video. Whoever did their marketing sure knew how to run the gamut of styles to keep their hateful, spiteful members happy. I wondered briefly about hiring them for HEX once I got it re-opened.

Cernun flinched at his adoptive name. The alliteration alone must have brought forth on onslaught of playground bullies in his youth. His hand grasped tightly to mine.

"Jason," he glared.

Jason held up his gloved hands in a feigned surrender as an evil smirk twisted across his cheeks.

"Careful now," he said. "Don't try and throw me against a wall. I'd hate to see the window of this fine establishment broken again."

It was almost a confession. I could feel the heat rising in Cernun's body, and I clutched tighter to his arm to warn him against doing anything stupid. But if I'd had access to my powers, things may have been different from my end.

Jason was about six years younger than Cernun, but the hard lines on his thin face made him look older than he was. A thinning mop of mouse brown hair with too much pomade helmeted his crown and tried to hide the wide extrusion of his ears. His Adam's apple, strong and protruding, rubbed against the collar of his buttoned shirt, turning red and irritated in the cold. The streetlights exaggerated his features, leaving him as sharp and hollow as most humans viewed the night. He had that obvious *I don't get my hands stained* look, preferring to hire others to do his dirty work.

"What are you doing here, Jason?"

"You didn't miss your little brother? How many years has it been? I think the last time I saw you was… It must've been in the hospital when you broke Brian's arm. Aside from that little video that went around a few years back anyway. Is this the devil-born hag that saved you?"

"You owe me money for what you did to my shop," I blurted.

Jason smirked again. He really thought his shit smelled great.

"Oh, did something happen to your little heathen salon?" he asked with a sneer. "I hope no one got hurt. But, you know, it's bound to happen when your kind lays carnally with Satan Morningstar. 'For whomever does these things is detestable to the Lord; and because of these detestable things, the Lord your God will drive them out before you.' That's Deuteronomy since I doubt you learn these things at your little bonfires in the woods."

Cernun's arm shifted as if he was going to go for a sucker punch, but I held tight to his hand. The last thing I needed was another boyfriend gone for the night, sleeping it off in a human jail cell, as satisfying as the sound of his knuckles hitting Jason's chin would have been. Seeing me stop Cernun only served to urge Jason on.

"I just wanted to let you know I'm in town for a bit," he grinned. "Thought that's what a good brother would do while he had the chance. And figured a heads up on a reckoning doesn't mean the reckoning won't still come."

His words slithered from his tongue like serpents readying their fangs to bite. Every word offered apples or persimmons or pomegranates. Every fruit was spoiled from its core.

"What the fuck is that supposed to mean?" Cernun asked.

Every cell in his body wanted me to release him. Every cell in his body was glad I had his hand.

A blue SUV pulled to a stop beside us, and the driver rolled down the passenger side window. I gave her a quick hand signal to give us a moment, and she rolled the window back up and turned on her music to wait. Jason scoffed and adjusted the cuff on his gloves.

"Soon, everyone in the world is going to know exactly what demons your kind are. What kind of devil you are," he said. "And when that happens, God help you."

He pursed his lips and scrunched his nose as he smoothed out the lapels of his overcoat.

"Mom and Dad say 'hi.'"

And with that stab of the knife, he turned to walk away, moving casually through the streetlights and whistling a hymn.

The Broomer ride back to Cernun's place was quiet. Our driver tried to make small talk, and I did my best to answer her as I watched the conversation with his brother play over and over again through Cernun's mind. I saw the could have, would have, should haves play out as he attempted, unsuccessfully, to make the encounter end differently. To seem bolder or less shocked, less angry or unbothered by his brother's presence.

He fumbled, dropping his keys twice, as he tried to unlock his front door. His broad chest heaved with deep breaths of fear and regret.

"Not exactly how I expected to meet your family," I joked as I closed the door behind us.

Cernun was better with the levity, but I was hoping I could help quell the anxiety that ravaged in his brain.

He grabbed my biceps and kissed me hard. It only took a moment for me to melt into his lips, savoring the taste of him. I tried to wrap my arms around his back, but he kept them pinned to my side. Our mouths parted, and I immediately wanted him to kiss me once more. I stared into his eyes as they squinted into a new-found fury. Angry and horny were so close on the spectrum after all.

With a grunt, he tossed me to the couch. His body writhed on top of me as his lips found my cheek, my ear, my neck. His hands pulled clumsily at my belt, but he gave me little resistance as my hands guided his chin back up until we were face to face.

"If this is what you need right now," I cooed, "you know I'm always down. But we can also… talk."

"Fuck talking," he growled. "And fuck me."

His shirt was over his head and across the room before the words even reached my ears. Instinctively, my hands reached up to caress his hard, muscled chest. His tattoos told stories of the past that mattered—not the one that had confronted us—as the bright, colorful images peeked between my fingers. The gentle brush of his chest hair felt soft against my palms. His pushed my shirt over my stomach, and grinned as he managed to free my belt from the loops and open the fly of my pants. I scraped my fingernails down his abs and tugged at his waistband. Already, he was hard. His cock bobbed in the air between us as I pushed down his jeans.

I smiled as I clutched his ass and guided him toward my lips. Even without my aura at play, the emotional connection between us—the sexual desire—was palpable. It swam the length of my body. It almost felt like I was connected to my power again.

His aura, though, was working overtime. It pulsed around me, teasing my skin with its warm, intricate vibrations. I was flying, laying there with my back against his couch, and I suddenly understood why so many witches warned against using our auras on humans. And why so many humans became familiars who kept coming back for more. The push of him was intense and glorious—more so even in the absence of my own. I would have fallen in love again if that were possible. Or, at the very least, lust.

He throbbed as he passed my lips. My tongue traced around the tip of his dick. I let my mouth make up for my aura's absence. He moaned as my head rocked back and forth on his member. His head fell back in ecstasy. His thighs tensed and tightened beneath my grip.

Just when I thought I had him, he pulled back and worked his tongue over my mouth, tasting the two of us there with a wicked smile.

"I said 'fuck me.'"

He leaned back and pulled a bottle of lube from the drawer of the end table beside his couch. Leave it to Cernun to always be prepared. His hand was slick and smooth, and the friction from his working the lubricant onto me almost sent me overboard. He bit his lip as he held me taut, then guided himself down to take me—all of me—into him.

I gasped. My breath shuddered as he rode me slowly, increasing his speed as my hands reached out to massage his arms, his neck, his nipples. His aura rippled around us, tugging and teasing every inch of me until I didn't think I could take it anymore.

We came together, and he collapsed on top of me in a heaving, sweaty mass. I was still inside him when he lifted his head to kiss me again.

"I love you," he said. "No matter what else: I love you."

"To the stars and back," I smiled, and his lips met mine once more.

CHAPTER 9

While I showered, Cernun "whipped up" a quick meal for us to settle our stomachs with a late dinner. Creamed corn and butter beans and a couple fried pork chops that tasted just like my mother's. Crispy and tender and with an extra heaping of black pepper which added enough spice to offset the heat of the long southern days.

"I called her a few months back for her recipe," he grinned. "I was going to make them for you for Valentine's Day this weekend, but I figured we both kind of needed some comfort food tonight."

"This was too much trouble," I said as I spooned another bite of the perfectly seasoned beans into my mouth. "Thank you."

"The corn was canned," he shrugged and reached across the table to hold my hand.

It was a pretty romantic scene: the two of us doused in candlelight as we sat across from each other at his large, dark walnut dining table that was made for entertaining. An ornate damask wall covering that featured orchids, yarrow, and twisting lobed leaves in black and dark grey spread across the walls behind us; and thick, heavy drapes skirted the floor beneath the large pair of windows that overlooked his resting garden. The whole house felt warm and cozy and primed for some sort of forever.

Like the promise of home was all bought and paid for. It was a feeling I could get used to.

I helped him scrape our leftovers from our plates—though there weren't many—into his composter and dished the rest of the food he'd made into a glass, compartmented container to stash in the fridge and reheat later. It was obviously a meal for Learco, though neither of us said so out loud. It made his absence all the more real. He made an iced latte for me and a cortado for himself as I started the dishwasher. We chose a movie we'd both seen a million times and snuggled close to one another on the couch. Tonight was all about comfort. The Fae knew we both needed it.

Even with the coffee, I was already dozing against Cernun's shoulder when the doorbell rang just before 3AM. I paused the movie when Learco slowly entered. He swallowed hard as he stood at attention just inside the door. His face was still, but his eyes told another story as they practiced what to say.

"My agents have confirmed that Jason Marshall is indeed in Atlanta," he proclaimed when he finally spoke. The calm, professional clip of his words was heartbreaking. Each vowel was a knife against my skin.

"I know," Cernun sighed. "He accosted us on the street outside of HEX."

"He did?! Why didn't you—? Nevermind."

Shit. Was this another omission? We should have called him right away. But he was working. And after the way he left, the last thing either of us wanted to do was bother him with our needs.

"Since he is here," Learco continued, "I thought it pertinent for us to complete the ritual to protect your property. The two of us can handle it since Darragh is out of commission. Temporarily."

His eyes paused briefly on mine as he said my name but winced and darted away almost as quickly as they'd settled. My mouth gasped open, but no words would come. There was so much I wanted to say, but none of it felt right. Not a single syllable my brain could conjure seemed apologetic enough. I could not convey the sincerity of my grief. I hoped my face would. It had a tendency to telegraph my every thought. Though I knew that wouldn't be enough.

Cernun checked his watch and nodded. It was five 'til the spelling hour. Learco had left no room for small talk. For apologies. His face looked hollow but beautiful as desire and humility fought their bouts behind his features.

"I'll get the ritual room ready," Cernun said. "Everything should still be laid out from last night."

He smiled weakly before he disappeared down the hallway. Learco remained where he'd chosen to stand when he entered. IIis chin raised as his eyes searched the ceiling. When no words would come, I finally went with what my mother would say.

"Have you eaten?" I asked, surprised at the frog croaking in my throat. "I can heat up the leftovers in the fridge for you. We—well, Cernun made you dinner."

The words started strong and fast but became weak and spaced out as they spilled from my lips. They seemed too simple, so unrefined, as they clung to the heavy air of the room, searching for holes in the atmosphere—for any way to break through the tension between us.

"I am here because this property needs protecting from Jason Marshall and his Defend Mankind From Magic goons." Each word took on a harsher slant as it snarled from Learco's mouth, pushing from professional to so sore it radiated. "I am not here to talk." Then, suddenly softer, his eyes meeting mine once more, he added, "I'm not ready to talk."

I nodded as Cernun popped his head back into the living room.

"All set," he called.

Learco marched across the room as my face folded in on itself. He paused at the threshold and tuned to face me. His face cracked as he took in my doe-eyed, needy expression.

"Darragh," he sighed. "We are going to get through this. Somehow. It just won't be tonight."

I clenched my lips and nodded my head. I had to give him the time he needed with this. But it gave me hope to hear his words.

"I'll leave you guys to it," I whispered, but they were gone.

I woke still on the couch with a blanket draped across me and a note from Cernun folded neatly atop the coffee table.

"Good morning, Love," it read. "Learco left after the spell, but said he'd call us both later. I'm off to HEX to get things situated there. The house is protected now, so you should be good here. Hopefully even from the Fomóraiġ. There's eggs and bacon in the fridge. And feel free to take another stab at the espresso machine."

I was hoping to catch them when the ritual ended, at the very least to say goodnight, but I must have passed out pretty hard. It was great that the property was now protected, especially with Jason and his DMFM lackeys setting their nefarious sites on Cernun and Atlanta. But I couldn't spend all day cooped up in the house. I had a to-do list a mile long. Well, it was only two points deep—find Madison to help prove their innocence and regain my power—but each of those points stretched as high and far as the Appalachian Mountains. Bacon and eggs did sound nice though. And coffee. Lots of coffee.

I couldn't risk going to the archive room at the MAW HQ, not with Learco still upset from my omission, but the University Library at the MAW-sanctioned Georgia Thaumaturgy Institute where Madison studied was world-renowned for its collection. Of course, that also meant that it was staffed by Moral Authority agents and most definitely restricted to the MAW edicts of acceptable tomes for public consumption. So that was out too. Plus, I doubted Madison would be reckless enough to hang out on campus when they knew they were being hunted.

The bigger state schools all had Magical Theory departments now, despite some politicians attempting to cut funding for them, that welcomed powered and non-powered students alike. They didn't teach things like spells or control, but focused instead on history and philosophy, the hardships and contributions of spellcasters throughout the ages. Those witches whose aptitude tests couldn't get them into GA Thaum—or those who didn't care for the MAW knowing all their business—as well as humans with innate or morbid interests in our kind filled those classrooms. It was just as likely I'd be recognized there, but less likely I'd be thrown out. Plus, even though books had to be sanctioned, that took time, effort, and energy. I'd seen the paperwork stacked high on some of his underlings' desks when I'd visited Learco at work. That meant there was the chance of some codex slipping through the cracks and waiting on their library shelves before an agent whisked it away to the archives. I figured that was probably my best shot. And I could get to Georgia State University on foot from Cernun's.

A MARTA train passed overhead as I trotted up Hill Street and took a left onto Dekalb Avenue. Or maybe it was Decatur or Marietta Street there. I always got confused about where the streets changed names. A cold wind chilled me as I walked across the bridge over the 75/85 connector, and I shivered. The gold dome of the Capital Building glared at me in the February morning sun. I hadn't been back there since Cernun, Learco, and I had formed our coven to defeat the Gowdies and Samara Byrne. I could still see Adrian Gowdie's reanimated corpse, shot through with a jolt of Samara's power, barreling down on me. It had been a harrowing experience, but at least something good had come from it. Until I fucked that up.

Samara had had years inside the MAW HQ to search the archive room, learning to increase her power to accomplish the necromancy spell she'd found in the Gowdie Grimoire. I'd have to make do with whatever the University had managed to get their hands on.

I piggybacked in after a student swiped their admission card and plastered a huge smile across my face as I beelined toward the desk beside the library entrance. I'd practiced what I was going to say the entire walk over, making sure it sounded legitimate and convincing enough to get me through the doors. The security guard at the desk squinted her eyes and tilted her head at my approach.

"Greetings," I called out, thinking it sounded more collegiate than a simple hello. My voice was more forceful than confident, like an actor playing to the cheap seats, and I told myself to rein it in a little. "I've been summoned to give a guest lecture to the Magic Theory 1101 course. You may recognize me as the witch who exposed magic to the world from that viral video a few years back."

The guard huffed and pursed her lips, looking at me in question, but letting me continue.

"At any rate, my guest pass credentials are still processing, so as of this moment, I find myself without the necessary card to grant me access to your fine institution. However, my lecture is this afternoon, and I am in dire need of this library as I would like to verify and cite some of the many fine points of my lecture."

She crossed her arms over her chest and leaned back into her chair. One of her hands flourished in front of her, asking for more.

"You see, there is so much great history within the world of witches. Most of it is handed down through word of mouth, from parent to child and so on—much like the ancient oral traditions of African or Indigenous American tribes. But, in the name of accuracy for your students, and to keep solely within the allowed circumference of the Moral Authority of Witches guidelines, I thought it pertinent to verify said facts before presenting them to your students."

If the thesaurus that had landed on my tongue didn't get her, I thought for sure the references to oral traditions or the MAW would convince her to let me through. She paused for a moment, looking me up and down once more before she huffed and leaned forward in her chair. She looked side to side conspiratorially and cupped a hand beside her mouth, urging me toward her with the other. I leaned across the riser and opened my eyes earnestly.

"You know we're open to the public, right?" she laughed. "Just need a state ID. Don't even need to be Georgia's."

I blushed the color of the ragged poinsettia she had neglected on the side of her desk and pulled out my driver's license. I didn't own a car, but I kept it up to date for the occasional trips back to my parent's farm. She darted her eyes between the picture on the ID and my face, back and forth a few times, hemming and hawing just to mess with me.

"Enjoy the library, Mister Cullen," she finally said, eyes beaming and a sarcastic smirk to at least tell me I'd brought some life to her day. "It closes to visitors at 8PM."

I wandered the stacks with my eyes raised in wonder. Libraries, I thought, were such magical spaces. Book stores too. I'd often dreamed of adding a selection of tomes to the shelves at HEX. Even if they didn't sell, the rich, worldly aroma of yellow-stained pages and the hefty, hearty sight of thick leather covers would add some gravitas to my little shop. But I supposed it was a good thing I hadn't gotten around to it yet. Those ancient books would have gone up like kindling in the attack. Well, that and the MAW would have severely limited my selection.

I reluctantly sauntered past the fiction section to the more severe and stately non-fiction works. Centuries of knowledge was packed onto those shelves. Almost like witchcraft itself, each page offered insights into worlds that were, worlds which would be. Humans had a saying that science was just magic explained. I thought it was the explaining that made the magic.

I avoided the computers with their digitized card catalogues—too many students were cloistered around them anyway—and decided I could search out the magic books for myself. They wouldn't be hard to find, even without my magic. Those sorts of books always carried a mystical air about them that was obvious to anyone who came near. Too, a leisurely stroll through the shelves worked wonders for my mood.

In a rear corner of the library, tucked behind the works on Religion and Spirituality, I found them. I couldn't help but sigh in disappointment. Where I'd expected shelves brimming with untold marvels, instead there were just a few ratty reproductions and a sign denoting Magic and the Occult that someone had defaced with a drawing of a bunny popping out of a top hat. It was actually a fairly good rendering, if altogether inaccurate.

I cleared my throat as I ran my fingers down the spines of a few of the books. Nothing came to me. No immediate jolt of power, of understanding, of connection. True, I was still cut off from the magics at the core of my being, but I'd hoped for, at the very least, a spark.

"Darragh?"

I turned quickly to find Verne smiling from a few paces behind me. His arms were laden down with that student-under-pressure stack of books I'd seen in so many movies. I'd forgotten he was in grad school here. His sheepish grin was sweet as he moved to my side.

"I thought that was you," he said. "I can't believe what happened to HEX! Is it true it was those Damn Mother Fucking Maniacs?"

It took me a moment to work out the DMFM acronym from his colorful language. His tone was sympathetic and well above a library whisper.

"Yeah," I said. "Cernun's there working right now though. We'll have the doors reopened in no time."

"No worries," Verne shrugged. The books shifted in his arms, and he readjusted his stance to keep hold of them. "It's giving me some time to catch up on my studies. Plus, I assume you're still gonna pay us for the hours we had scheduled."

I couldn't help but laugh as I nodded my affirmation. A nearby student shushed us, and I smiled. I really was getting the entire teen comedy treatment.

"I've got a study room booked for the next hour," he said, nodding his head toward the row of small conference spaces adjacent to the nearby open tables. "If you want to chat. I could use a little break before I dive back in."

It didn't look like I was going to find anything remotely close to what I needed as I glanced back at the shelves. He smiled as he turned, then loudly shushed our shush-er while I followed him to the door.

The study room was small and basic—a central table, a few

chairs, and sound panels on the walls. It was designed for three or four at a time to have earnest discussions about their classes, but most students—like Verne—utilized them solo to spread out further than the communal tables allowed.

His books thudded as he dumped them to the table then spread in a kaleidoscopic array between us. I closed the door and took a seat opposite him. The chair was uncomfortable, I guessed to keep students from sleeping during late night study sessions.

"My parents think I should quit and move back up to Ellijay after the attack," he said, frowning. "They don't seem to get that we're more accepted here in the city than we are there though, despite shit like the DMFM. I try to tell them it's really rednecks from out there booming through here with their hate, but they don't listen."

I held my breath in a grimace. A lot of small town and country witches—my parents included—fretted over our city exposure while they stayed "safe" where they were. But many of their neighbors didn't even know their true nature. I did not want to live like that ever again.

"Don't worry," he quickly added. "I'm not going anywhere."

"How did they hear about the fire?" I asked, gulping down the words in wary anticipation. So much of my clientele weren't witches, and if the humans thought my shop was dangerous— in more than an enticing, magical way—it wouldn't matter how quickly I could get the doors back open.

"Oh, it wasn't on the news or anything so the lay folk won't know," he said to my quick relief. "But Mom and Dad have a phone tree, and you know how witches are. Gossips. Every last one of us."

"That's how we spread our power," I joked.

"That and sex," he laughed, tilting his chin and blowing a mock kiss to a gaggle of young women nonchalantly watching him and blushing from outside the window of the conference room.

He wasn't wrong. There was definitely a sexual freedom that came from being a witch. Perhaps it was the centuries of persecution for just being who we were that unbridled our desires in other forms. And judging by the obviously giggling of the girls, Verne seemed to be very popular with the ladies on campus. I could see why. He was a good-looking young man with broad shoulders and a goofy smile that served him well. Plus, I bet his aura push was sought after at the mostly human school.

"Well, I'm glad you're not going anywhere," I said.

Still distracted by his audience, Verne shrugged.

"I like my job," he said. "And the perks of being a powered student at a non-magic school. Even with the hours of actual work that entails."

I smiled as he pushed at his books to sort them into piles—practical, research, and extraneous. They were mostly benign. *Histories of the World; The World in Literature; An Omnibus of Oral Traditions.* But one in particular caught my eye.

"It's actually good that I ended up with this week off," he sighed. "I've got a term paper I haven't even started on. How're Stacey and Mads, by the way?"

I startled back to attention. I guessed witches weren't the gossips he thought we were if he hadn't heard what happened yet. That was a small victory, I supposed.

"Stacey's good," I said. "I talked to her earlier this week after I called you, and she's just as happy working on her sachets at home with her soap operas blaring. Madison's… going to be okay too."

"That's good," he smiled. "Silver linings and whatnot."

"Better than gold sometimes," I agreed. At least verbally.

A part of me had been hoping he'd heard something from or about Madison to at least get me started on my search for their new hiding place. All of me was certain they'd had nothing to do with Angel's death. Or the new murder of the male witch across town. No matter how the evidence pointed. But, if I wanted to prove it, I needed to find them first.

"I'm glad I ran into you," I said. "It's weird not seeing you all at the shop several times a week. Hell, it's weird not having a shop to see you in."

"We'll be back at it soon enough," he sighed.

I could tell the weight of his assignment had finally set in. He'd moved past the need for distractions and was starting to crack the spines of the tomes. I was overstaying my welcome, but he didn't want to be rude.

"I don't want to fuck your flow," I said timidly, "but do you think I could borrow one of these books for a day or two? I mean, not if you need it for reference, obviously."

I held up the book with an overly wide smile. Its kelly green, clover field of a cover with silver metallic writing glinted in the overhead fluorescent lights.

"Go for it, man," he smiled. "Nothing in there for me anyway. It's not like Faeries are real."

"Of course not."

My eyes widened as my smile stretched further until it met my ears, but he wasn't watching me anyway. Like me prior to meeting Balor, most younger witches didn't believe in the Fae-folk anymore. They were simply stories our grandparents told us to make us behave; folklore passed down as parable, not fact. And if Cernun, Learco, and I could figure out a way to get out of our bargain and prevent the Fomóraiġ from crossing through to our reality, it could stay that way.

"Thanks," I said, tucking the book into the tote I'd brought just in case I found something worthwhile. "I'll get it back to you soon. And I'll give you a call when we're ready to reopen. I'm thinking sometime next week."

"That's cool," Verne smiled, but he wasn't paying attention. He was already elbow deep in James Joyce.

I smiled and tapped the table as a goodbye as I stood to leave. He waved absently while he jotted quotes and page numbers in his notebook.

The library was busier now as I made my way toward the exit. The students nearly hummed as they jostled through the shelves in search of the knowledge they were paying the big bucks for, hoping for some insight that would change the world for them. Or change them enough to face the world. I supposed that was why I was there too. And hopefully, the book in my bag would have what I was seeking. Or at least lead me in the right direction.

I could tell a few of the students recognized me as the witch who revealed magic when I set my gait in a straight line for the door. The whispers were obvious, but I was long since used to them. Even Madison and Angel, the first time I met them, had fan-theyed out over me. It always made me a little uncomfortable. Cernun insisted I should embrace the fame, but I was certain it was infamy.

As I neared the exit, a blood-curdling scream sounded from the rear of the library followed by the blaring tone of the building's fire alarm. Students rushed toward the exit, but, on instinct, I ran toward the noise. Even without my power, my gut reaction was toward danger. That was probably something I needed to work on.

A young woman slammed into my shoulder as she made her way outside and froze like a deer in headlights as she saw my face, then took off running once more. She looked familiar somehow, but there was no way I could have known her. I shook it off and continued to where the scream had sounded.

A thick plume of black smoke billowed toward the vaulted

ceiling, and I listened as the huff of a fire extinguisher pulsed out its condensed and pressurized water. As I reached the rear of the library, Verne—extinguisher in hand—and a few other students stood aghast. The entirety of the Magic and the Occult shelf—which, albeit, had been limited—had gone up in flames before Verne was able to put it out.

But that wasn't the real problem. That wasn't what had elicited such a horrendous scream.

No, that lay on the floor before the stack.

The witch's body was limp, yet still twisted as though she had been pulled through a jet engine. The blood around the wounds where the bones of her ribcage jutted through her skin had long since dried to a crimson black and began to flake away, leaving the muscle raw and exposed. Her lower jaw jutted past her nostrils; great fangs pointed up and pierced through her cheeks. One of her feet looked like a flipper, scaled and muted and dead.

Shit. A third body. And in a very public, very human arena. The students who'd remained inside during the fire alarm gasped even as their fingers fumbled with their phones to snap pictures, ready to share their horror with the world.

The MAW would not be able to keep these murders quiet any longer.

CHAPTER 10

I did my best to ensure the integrity of the scene for the ten minutes it took the MAW to arrive. Putting on my "adult voice," my arms acted as a barricade as I shooed the gaping horde of students away from the body and instructed them to sit quietly at one of the large, oak study tables so they could give witness when called upon. Verne wanted to help, I could tell, but his body was frozen where he stood. The empty red canister he'd used to douse the flames lay dormant at his feet.

Two of the librarians who'd initially fled the building reentered the scene, but upon seeing the magically manipulated body of the young woman—and potentially recognizing me—they clustered near the students and deferred the matter to the witches. As much of a witch as I was without my magic. Foam and ash and other remnants of the lost tomes fell from the shelves to contaminate the body. But from what I could tell of the dried blood and pliable limbs, rigor mortis had set in and gone. The poor girl had died long before today and definitely not here.

Learco and his agents entered the library like a calvary of horse hooved soldiers, clomping through in a forceful show of exactly who was in charge of the situation. Startled by my presence, his step faltered a bit before he regained his composure.

I winced and waved timidly.

"What the hell are you doing here?" he asked under his breath when he reached me.

A few of his agents had already spelled a barrier around the body and the fire while others had formed a line near the waiting students. They stood at attention and waited for his direction.

"Research," I whispered back through gritted teeth.

I opened my tote to show him the spine of the book I'd borrowed from Verne: *From Changelings to Succubi: The Fright of the Fae Folk In Our World*. He twisted his lips into a frown.

"This is not good," he said. "Three witches dead, and one found here."

"She didn't die here," I blurted, and he tilted his head in question.

"What I mean is, it's obvious she was moved." I was trying for helpful. Fuck, I hoped he thought I was helpful. "I didn't touch the body. No one has since we found it. But Verne did have to put out the fire. Everyone who stayed when the alarms sounded is waiting at that table for interrogation."

I'd handled the scene in the way I thought he would. I crossed my fingers that could give me some brownie points. At the very least, it was proof that I was trying to make amends.

"Thank you, Mister Cullen," Learco said stiffly. His ragged breath told me he wanted to say more, but the words just wouldn't come. "If you would like to wait in the—"

"Darragh Cullen!"

Learco froze as I turned to face the booming voice that had called my name. A heavy-set man, eyes black and brimming with the kind of mirth that only came with self-determined importance, sauntered toward us. His gray woolen trench coat flapped at his sides, and he held a matching bowler hat in his small, thick hands. A band of chestnut hair circled his otherwise balding head. Thin lips twisted into a semi-smile.

"At last, we meet," he said and extended his hand between us.

His words carried the nasal, clipped cadence of the Northeast.

"Leland Hyde," he said as I grasped his hand in the firm shake my father had taught me was a sign of respect.

I felt my muscles tense as he spoke his name. So this was the infamous Leland Hyde. A fixer of sorts of the highest rank within the Moral Authority of Witches, Leland—like those who'd held his rank before him—was the monster who hid under young witch's beds and sliced off their toes if they dared to step out of line. He was the person called when the MAW's local intimidation tactics proved fruitless, and many of those witches never saw another full moon. Hell, he was the one Learco's traitorous old assistant, Samara, had been given to after she summoned the dead and nearly blew up the state capital building in an effort to steal Learco's station for herself. His new assistant—Rafael, wasn't it?—wouldn't even look toward the man directly.

"I was just thanking Mister Cullen for his efforts in preserving the scene before we could arrive," Learco said. "And suggesting he wait for questioning in one of the conference spaces over there."

"'Mister Cullen?'" Leland guffawed. "Come on, Clarke. Everyone in the order knows you two are boyfriends."

Learco's entire body went stiff as he closed his eyes and sighed.

"It's complicated," he said.

"Is that so? The head of the southeastern division dating the witch who exposed magic and broke nearly every single one of the Moral Authority's tightly held conventions? I can't imagine how that would be complicated."

Sarcasm notwithstanding, it was Leland's curt tone that made me bristle. I smiled weakly.

"I'm here as a witness, not a boyfriend," I said, trying to quell the awkwardness of the situation.

"And what was a witch in his forties doing in a human university library?"

Leland's tone wasn't the least bit accusatory. It made the words bite even harder somehow.

I looked at Learco briefly before I spoke. As far as I knew, he still had not informed the MAW about the bargain we'd made with Balor to bring the Fomóraiġ back into our reality. As far as the MAW knew, the Fomóraiġ were still simply fairytales.

"I was visiting with my employee, Verne," I said, nodding toward the still frozen witch lingering just beyond the agents' protective circle. "After the fire at my shop earlier this week, I just wanted to make sure he was doing okay."

It was half true, at least, even if it wasn't the full story.

Leland wet his lips and smiled. His demeanor was all at once intimidating and dismissive. I could tell from the way he shifted his eyes that he did not miss a thing.

"Ahh, yes," he said. "The Defend Mankind From Magic attack on—what do you call your little store? HEX? Seems like you manage to squeeze yourself right in the middle of quite a few unsavory circumstances, Mister Cullen."

"Luck of the Irish, I guess."

If he wanted to rely on sarcasm, I could give it right back.

Learco cleared his throat as Leland let out another hearty laugh.

"I can see why you like him, Clarke," he said. This time I wasn't sure if he was taunting us or not.

His demeanor stiffened as he pushed past us to take in the carnage that had brought him here in the first place. I smiled timidly and shrugged as Learco's eyes widened, urging me to step away and wait.

"What do you make of this, Clarke?"

Learco moved to Leland's side apologetically. It was a site

to behold. I'd only ever seen Learco as self-assured, positive his every step would land where he wanted it to take him. To see him cowering in Leland's presence was strange.

"I've not yet had an opportunity to fully survey the crime scene," he said.

As they were speaking, I saw the opportunity to slowly step away. But Leland was having none of that.

"Cullen!" he bellowed. "What do you think?"

"Uh—" I stammered, walking shyly forward to stand beside him. "She wasn't killed here. She's been dead for at least twenty-four hours judging by the lack of rigor in her limbs. So that means the body was placed here, and the fire was started to draw attention to it. Either the killer's getting cocky, or he wants to be caught."

I used male pronouns purposefully, refusing the gender-neutral words that belonged to Madison, but Leland paid that no mind. I bit my lip as I hoped the statements had gone over well, dialogue I'd borrowed from those true crime dramas my parents liked to watch when I visited.

"See? This is why I keep insisting he would be an asset to our organization," Leland smiled.

Learco had asked me a few times to consider joining the MAW. Hell, our first real meeting—before everything went crazy, before we even started dating—had been a fancy meal and a pitch to become one of his agents. Was that pressure from Leland Hyde the entire time? Suddenly the ask felt less like flattery and more like keeping their enemies closer.

Leland nodded, and the guards took down their circle to let him investigate the scene close up. He huffed as he eyed the blackened laminated paper documenting the section and ran his finger through the ash on the shelves. It had gone up so quickly, the wooden stacks themselves were barely more than singed. The books, though, were lost. Not that there was anything of real worth there anyway. But it was still heartbreaking to see.

He flung the tails of his trench coat out behind him like wings as he squatted his girth to get a closer look at the body. Learco's eyes darted to mine, and I raised my hands in the universal symbol of *I have no fucking clue what's going on either.*

"When did this happen?" Leland asked, still examining the corpse.

Learco urged my answer.

"My best bet is right around 11:50AM," I said. "Verne and I had been in the Magic and Occult section just prior and had only stepped into the study room to chat for about ten minutes. I was headed toward the door when the fire alarm sounded."

"That's right," Verne said, suddenly finding his voice. "Darragh had just left when I heard the alarm. I ran out of the study room to leave—thinking it was just another drill—but when I saw the flames, I grabbed the nearest fire extinguisher to put them out."

Leland swiveled sharply and eyed Verne up and down. His gaze lingered on the spent canister by his feet.

"Quick thinking, kid," he finally said. "You see anything else?"

"No," Verne demurred. "I had my head stuck in a book. But… thing is, I didn't *feel* anything either. No one cast a spell in here. There wasn't a single twinge of power."

Leland looked to me for confirmation, but I just shook my head with a shrug. I hadn't felt anything, but, being cut off from my power, I wouldn't have sensed any sort of pull anyway. Still, I didn't want to let him know I couldn't conjure. That would lead to a world of questions neither myself or Learco wanted to answer.

"An accelerant was definitely used," Leland said, rubbing his fingers together where he'd swiped them through the ash. "But the body? That's the work of all kinds of forbidden magic. So, the question is, why would someone use their power to kill this witch, but then not rely on magic to stage this scene?"

Learco's mouth gaped as he looked at me wide-eyed. I could not help but shudder. If I was right about the time of death from the decomposition of this body, the three witches had been killed while I still had access to my magic. And now that I didn't, this body was dumped, and the fire was lit by non-magical means. In a very public place with a very present me. I knew Learco wouldn't believe I was the killer, but it certainly seemed like somebody wanted it to look that way.

"What are you two not telling me?" Leland asked, the sharp, jovial lilt in his voice suddenly harsh and narrow as he watched the worry play out on our faces.

Shit. If someone was trying to frame me, Learco and I needed to tell Leland the truth—or at least a version of it—about my lack of power. I'd already experienced how ommission backfired. A lesson learned too late if looking at my lover's wounded expression was to be believed. But at least I was learning.

I took a deep breath, face scrunching as I turned to look the MAW's resident punisher in the eye.

Cold and empty, the white florescent light on the solid white walls and white lacquered table made it feel like I was sitting outside of time and space. The harshness of the overhead glow made the shadows cast the deepest of blacks, nearly as dark as Cernun's hair, and only served to amplify the perception of absence. Like there was light and dark, good and bad, and nothing in between.

I'd never seen the inside of the MAW's interrogation rooms before. It was not a pleasant experience.

"You really can't access your magic?"

Leland was still shocked as he paced the floor in front of me. I was glad Learco was there on the opposite side of the table and also glad they placed him opposite me instead of beside me.

"I can't," I admitted. "I can feel that it's there, but I just can't access it."

His pacing was a bit unnerving. I imagined it had started as an interrogation technique to throw his opponent off-guard. Now though, his frantic stepping back and forth seemed more like habit than offense.

"I've never heard of this before. Have you?" he asked.

I was glad he hadn't drawn a correlation between the magic and then the non-magic of the crime scene and my powered and then non-powered state. Or, if he had, he assumed it was just as absurd as I felt it to be. I really hoped it was the latter.

"We think it may have something to do with the trauma from the fire," Learco offered.

It felt good that he was trying to be helpful. That had to count for something, right? Though he'd already assured me it wasn't, it made me believe that all was not lost.

Leland took a seat in the chair next to Learco with a heavy thud. The girth of his stomach rubbed the edge of the table as he leaned forward to rest his elbows atop it.

"How does it feel? Being cut off?" he asked. He seemed genuinely, empirically interested. Almost as if he thought my loss of connection to my power was more important than the murders.

I shrugged.

"I honestly didn't notice it until we tried to perform the ritual to protect Cernun's house from the DMFM," I said. "And even that is a blur."

"We had just begun the rite," Learco explained. It was great that he'd found his voice again, even if it was the cold, professional tone he used when performing Moral Authority business. It had not felt right seeing him capitulate to Leland Hyde. Maybe the shock of seeing me at the library crime scene was finally wearing off, but I wanted to believe it was my presence making him stronger. "The three of us were calling the corners to form our circle when Darragh froze. His eyes went dull. Glassy. Like taxidermy. He stopped speaking, breathing. It was as if, suddenly, no one was home. His mind had left his body completely. It was incredibly frightening. And then he passed out."

Learco's voice cracked as he pulled forth the memory. I'd had no idea the moment had been so intense. I thought I'd called my element and simply passed out from the friction of what should have been and what did not occur. My brow furrowed as I looked across the table to him. I wanted to reach across and hold his hand, to thank him for taking care of me when it happened. But that would not have been appropriate, even if he wasn't upset with me.

"When I woke up," I added, "it felt like someone had slipped one of your magic dampening amulets over my head. Everything was fuzzy and sharp. Like a fountain gurgling inside of me, but it's attached to a live wire."

"But there's no charm," Leland said. "No spell sign around you whatsoever. Not an ounce of magical residue."

They were statements, not questions. I watched his eyes as his mind attempted to weave this information through the years of knowledge he'd acquired at the MAW. He seemed truly invested in figuring this out. A part of me wanted to tell him about my encounter with Balor so he'd truly have all of the information we did, but I held my tongue.

"And what happens when you try to conjure?"

I shrugged once more, wincing this time to showcase the combination of grief, loss, and pain that overwhelmed me when I tried to touch my power.

"I feel a jolt," I said. "Almost like the absence gets more intense. Like my magic wants to reach me but we are vibrating at opposing frequencies. It hurts like a hell for a minute. And then… nothing."

"Fascinating," he said. "And you've found nothing in the archive room to explain or cure this predicament?"

That question was for Learco. The look of sorrow on his face made me want to leap the table to wrap him in my arms, to let him know it was okay. My timid smile would have to do in lieu of my arms.

"Not as yet," he sighed. Even if he had discovered something, we couldn't let Leland know our search encompassed the Fae. "Though I have been a bit preoccupied with the murder investigation."

"Ah, yes!" Leland guffawed, slapping his knee and leaning back in his creaking chair as if he'd just remembered the real reason he was in Atlanta. "The young, dead witches. Dirty stuff, that is."

I was beginning to wonder why Leland had such a scary reputation. Between his boisterous laughter and witty sarcasm, he was exactly the type of guy most folks would want to spend an evening in the pub with, drinking beers and shooting darts. Though something told me those very same darts could meet the center of a pupil or the space between two vertebrae in the blink of an eye if things turned sour enough to leave you on his bad side. Still, I kind of liked this Leland. And I could tell Learco was growing more comfortable in his presence too.

"So… What's your working theory?"

Maybe I spoke too quickly. Learco glanced uneasily across the table, unsure of how to answer with me sitting there. But Leland obviously did not give a damn about pomp and protocol. He was definitely my kind of guy.

"We have one suspect currently," Learco finally said.

"Ah, yes!" Leland followed. I could see the rolodex of information spinning behind his eyes. "Madison Ridge. A young nonbinary witch in their third year of studies at Georgia Thaum. Bright and gifted according to their records. And, I believe, an employee at your little store."

This time, as his eyes lit on me, the glare of accusation was fully present. My heart leapt into my throat.

"They are," I said. Learco refused to meet my eyes as I peered across at him. "And… they have been obsessed with the ancient spells of transformation. If those even exist."

Now was not the time to hold anything back, at least when it came to the murder investigation. My breath caught as I remembered the look of pain on Learco's face when he discovered what I'd hidden from him.

"I don't think they did it though," I quickly added.

Learco remained silent and stone faced. His fingers tapped a syncopated rhythm on the table. It was obvious to everyone in the room he disagreed with my assessment.

"I studied your reports on the plane ride down," Leland said. "Madison's spell sign was found all over the first crime scene, with the only other residue being that of the victim. Pretty damning evidence there if you ask me."

My face crumbled as he stared me down. Maybe I really was a horrible judge of character when it came to hiring employees. First, I'd taken in—and even taken as my protégé—a young man so power hungry he'd attempted to kill me and two others, and then my hire to replace him had turned out to be a murderer. Would Verne and Stacey be the next to incite city-wide massacres?

"Madison's spell sign was not present at the scene of the second murder," Learco finally said, allowing a bit of my breath to return to my lungs.

That was great! That got them off the hook!

"Sounds like it's fifty-fifty to me now," Leland said. "I'd say the two of you need to find the actual scene of the third murder to rule Ridge out completely."

Learco's jaw gaped as my words floundered. An agent knocked against the window of the door and pointed to Leland when Learco remained frozen.

"I—I don't work for the MAW," I finally spat.

"Great!" Leland laughed, slapping his thighs again before rising to his feet. "Means we don't have to pay you. You fellas stay here and figure out your course of action, and I'll be right back."

"You just couldn't stay home and stay out of this, could you?!"

The door had barely closed when Learco leapt to his feet and punctuated his words with open palms against the table. His pain lit through with frustration was evident throughout his body. But I was as shocked as he was. This was the last thing I wanted to happen. It was one thing to date a man affiliated with the MAW, but I sure as fuck didn't want to be the affiliate.

"This is not how you make things up to me!" he yelled.

"I didn't know someone was going to dump a fucking body at the human university library at lunch time on a fucking Thursday!" I insisted, standing to meet his eye, but refraining from playing drums on the table between us.

He still had every right to be mad at me. I was the one

who withheld important information from him—details whose revelation could have prevented three murders—but this, today, was not my fault. I didn't want to be here any more than he did. And I certainly didn't want to end up on the Moral Authority's payroll.

"Fucking Fae!" Learco exclaimed. He'd picked up Leland's pacing habit. Maybe it was something about the interrogation room. "Trouble just seems to follow you around like it's getting free rides on your coattails."

I had no response. What he said wasn't so far from the truth. Traced back to its root, everything that had happened was my fault. I exposed magic to the world. If it had not been for that, Aiden and his father would never have targeted Cernun, Learco, and me in an attempt to gain power for their family line. We would not have made the bargain with Balor to bring the Dark Fae into our realm. The Defend Mankind From Magic maniacs would not have the power they held, their numbers growing all the time. And witches like Madison would not have become obsessed with ancient spell craft—spells that had seemingly lead to the deaths of three young witches now.

But good things had happened because of that revelation as well. Without it, our kind would still be suffering in the shadows, hiding, and terrified of revealing who we really were. The Moral Authority would still be just a shadow organization, operating in darkness with no real-world repercussions. Okay, so maybe that was still what it kind of was. But there would be no such thing as magical universities to teach our young witches more than what had survived in the family Book of Shadows. There'd be no witch museums like MA'AM preserving the artifacts of our histories. We'd not be free to express ourselves, to love ourselves, to be proud of our very being. And I wouldn't have met Learco.

Even if he was mad at me, even if this was the end of our

romantic relationship, I was truly happy he had been a part of my life.

"I asked for time," he said. "That's all I asked for. And you couldn't even give me that."

"I didn't expect for this to happen."

My voice was softer now, quieted by the sorrow that had overtaken my fear. I wasn't ready to accept that we were over, but I had to trust the cards that had been laid out on the table, no matter how the tarot deck had been shuffled.

"You never do, Darragh," he said, shaking his head and speaking more to himself than to me. "You never do."

The door jolted open as Leland strode through with a bemused grin plastered to his rounded features.

"If you two are done with your little lover's quarrel," he said. "Perhaps we can get down to business."

"We're not quarreling," Learco said as he moved to retake his seat.

"Please," Leland laughed. "I could hear the two of you bickering like magpies halfway down the hall."

He tossed a manilla folder onto the table between us and lingered expectantly beside the door. When neither of us moved to touch the folder, he sighed heavily and leaned forward to push back the cover. Grainy, washed-out images of the University Library stared back at us. I recognized the tall stacks and the 90s office-style carpeting immediately.

"What are we looking at?" Learco asked.

"Surveillance photos from the video feed at the library," Leland said. "Humans are slow, especially when it doesn't directly concern then, but they finally sent them over. Two of their cameras in the area weren't even working, but this one gives us some idea of what went down."

Learco leaned in to study the photos, and I had to stifle my smile when he turned them outward for us both to see. The view of the Magic and the Occult section was partially obstructed, and the quality was horrible, but I could plainly make out the area on the floor where the body had been dumped. In this photo, though, it was me talking to a stack a books, peeking out from behind another shelf. By the second still, I'd followed Verne off to the study room. The third saw just the books. It was in the fourth where the action happened.

I squinted to make out the figures—five of them: four standing and the fifth in a wheelchair, shrouded in an army green blanket. No one's face was visible from the angle of the camera, but it was obvious, even in the crude frame, they had purpose, intent. They may have been still, yet the photo brimmed with life. With one obvious exception.

Learco swallowed hard as he shifted to the next picture in the stack, like a flip book of action, right before the stick figure became whole and started dancing. As one figure doused the books in the section with whatever liquid they held in their flask, another dumped the body from the wheelchair. For some reason, the blurry aspects of the printed photograph made the young witch's corpse look even more gruesome than it had in person. Her twisted flesh was highlighted. The exposed bone formed flares in the image. The places where her skin turned to beast looked superimposed.

The camera captured the foursome posing the body, then using a disposable lighter to ignite the gasoline they'd doused over the books.

It was the final photo in the stack, however, which told us the most. Captured from an exterior angle and blown out a bit by the midday Winter sun, we saw our wheelchair bound witch, still wrapped in her blanket but with just a hint of her newly finned foot extruding along with three of our fire starters being welcomed by their compatriot through a fire exit. A quick in and a quick out from the alley with no one the wiser. They kept their heads low, with baseball caps shrouding their features. All except for the young person who was opening the door. Their face we could see clearly.

And it wasn't Madison.

"They look familiar," I said as I pulled the photo close to study her long blonde hair, her soft, round features. She looked so young and innocent. It hurt to believe she'd been caught up in such horror.

"She does to me also," Learco said as I handed him the photo analyze. His brow furrowed as he tapped the edge of the picture, willing it to speak.

I wracked my brain to place her somewhere. I was certain I'd seen her before. But the memory was as grainy as the photo.

"Pull out your phone!" Learco demanded.

That was it! That's where I'd seen her!

I scrolled through my photos to the last three I'd taken, and there she was, running from the Molotov cocktail that had just ignited inside my store. Her features were blurry, but unmistakable. She was even wearing the same denim jacket with the punk-inspired back patch.

Suddenly, my brain flashed on an image of her, one more clear than either of the surveillance photos. I saw the surprise, the utter fear in her eyes as she bumped into me while she was fleeing the scene after I'd turned back toward the scream. I had no doubt it was the same person.

Defend Mankind From Magic had dumped the body and lit the fire. I was certain of it.

CHAPTER 11

"Even if it was those fucks who set this scene, there's no way they murdered this witch. Not with how her body was mutilated."

We were back in Learco's office. Leland had sent us there with a hearty guffaw and a "See? You work good together!" before heading off to torment some other MAW agents. Without his presence, Learco was already back to his former, self-assured self. And he looked damn sexy sitting behind the walnut expanse of his desk, even if it was brimming with photographs of mutilated witches.

"I don't think the DMFM would work with a witch," I offered. "It's not their M.O."

"Nor do I think a witch would ever work with them," he added.

I could tell he still hadn't fully forgiven me, but the conspiratorial camaraderie of working on a case might just bring him around. He huffed as he stood and crossed the room to his bar cabinet—a fine, antique wood which matched his newly carved desk perfectly—and pulled out two crystal rocks glasses. He poured me two fingers of whisky and himself a shot of rum without even asking. Just like old times. Well, the "old times" of only a few days before which now seemed so far away. I smiled with all the sweetness I could muster—short of saccharine falsity—as he handed me my glass.

"This doesn't mean everything is okay now," he warned, staring deeply into my eyes for the first time all night. Damn, it felt good. "But Leland was right. Your impetuousness has a tendency to compliment my rigidity. And I don't want more witches to die because I'm too stubborn to see that."

"Heard," I smiled. I knew he was coming around. I still had a lot of work to do to prove that I trusted him—to prove he could trust me, but this was a start. "Plus, I don't mind complimenting your rigidity."

He rolled his eyes at my innuendo, but I could see a faint smile tickle his lips. I took a swig from my glass, grateful he'd started keeping the good stuff on hand when we started dating. It was such a small, sweet gesture on his part. I kicked myself for not having noticed it before.

"Okay," I said, forcing a stern look despite the smirk that fought with my cheeks as I leaned over the desk. "What do we know about the victims? Is there anything that connects them? To each other. Or to Madison."

"I'm serious, Darragh," he said. "This isn't a backdoor to fixing what's broken with us. We are focusing solely on the case."

"I know. That's all I'm doing."

At least a part of me meant it. I could put my feelings aside for one day to solve the brutal slayings of young witches. And if it happened to prove to Learco that I was trustworthy, if it managed to bring the two of us a little closer together, then who was I to stand in the way of fate?

He squinted as if he didn't believe me but pulled the red folder I recognized from when he'd shown us Angel's crime scene photos from his desk drawer nonetheless. His notes were meticulous, scrawled in his condensed, well-practiced hand and noting every fact, every observation from the case. He studied them silently, then turned to the black folder Rafael had slipped him on the way back to his office.

I'd expected a lot more cloak and dagger within the halls of the Moral Authority of Witches. Instead, it was folders and forms and bureaucracy. The color-coded folders may have said "For Eyes" in bold black letters, but the stamps, stickers, and signatures were done by hand and not power. Or at least not our kind of power.

"You already know about the first body found," he said when he'd finished reading, pushing the folder toward me in case I wanted a refresher of the awful scene. "She appeared to be the first victim, discovered Monday morning in her off-campus apartment by a cleaning crew her parents hired out for her. The victim was found nude atop her bed. The only spell signs present were her own and those of Madison Ridge."

I noticed he referred to her as "the victim," even though we had both met her and spent a little time with her when she visited Madison at HEX. I supposed it made it easier to focus on the facts instead of the dead. That was one of the—many—reasons I did not think I could ever work for the MAW. With the exception of a few twenty-something trysts with some questionable men, I'd never really been able to separate the person from the body.

"Forensics places the time of death sometime between 3 and 4AM the previous evening. However, judging by the decomposition of the victim discovered by you today at the University Library, it's possible that our first discovered victim was actually the second murder. Though I won't have that report until the hour."

I nodded and checked the clock on the wall. It was already pushing three in the afternoon, and I hadn't eaten lunch. I wondered if I could entice Learco over to that cute little pub nearby.

"The second victim—one Daniel Shelley—was a twenty-eight-year-old male working in marketing at a witch-led firm in midtown. His bosses became concerned when he spent the early part of the week changing all of his pitch decks to include images of"—he checked his notes—"'red and yellow clouds' and speaking of the 'wild things coming.' So, when he didn't show up for work that morning, they contacted us with their concerns. Granted, with the search for Madison and the investigation of Angel's death, it took my agents a bit longer than it should have to arrive at his West End apartment. Forensics, again, places the time of death sometime between 3 and 4AM the previous night."

The idea of red and yellow clouds seemed somehow familiar to me, but I wasn't sure why. They swirled in my head like a dream I couldn't quite place. I shook it off as I took in the photos Learco handed me.

Daniel, too, lay prone on his bed, twisted beyond recognition by whatever curse had been placed upon him. His limbs, maligned and akimbo, were shattered; bone spurs jutted to leverage him off of the mattress as if the whole of him had been impaled on spikes. Elk-like antlers protruded from his forehead and his skin sagged away from his features with the rips. It was truly horrific.

"What do you think he meant by the 'wild things coming?'" I asked.

"Our best guess, all things considered, is that whatever spell is causing these deaths takes its time to work through the system."

"Like it's trying to prime them for the transformation."

"Exactly." I couldn't help but notice the slight twinge of a smile as Learco noted my engagement. I had to admit it felt good—not just working with him, but also examining the pieces of the puzzle, putting them together where they fit, no matter how horrendous the image they created. "He knew what was coming," Learco said. "His power sensed it, even if he couldn't ascertain what it meant."

"But no spell signs but his own were found in his house, right?"

"They were not." Learco's partial smile reformed its frown. "Though, if the spell took days to materialize, it's highly possible it was placed on him elsewhere and simply carried back to his home."

That made sense, but I still felt like some residue of the witch who cast the spell would still be on the body. When I said as much, Learco nodded.

"Depending on the potency of the cast, spell signs can be present for up to two weeks—both in the space of the ritual and upon the object or person to whom the spell was attached," he explained. "It is troublesome to find only his own. Even if the spell did occur elsewhere."

My mouth twisted as I thought it through aloud.

"The likelihood of three separate witches not within a coven stumbling upon and attempting the same spell—especially one like this—is nil to none," I sighed. "Do you think it's possible our murderer is forcing these witches to perform the rite themselves? That would explain why only their own spell sign was present."

"It's possible," Learco considered. "But to force a witch to perform magic without the force of one's own power seems improbable."

"Maybe the killer kidnapped a loved one? Or threatened their mom?"

I'd seen enough of those procedural dramas on TV to know murderers liked to play dirty.

"You're delving into speculation," Learco grinned at my obvious eagerness. "We have to stay with the facts at hand."

"Fine," I moaned, pulling myself back from my ever-expanding fantasy. "What do we know about the third body?"

"The latest victim, whom as I said I believe may be the first, has not been positively identified. However, a young witch from Jonesboro, just south of the airport, was reported missing last weekend when she failed to return home after a night out here in the city with her friends. Here name is"—Learco reopened the black folder he'd been handed as we walked in—"Jenna Camp. Agents are on the way to her home now to investigate. And forensics should have a confirmed ID and time of death shortly."

I sighed and leaned back in my chair, placing my hand over my mouth as I thought through the information.

"But we can probably guess that it's her," I said. "And that the time of death was between 3 and 4AM. If that's not too speculative."

Learco smirked but nodded. The whole of the case was laid out before us, and it wasn't very much to go on. Whatever witch was responsible for the deaths was certainly a powerful one— though not powerful enough to manifest the transformations into beasts we were both sure was the intention. In the end, it all came back to the ancient rites Madison had been so insistent we investigate. We both saw as much, but Learco did me the courtesy of not openly accusing them. Not again anyway. Still, it really did not look good for Madison, wherever they were.

I sighed heavily as I finished the whisky in my glass.

"Your job really is like one of those cop shows, huh?"

Learco smiled and leaned back in his seat, crossing his arms over his chest. The way the tight, fine fabric of his button up bulged across his pecs and over his biceps made me bite my lip. My eyebrows bounced suggestively before I caught them.

"Not normally," he said. "More often than not it's preventative presence or fining some grandma because she spelled the neighborhood kids to stop letting their dogs shit in her yard. That and schmoozing with the moneyed elite to keep us afloat."

"You like the schmoozing though," I laughed. "I remember

your fancy, always reserved table at the Dove and the Crow quite well."

"One of the perks of my position," he shrugged.

An amused expression swam, like relief, across his face. It was nice to see a genuine smile he didn't try to pull back. I leaned forward, wishing there wasn't a desk between us.

"You had the chef prepare the same Irish meal my mother made for every single one of our major celebrations!" I mused. "And it was fucking amazing."

Learco grinned as a faint blush coated his cheeks.

"We do our research," he said. "Plus, after I met you at the Botanical Gardens, I kind of wanted to make it special."

"I went into it thinking you were going to flame me!"

"I still might," he joked. At least I thought he was being funny. There was humor dancing behind the mischievous glint in his eyes. Right?

"I also thought it may have been a date," I added. "After meeting you at the Botanical Gardens, I kind of wanted it to be."

The red in Learco's cheeks intensified briefly before he shook his head and tapped his palm on the desk.

"No," he scolded. "We are not doing this. Right now, we are working together to solve this case. This is not about us. This can't be about us. We need to figure out who is killing these witches so that it does not happen again. And to ensure Madison, if innocent, goes free, we really need to find them."

It was a nice gesture on his part, allowing the space for Madison's innocence. Even if he wasn't ready to talk about or move on from our spat, it showed me there was room for grace in the future. I smiled, nodded, then stretched my limbs back into work mode.

"Have you even eaten lunch yet?" Learco asked. His voice was softer now. Sweet even. "We should get you some food."

I heard my stomach growl, but my hunger was the last thing on my mind. Learco was right. The lack of a second spell sign meant nothing if the magic had been placed on the victims at a secondary location and given time to work. Especially with as mutilated as each of the corpses were. Time and the transmogrifying elements could have diminished those spell signs to nothing. We couldn't use it to rule out Madison. And with the signs at Angel's alongside their insistence on discovering the old spells, they seemed nestled right in the core of the murder spree. But there was another possibility.

A horrible thought raged through me. Jenna, the potential third—or first—victim, had been missing for days before her body was dumped by the DMFM for us to find. And now no one knew where Madison was.

"What if Madison's not in hiding?" I gulped. "What if they're a victim too?"

I phoned Cernun from the backseat of one of the MAW's black sedans as we barreled down the highway from Buckhead back toward more familiar streets. We'd decided we could grow two trees from one seed at Aunt Paulina's: lunch and a second chance at talking to Katrina to try to figure out where Madison could have gone. I'd also convinced Learco to bring Cernun in on the new developments, particularly with what was going on with the new connection to the DMFM. It would feel good to have the coven back together again. Sort of, anyway.

"Hey, Love," Cernun whispered through the line. Our car wove seamlessly through the regular traffic congestion where 400 merged with 85 as if by magic. "I was just about to call you. The boys have been here since six, so we're wrapping up for the day. Want me to stop at the market to pick something up for dinner?"

"I'm with Learco," I said, then to Cernun's quiet astonishment, I added, "Not like that. There's been another murder. Meet us at Aunt Paulina's. We can go over everything there."

Learco side-eyed me as I finished the call, but he didn't comment. He clutched the newly acquired forensics report in his hands. The paperwork only served to confirm what we already knew. The dead witch who'd been dumped at the library was indeed Jenna Camp. She had died between the hours of 3 and 4AM on Friday night/Saturday morning, making her the first known victim. We had a witch serial killer on our hands.

Rafael, from his perch in the front passenger seat, looked as worried and overwhelmed as I felt. Murders like these were a lot to take in, much less within the first two weeks on the job. If he made it through it all with his sanity intact, Learco may have finally found the right assistant.

"She didn't die at her apartment," Learco said as he reviewed the pages. "Agents found her car abandoned in the median just north of the airport. We believe she was driving home from her night out when the transformations began to occur. She must've had time to pull over and exit her vehicle."

"So she died there. Next to the highway. Alone," I sighed. "No one—no magic to protect her."

Learco grunted as he closed the file. He shifted in his seat to look me squarely in the eye.

"We're going to find Madison," he assured me.

I was far from certain. So much pain had littered the last week. And I didn't even have access to my power to safeguard those whom I loved. Or to defend myself. My eyes fell to the green spine of the book on the Fae legends I'd borrowed from Verne, still nestled inside my tote. I'd been hoping to find some parable in its pages that could tell me what to do or, at the very least, mentioned the thorn Balor had used to mark me. If I could find the root, so to speak, I could cut the chains of the spell. But all that would have to wait.

We careened into my neighborhood, and the car idled in the fire lane in front of the restaurant to let us exit. Rafael leapt out to open the curb side door and held a stoic expression as we bumbled out. My home shone in the afternoon sun from just up the street. Damn, it would feel good to retreat there, to snuggle up in my own bed, to have my own things surrounding me, to cut off ties to the outside world. But that would have to wait as well.

Paul raised his eyebrows at me as we entered, then nodded toward the back booth where Cernun was already waiting. Katrina sat on the opposite side of the restaurant, rolling silverware at a two top. She barely looked up when we walked in. The sunlight on her closely shorn, blonde hair looked like a halo against the window.

It was that golden hour between lunch and dinner service when the bar got to rest and reset for the night ahead. I was glad it was empty. That would make it much easier to talk about the things we needed to discuss. As always and like magic, Paul had our drinks in hand and was walking over to us before we'd even joined Cernun at the booth. I slid in next to him, and Learco took the bench across the table. Rafael waited by the entrance and tried to appear as if he wasn't mystified by the local art and scantily clad pin-up girls that covered the walls.

"Don't you go making her upset again," Paul warned as he slipped the beer, red wine, and Old Fashioned between us. "You might be my favorite customers, but she's my flesh and blood."

"We do need to talk to her if she's open to it," I sighed. "But we'll try not to piss her off."

Paul frowned. His lipstick was already smeared across his chin, and his wig was set a little further back than it should have been. He paused as he tapped his fingers on his tray, then shrugged.

"I know y'all are just trying to help," he frowned. "I'll ask her if she's willing, but it's up to her when and if she comes over. You having the usuals?"

Learco and I both opted for the burger and fries, but Cernun went with a side salad and some tots.

"Best of both worlds: healthy and decadent," he laughed as Paul sauntered off to put in our order. "Now what's this all about? Are we making up and playing nice?"

"Playing nice," Learco smirked. "We'll see about the making up later. Leland Hyde has recruited the top witness in the latest body found to assist on the case."

I grimaced as we filled Cernun in on the day's happenings. His face fell. It was a lot to take in, even without the accompanying photographs. He sighed heavily as he viewed the pictures from the library's security system.

"That's my brother," he said, tapping one of the clouded figures in the image. "That's Jason. I recognize the coat. And the holier-than-thou stance."

Faerie shit! I can't believe I hadn't noticed it before! Though his face was shrouded, he wore the same knee length wool overcoat and kept his shoulders pulled back in that above-it-all manner. Even though I couldn't actually see it, I imagined his smug face staring down at Jenna's mutilated body.

"Fuck," I said. "'Soon, everyone in the world is going to know exactly what kind of devil you are.' He said that to us on the street."

Cernun frowned as he remembered the encounter. The violence in Jason's words was just the beginning. He'd promised as much. Had we been wrong? Was a witch—and a powerful one at that—actually working alongside the DMFM?

Cernun bit his lip while he gathered his thoughts. He groaned as he pushed the photos away.

"What if they found that poor witch's body on the side of the highway," he said. "The way she was deformed, the way she was killed… Magic is the only explanation. They could have seen it as an opportunity they were all too willing to grab onto."

"And they decided to display the body in a very public, very human place," Learco continued when Cernun stopped speaking.

"One with plenty of kids with lots of cell phones and social media sites to make sure when this got out there, it stayed," I finished.

That would explain how Defend Mankind From Magic became involved. And it made the most sense. They were organized, but dumb luck was more likely at play here than orchestration. Even if I didn't put it past them to utilize the same magic they hated—or envied—to kill a few of our own. I thought an answer would be comforting, especially one that didn't involve a witch—murderer or not—aligning with those hate mongers, but it was not.

Katrina approached our table with our plates and a mad as a midnight rooster scowl on her face.

"Darragh. Cernun. Fucking MAW," she said as she slid our meals between us. "What do you want?"

Learco motioned for her to take the empty seat beside him, but she crossed her arms over her chest, letting her tray dangle at her side like a weapon, like a shield. I slid my burger across the tabletop and moved to sit next to him as she took my vacated place beside Cernun. My hand gripped at Learco's thigh in comfort before he pulled it away.

"You here to accuse more witches of witchcraft since you

can't do your fucking job and find the real killer of Madison's best friend?" Katrina barked. "Or do you think I'm still hiding them somewhere since this happened?"

She slid her phone onto the table. From her newsfeed, a picture of Jenna's mangled body stared us down.

"We're just trying to find Madison," I winced. "We don't want this to happen to them."

"I already told you I don't know where they are."

Katrina swiped her phone back and crossed her arms over her chest. Her chin jutted forward in a stubborn pout. She raised her eyebrows, daring us to question her further. I admired her cocksure defiance. It was something a lot of rural queer kids possessed. Growing up in the middle of nowhere made us strong, self-reliant, and confrontational. There was a different strength to finding our tribes in the cities though. I was glad I'd been able to inhabit both.

"Katrina," Learco sighed. His voice was low and calm, but sympathetic and urgent. "I know I'm not your favorite person right now. Hopefully that's not because of me, but due to the organization I represent. But right now, the Moral Authority of Witches and my agents have the best chance of finding Madison—alive—and putting a stop to these senseless killings. But we need your help to figure out where to start. Did they say anything while they were with you that could help lead us to them?"

She huffed, but I could see that her resolve was waning. Her fingers tapped against her elbows, and her shoulders were not quite as tense. Her eyes glazed as she thought about Madison. Her affection for them was obvious, even if their first date had not gone exactly as planned. I knew from firsthand experience how intense situations could bond a couple. Or a threesome. I glanced at Learco with a sigh.

"You've seen the body," Learco tried again, nodding to her

phone between us. "There are two other young witches just like that in our morgue."

He paused a moment to let the realization that Angel's was one of those bodies sink over her. I knew he'd wanted to avoid affirming the library body as real—as actually magically manipulated—but I admired him for doing what he had to do. He took a sharp breath before he continued.

"I'm not here to debate Madison's guilt or innocence. But I do know I don't want them to end up like that."

Katrina's resolve faltered. Like me, she hadn't believed Madison to be capable of murder, but the sudden potentiality of them becoming a victim made the search all the more urgent.

"I don't know," she moaned, angry at herself now for not being able to remember anything useful. "I was at work a lot of the time they were there. With what they were going through, I should have stayed with them. But they insisted things needed to look normal. When they were gone, for a minute I thought I'd let something slip when you were looking at the security cameras, and you'd turned them in."

"I didn't," I sighed, then, to Learco's grumble, added, "You didn't."

"I know," Katrina whispered.

It felt good. At least our relationship wasn't ruined. That was something. But we still needed to find Madison.

"Is there anything they said?" I asked. "Anything at all. Even if it doesn't seem pertinent."

Katrina shrugged.

"When I was home, they spent most of their time worrying about you. Thinking their insistence on having you help them research those spells was why the MAW was at their dorm. Until I told them I'd seen you, they were convinced you'd been snatched up and flamed." She turned pointedly to Learco. "Y'all really need to work on your public relations if this is how young witches see you."

"I agree with that wholeheartedly," Learco responded to her obvious surprise.

"After we saw the news about Angel," she continued, "they really just talked about that. How they couldn't believe their best friend was dead. How they should have done something to stop it."

"What do you mean?" Cernun asked. "How could they have done something?"

A frown spread across Katrina's lips as she tried to remember their conversations verbatim. Paul watched with an eagle eye while pretending to polish glasses behind the bar.

"They told me Angel had been acting strange. 'Wild' was the word they used. That she'd been talking about 'going wild' or 'getting wild' or something like that for days before her death."

"That syncs with what we know about Daniel from his boss," I interjected.

"I just assumed they meant Angel was acting out. Being a rich little rebellious girl in her junior year of college. I honestly didn't think much of it."

"And you're sure they didn't mention wanting to leave. Or anywhere they would go?" I asked.

I tried to hide the desperation in my voice. I couldn't bear it if something bad were to happen to them.

"No," Katrina winced. "Nothing. They were antsy, but not in that wild hair up your ass way. More in a helpless way."

I frowned. I understood that helpless feeling all too well. But what could have driven them to leave the safety of Katrina's hideout? Especially with the MAW hunting them down. They were a smart witch. The last thing they'd do is place themselves in more danger.

"Thank you, Katrina," Learco said, and she nodded.

"You have to find them," she commanded as she stood and grabbed her tray from the adjacent table. "You eat up, and then you find them."

I fished a fry from my plate and tapped it against the ceramic. I was starving, but now the thought of food made my stomach turn. There was so much to do. The weight of the week was heavy on my shoulders as it settled there for me to lift. A Sisyphean undertaking even with my magic. And here I was, homeless—sort of—and disconnected from my power on top of it all.

"You heard the girl," Cernun said as he watched my hesitation and listened to my stomach growl. "Eat up. We've got a lot more on our plates when we're done here."

CHAPTER 12

The car slipped silently across the asphalt as we made our way to Learco's high rise condo in Buckhead. It wasn't the usual penthouse that came with his position—he'd forgone that perk for a slightly more "modest" three bedroom, four and a half bath on a lower floor—but the Moral Authority had insisted he remain in the building due to its proximity to their HQ. I also presumed it was because the building staff as well as the other floors were littered with agents who could be on hand at a moment's notice, but Learco had never verified as much.

The building itself was beautiful. Its white, minimalist facade towered above the trees like a monolith, a beacon to the area's rich and elite. Even from the street I could appreciate the balconies and outdoor patios nestled within the structure to give even those who couldn't reach the ground an opportunity to connect with nature. Plus, though I'd only been to his place a handful of times, I remembered the view from Learco's twentieth floor suite to be exquisite.

The doorman retained a calm, vacant expression as he welcomed us to the building.

"Mister Clarke. Mister Cullen. Mister Kyteler," he said.

It was his job to memorize each of the residents and their

frequent guests. And I would not have been surprised if Rafael had called ahead while we traveled.

"Thanks, Jeeves," I joked, but he didn't even crack a smile.

It was Learco's suggestion—moving the discussion to his place—as we wrapped up our meals and the early drinkers and dinner crowd began to swarm into Aunt Paulina's. I knew it didn't mean anything, not really, but I'd always been taught not to look a gift horse in the mouth. Or approach a donkey from behind.

"You know he's probably heard that a thousand times," Cernun quipped as we waited in the fobbed lobby to ascend to Learco's floor.

The elevator hummed when we left the ground. If I'd still been connected to my power, I would have felt a subconscious pull in the opposite direction, gentle and easy to overcome, but still guiding me back toward the earth all the same. Like a compass always pointing due North. Or a bird flying South for the Winter. Now, though, all I could feel was the vibration of the metal as the cables guided us upward.

"I know," I smiled. "But I figure eventually he has to react. Even if it's just an eye roll. And I want to be the one to make that happen."

"He's not a guard at Buckingham Palace," Learco smirked.

I'd watched him ease back into himself throughout our meal. He hadn't seemed to mind me remaining beside him even after Katrina left. At one point, our elbows had met, and he hadn't pulled his away. But I was trying not to read into that.

"Oh, really?" I replied. "And here I was certain you were the Queen."

Learco had painted the normally white walls of his space black which only served to bring out the white marble accents and the wide plank wood flooring in stark and comforting ways. A collection of artworks by Caribbean and African artists were individually lit along the long hallway between the foyer and the living room. The one used for entertaining, that is; a second living space held his television and a couch actually comfortable enough to sit on for longer than half an hour.

As we entered the real living room, I stared at the knit blanket still crumpled into a pile on the sofa. It was obvious Learco had chosen the couch instead of his bed the night before. I understood completely. I did that too when in the midst of relationship troubles. My bed just felt so vast and empty even if I wasn't used to it being shared nightly by my lover. The couch embraced me, although it did wreak havoc on my back.

The coffee table was covered with ancient texts and notecards, each splayed out and toppling over one another as they begged for new eyes to read them. He'd been working late and working intensely. I scanned over the books and noticed they were not about transmutation or the murder; they were each—all of them—centered on the Fomóraiġ, on Balor, and on the loss of a witch's power. He'd been working late, yes; but he'd been working for me. My heart ached a bit as I took in the display.

"Pardon the mess," Learco blushed. "Research." Neither of us mentioned what the mess contained. "Why don't we continue our discussion on the terrace? The sun's near setting, and, since it's chilly, I can get the fireplace out there going."

Though he often tried to hide it—designer suits aside—it was quite clear that Learco had come from money. If his ease at moving in those circles had not made it obvious, his personal collection of bejeweled masks and antique pottery did. Most of his biological family were scattered around the islands throughout the Caribbean Sea, though his niece had visited twice in the past six months as she tested for her MAW University placement. Having an uncle as Director of the Southeastern Division should have made her a shoo in for a prime spot, but, though she agreed to let him tutor her, she had chosen to test under an assumed name to get no preferential treatment. I really admired that about her. I saw the same determination of self in Learco.

The chill of the late evening air was its usual brisk as we stepped onto the terrace, though, this high up, the shivering breeze that dusk usually brought with it was much crisper. I shivered as I leaned against the railing to look out across the City in the Forest. Cernun draped a throw over my arms while Learco busied himself with the fire.

Even in the midst of Winter, the expanse of treetops wove like green waves across the hills before me. The clustered high-rise buildings of Downtown and then Midtown rose like castles through the thickets and gave the whole city the feeling of being Camelot. Or Oz. The setting sun sent passionate wafts of saffron and rose to dazzle anyone who dared to look up; and, to the East, I could see the fast-encroaching navy of night spread her wings from the horizon. I listened as the fire sparked then roared from the fireplace and relished in the sudden warmth that shrouded the right side of my body in its glow.

It was altogether a perfectly romantic evening. An outdoor terrace high above the city; fire blazing in its pit; a trio of wine glasses at the ready atop the glass patio table. Or it would have been if I hadn't fucked that up.

And if we weren't investigating a trio of gruesome murders.

I shook myself back to reality and turned to join the others sat around the cushioned, wicker outdoor furniture set, but I froze as my eyes landed on the fire. Thick red plumes, like feathers, danced, keeping an ecstatic rhythm as yellow flickers hypnotized me. There was something familiar there. In the colors. In the motion. I just couldn't place it. I listened as it called me to remember. To forget.

"I do still have your whisky, if you'd prefer."

I snapped out of it to see Learco hovering the neck of a bottle of Tempranillo above a wine glass. He'd already poured one for Cernun and himself. Maybe the romance of the evening was not completely lost.

"Wine's fine," I smiled and took my seat. "Thank you."

I held my glass up to toast, but Learco placed the bottle on a side table and pulled out his phone to review his emails. Cernun winced as he shrugged. I wasn't out of hot water just yet.

The ruby red wine tingled as it made its way across my tongue, its tannins and acidity rounding out the robust black cherry and tobacco flavors. I wasn't sure why I didn't drink more of the stuff. Red wines had the same complexities of flavor I cherished in a good whisky. Of course, they went down a hell of a lot faster too.

Learco cleared his throat as he placed his phone on the table.

"I think it's fairly safe to rule out the DMFM as an accomplice in these murders," he said. "Traffic cam footage places the red hatchback of a known member in the vicinity where the first victim's body should have been discovered in the early hours of the morning following her death. The area itself is unmonitored, so it's not concrete, but timing from the surrounding cameras suggests the vehicle stopped for long enough to find and stash the body before continuing further on 75."

"Fucking Jason," Cernun groaned, shaking his head as he dropped the file folders he'd been perusing to see if we'd missed anything in the crime scene photos.

"At least that's one assumption confirmed," I offered.

Learco nodded stiffly before he continued.

"So far it seems most people just think the photos of the library body"—he still refused to speak the victim's names—"are a hoax, manufactured and staged to get likes on the internet. Except for those with ties to the DMFM, that is."

"But they're going to believe what they want to believe

anyway," Cernun said. "Especially if it's disparaging to us."

"Indeed," Learco sighed. "Though something like this could help to bolster their numbers."

"It doesn't help that this time 'what they want to believe' is actually the truth," I frowned.

Learco nodded. "It's only a matter of time before the press picks this up and does their own investigating. The MAW may have its ties, but we stop short of interfering with the free press."

I squinted and cocked my head.

"These days, anyway," he quickly added.

"So where does that leave our investigation?" Cernun asked.

We all stared blankly at the space between us. Three witches were now dead, and there really was very little to go on. Aside from Madison, the MAW had produced no viable suspects, and it was becoming more and more evident—at least to me—that they were innocent. We were reaching a dead end.

"Here's something," I blurted. "Jenna—"

"Victim one."

"Died between three and four on Saturday morning, right?"

"Yes," Learco confirmed. "She was returning from a Friday night out with her friends when the spell took her."

"Okay," I said. I was getting excited. This had to mean something! I was sure of it. "And then Angel's death occurred during those same hours on Monday morning. Daniel was killed during the same time frame on Wednesday morning. Saturday, Monday, Wednesday. They're all two days apart. That has to be the length of time it takes the spell to fully enact!"

I was proud of myself as I took another swig of the wine and beamed across the table. I'd been able to figure out something Learco's legions of MAW agents hadn't even put together yet. Leland Hyde was right to bring me in. I still didn't want to work for them, but maybe it wouldn't be so bad to be a consultant.

Learco, for his part though, look horrified.

"Which means," he said stiffly, "another witch has already been cursed. And they will die in"—he checked his watch—"eight and half hours unless we can figure out who's behind this and stop them. And that's if there is a way to reverse the curse."

Shit. Somewhere in the city another witch was losing their mind, dreaming about "wild things" coming as their body prepared itself to break and twist into an amalgamation of beasts. Somewhere in the city a witch had no idea their bones were about to snap free of their skin as their skeleton broke its confines to adapt to a spell nature had no intention of supporting.

I couldn't help but picture Madison: alone and unsupported. Afraid to go to those, like me, whom they trusted because the MAW was out to get them. Lost and huddling as their mind shuffled through images of red and yellow horizons. Of beasts. Of death.

The terrace suddenly became a war room.

Learco, on his feet and on his phone, belted orders in a tone I wished he would sometimes use in the bedroom. But this was no time for that. Agents were dispatched to canvas the community, asking witches and mortals alike if anyone they'd come in contact with had presented the same signs as Daniel had at work in the days prior to his own terrifying death. Spells were being cast, but without a spell sign to center in on, the chances of them producing much, if anything, were slim.

Cernun scrolled through the newsfeed on his phone, searching for any mention of Defend Mankind From Magic to try to locate his brother. He wanted to focus on something he could control, and stopping their hatred from spreading was something. Plus, though it was a long shot, if they had seen anything when they absconded with Jenna's body, it could point us in the right direction.

I felt myself spiraling. I was helpless without my power. I sat cut off from the natural world. Even if there was nothing natural about this. All I wanted to do was stare into the fire. To get lost inside its flames. It felt like a feral thing come to claim me. As if, in the absence of my magic, it could swallow me whole. It sang lush lullabies, luring me into its warmth, promising sanctum.

"Hyde called in the archivists in Salem," Learco said, snapping me out of my trance as he dropped his phone back to his seat. "They are scouring their resources for any spells to do with shapeshifting or transmogrification."

"Smart," I said. "If we can figure out the curse being used, we may be able to work out a counter spell."

"But we still need to find the afflicted witch," Learco frowned.

It was a tall order, but if anyone could do it, it was the three of us. Still, the fire seemed so alluring. So comforting in its primitive power. Like it could take me. Like it could change the world.

"Jason just gave a press conference," Cernun moaned. "Only a few local stations have picked it up, but it's only a matter of time before this goes national."

He placed his phone on the table, propping it up on the stem of his wine glass as we snuggled close to see the screen. Learco's hand felt soft and strong against my shoulder when he nestled between us to watch. I imagined his fingers traipsing the contours of my skin, lingering in the anticipatory place between here and… there. Yes, right there. One more time.

By the Fae, I hated that I'd fucked things up.

Cernun's finger trembled as he hit play on the video he'd queued.

"We, as the people of these great United States, must come together to combat the scourge of demons who have overtaken our land!"

He had a biblical way with words, I had to give him that. Despite the pinched hatred in his eyes, Jason Marshall possessed a certain charisma when he spoke to the cameras. His capitulation of himself as an everyman, as opposed to being one of the masterminds behind an agenda of violence and hatred, played well upon his suffering persona. It was smart if not altogether wicked. If he could posit himself—and, by proxy, other non-powered individuals—as the victim, he could gain untold sympathy to his cause. No matter how evil it truly was.

"As you all know by now, my parents, God bless them," he continued, "took in one of these wretched creatures. Yes, Todd and Mavis Marshall rescued this demon, posing as an innocent lamb, only to be cursed by his vile, evil temperament."

Cernun stiffened. At least Jason hadn't said his name.

"And today," the DMFM mouthpiece preached through the tiny speaker on Cernun's phone, "we see what these Godforsaken fiends are all about!"

Images of Jenna's mangled corpse, her face and genitalia blurred, filled the screen as Jason spoke. The Magic and the Occult books raged with fire behind her like the pits of hell come to swallow her within their torment. Our own flames called to me from the closed quarters of the fireplace.

"We cannot let these creatures, these witches, terrorize our people with their magics any longer. It is abhorrent to the Lord Almighty. Defend Magic From Mankind has vowed—"

Cernun stopped the video.

"Fucking Jason," he said again.

"He sounds like a preacher on acid," I said, hoping it would bring some sort of comfort to the man I loved. One of them anyway.

"But that gets clicks," Learco frowned. Then, regaining his composure, he added, "Don't worry, Cernun. The Moral Authority of Witches will handle the DMFM. They want to up their stake in the game? We can move them from a nuisance to a problem."

It sounded scary, the casual way in which Learco announced his threat, but it seemed to appease Cernun. Slightly.

"It looks like he was on the steps of the courthouse downtown," I said. "Or the church next door."

"There are like five churches down there," Cernun growled.

"I have agents on the ground who can bring him in for questioning," Learco said.

"He won't come easily."

"We have our ways."

I was certain they did. And though I would normally be the first to call those means into question, I didn't want to rock the boat. Besides which, the way the flames were dancing—snaking forth with their yellow-red-yellow frills—was all too captivating.

I loved the way they swirled, like a dream, to fill my vision. I smiled as I leaned back in my chair to let the sight embrace me. I could see every bit of it—the flicker here that shot forth to become an inferno; the glimmer there which entranced the skies with its blaze. The fire which had always been. The storm which would always be. It was beautiful, wasn't it? The thing that would take us all.

Somewhere, far off in the distance, I heard voices calling my name. Familiar voices. Names I should have easily recalled. But they were so far away. And they would join me soon. In the flames.

Red and yellow. All this, and red and yellow.

It swirled around me like lost souls attempting form, like

wind attempting meaning through unspoken words. There was an uncanny valley between life and death—primary, primitive—where things were real and then they were not. Solid and then passed through to the beyond. Where power was formed. The source of it all. Burning through the ether in red and yellow flame.

But it wasn't fire. No, it was something else. The thing before the fire, before the air, before the water, before the earth.

There was a precipice. A cliff. Unsteady but firm.

Crumbling.

And I was atop it. There in the ether where everything was formed. Where everything that formed changed. A millennia of becoming. A moment of dissolution.

I breathed a ragged breath.

The nothing could take me, pull me into its red and yellowness. In the absence of my own, it had the power now. It was the power. And I was subservient to its will.

"There you are, clever witch. I was getting tired of waiting."

The voice was familiar, with a lilting boom that sent the air swirling around me, activating eternity with its words. It pulled the ether into being, gave it substance. Made it whole if not solid. I recognized the fire as that which I had always seen in Balor's eye. I could see it now: the depths of the pupil, the hazy prism of the iris. I was inside Balor's head, looking out to how he saw the world! It was beautiful. And horrifying.

"What do you want, Balor?" I called.

His laughter raged around me.

Twice before, when he had pulled me to his realm—or at least the space between ours and his—the whispering song of the other Fomóraiġ had been awful, washing me in the unease of their melody. This space though, with only Balor's thoughts and the silence in between, was so much worse.

I swallowed hard as his laughter came to an abrupt stop.

"Want," he said, his voice sounding from everywhere and nowhere simultaneously. "That's such a tricky word, want. You, clever witch, wanted to live, to keep your power from coursing through the veins of those impetuous Gowdies. And so you made a bargain. You entered into a deal to give you what you thought you wanted in that moment. But the wants of simple farmers… Oh, how they may change on the wind."

The ground shook violently beneath me. I steeled myself, bracing my legs hard against the crumbling rock. But somewhere inside I knew Balor was simply trying to scare me, not hurt me. It was almost like, as I was inside his mind, I could feel his thoughts. They were barely there—like smoke, like slivers of sheer fabric— seeping into me without his knowledge. I could nearly make them out.

"What are you talking about?" I called. "You gave us three years to complete our end of the bargain. We have not yet reached that time, so we have not reneged on our deal!"

"Yes, but I've grown so tired of waiting," he pouted, repeating the phrase for a second time as if that were reason enough for his actions. "And how you work against me! I can see it. Feel it. That's why I had to take your power. Lock it in a tower like a daughter destined to birth the one who would kill her sire."

I could see it now—my power!—wrapped thick with vines, but there, inside me. I could see it through his eyes. The whole of the magic he'd used to disconnect me from my power. And if I knew the curse, I could counter it!

It was a spell unlike any I had seen before. An ancient magic trapped in the mind instead of earthbound, its tendrils held a dull, lifeless weight beneath their sheen. With earth magic, I always knew how it moved. I understood the elements at play, working in tandem with my will to manipulate each strand toward a goal. Even my much rarer forays into key line magics were the same as each line coursed with the intrinsic pull of the world. Balor's curse originated from something else—somewhere I wasn't even sure he knew—and teemed with an alchemical power. Instead of using what was to push toward what could be, it moved nothing to something, ignoring natural and evolutionary lines. It was as fascinating as it was horrifying. But, at least while I was here, I could figure it out.

"You are something though, clever witch," Balor continued, carried away by his thoughts as if I wasn't even there, like I was just another of his memories—a daydream he was having. "Perhaps I was wise to claim you. To let you take my deal. Never have I seen a witch perform so much as a prayer, much less an aura push, once marked by my thorn. And yet you… But you work against me in your spirit. You come here, called to me by your power, and you stall yet again."

But I wasn't there. I knew it instinctively. My consciousness was—as Balor said—drawn in by the call of my power, but my physical form—my body—still sat on the terrace of Learco's twentieth floor condominium, frozen and entranced by the fire. A string of awareness connected me to my corporeal form. I had to be careful. Subtle. I had to work there and not here so that Balor would not be the wiser. I had to keep him distracted while I unbound his curse.

I felt my fingers twitch.

"How have I been working against you?" I bellowed. "The three of us have been researching ways to bring you through. So much of our magics have been lost. We haven't found the way yet."

Balor's scoff crumpled another foot of red clay from the cliff, and it took all I had not to jump away from the imagined warning. The ethereal hellscape ravaged around me—images of mine and Balor's histories intertwined and murky. Faces formed and dissipated. Bodies writhed in agony. For a brief second, I saw Madison, scared and alone and longing.

"Ah, yes," he said. "The Kyteler and the Clarke. Your little coven of deceivers. Working and toiling and bubbling and boiling. And yet you work against me. I've grown so tired of waiting. I should simply see myself through."

There was a madness to his thoughts. I recognized it as having always been there, idling behind his words, but there—in his mind—it converged with a frenetic energy. It worked to consume him— to consume us both—in its feral, unguided snarl.

I sensed him tug the string of awareness that still connected me to me. It strained against his pull. If he were to severe it, I would be contained there, forever a prisoner of his mind. I shuddered at the thought.

But my fingers! They were moving now in the real world. They worked an intricate weave, pulling carefully at the vines which meshed and intertwined to form a living tower around my power. I worked slowly, avoiding the thorns, avoiding Balor's attention, as I freed the first stem from the mass. It withered, decomposed, and vanished as if it had never been there to begin with. I felt the spark of my power, stronger now, begging to come back to me, to exist where it belonged. I began working another vine.

Balor's lunacy agitated the whole of the environment as it whipped through his brain. I was losing him, and I knew if he were lost, I'd be trapped with him. I decided to try a different tact.

"You made a deal with my coven," I called, stressing the pronouns to try to bring him back to himself, to try to differentiate us into two distinct beings. "You entered the deal, as did I, with agreed upon terms and agreed upon timing. If you so choose to renegotiate those terms, we must come to an amicable conclusion or else the bargain is voided."

Balor laughed, shaking the earth and dropping me to my

knees. I braced myself for a fall, but none came. A second vine pulled free from the tower.

"Our deal is solid!" he yelled. "And you will play your part, clever witch. That is a separate issue."

"How may I play my part without my power?" I asked, growing bolder as the vines loosened. "You obviously didn't think that through."

I knew I was taunting him, and I knew the risks of even mentioning my magic, but I rightly assumed his ire would blind him.

"I think through everything, simple farmer!" he screamed. "All of it. Every past. Every outcome. Find the means to complete your task in our deal, and your magic is returned. An incentive if you will."

The plane of his mind was shaking now, jostling in every direction at once. But this was anger, not madness. He had found his way back to himself. This was the rage which existed at the core of his fire.

"But you've grown so tired of waiting," I mocked. "Six months is just too damn long to go another day!"

A third vine fell from the tower. They were falling so much easier now. Just a few more to go and I would be free. I would be myself again. Fully.

"Six months?" Balor scoffed. "Over eight centuries I've been here. Trapped with my kin. Waiting. Waiting. Waiting."

I could see his recollection, feel the pain of his torment as the Fomóraiġ were expelled from our world. His thoughts, his memories, were laid out before me. I could see it all if I knew where to look, despite the disjointed nature of his mind. His past and his present were laid out before me.

"I will see myself through!" he called. "No clever witch, no simple farmer with their spells will stop me! The destruction of your own histories by your own hands shall see to that. I will be free! I will be free! I will be—"

His voice trailed into silence as the last vine fell free from around my power. I gasped as it surged within me, exploding forth to make me whole and pulling me back to my body, back to reality. I blinked rapidly as I clutched the arms of my chair, feeling heavy and solid.

"Where the fuck did you go?" Cernun asked.

He was crouched down in front of me, one hand on my heart, the other clutching my shoulder. Learco stood behind him, his face awash in a mixture of worry and relief. I breathed deeply and cleared my throat.

"Balor," I croaked. My throat was dry, and I could still smell the acrid scent of sulphur that had permeated his mind.

His words still echoed in my head, but this time they were my memory. My thoughts were my own. I was whole again. And I could feel the vibration of my power coursing through me.

"What did he do to you?" Learco demanded.

I smiled.

"It's what I did for myself," I said.

A quick thought sent my aura out to embrace the two men I loved. I didn't care that Learco was still angry. He and Cernun both deserved to feel the beauty of my emotions for them.

"You got your power back!" Learco gasped.

He didn't fight my aura. Instead, I felt his join the air around our bodies.

CHAPTER 13

The fire and our auras kept us warm even as our clothes came off. My skin bristled as first Cernun's then Learco's washed over me. I let mine lap against them with an ecstatic glee. It felt good to have it back, to be in control of my power again. But these two men, they felt so much better.

"This doesn't mean all is forgiven," Learco said, suddenly serious even as his spirit continued to pulse against the small of my back.

He looked so damn sexy in the glow of the fire. It swam his skin in enticing flickers of light and shadow as he stood before me. I could see his magic bound through with his sex like I was seeing us all with new eyes.

"We still have to talk everything through," he continued. "Figure it all out."

"I know—" I started, but he kissed me to stop the rambling apology from exiting my mouth.

The push of his lips intensified as his tongue worked its way to mine. I felt him throb against me, thick and perfect, before Cernun took each of us in hand and guided us, first one and then the other, into his mouth. Cernun's magic, too, wound through the air around him. I didn't even mind that it had taken an excursion into the darker recesses of Balor's mind to see it, or that it was fading now that I was once again my own. It was beautiful.

Lips still to mine, Learco let his fingertips trace intricate, excruciating designs across my chest. Slow and purposeful, my skin pricked where his touch had been and gone, longing for more. I let my body succumb to us, the three of us, the whole of us. Our coven.

One hand found the small of Learco's back—taut and narrow above the luscious curve of his ass—while the other wrapped the back of Cernun's head. Our auras meshed in a pulse of power I had never experienced before, even through all the times we had placed ourselves, naked and subservient, powerful and guided, upon the altars of one another's sex. As intoxicating as it was invigorating, I let it fill me.

My lovers did too.

As Learco's hand left my body, I felt his fingers twine with mine through the curls of Cernun's hair. Cernun growled and took us both, simultaneously, past his lips. Learco's thick shaft throbbed against my own as the warmth of Cernun's breath teased a tiny drop of pre-cum from me. His tongue worked the head of my cock before passing over to Learco's and back again. I moaned as our hands clenched to guide us deeper inside.

Cernun's mouth was quickly replaced by hands as he rose. Our lips met, the three of us, as we pushed and pulled at one another, begging to be closer. To feel. To touch. To discover.

"Turn around," Learco growled.

I spun and bent. My hands gripped to steady myself on the arms of the patio chair as Cernun moved to stand before me. His cock bobbed through the air in front of my face, and I wanted him. Smiling mischievously, he handed Learco a bottle before he let the head of his penis brush my lips. I didn't know where the lube had come from. I didn't care.

Learco readied himself and then me as Cernun teased my mouth with his dick. When finally he let me taste him, I was overcome with the sharp, pleasurable pain of Learco's member pushing inside of me. I gasped. I shuddered. The heat of Learco's body felt glorious on my back and he bent to kiss my neck, grinning wickedly at the sight of Cernun's hard dick in my mouth. When he rose again, I felt the whole of him fill me.

Cernun moaned as he pulled out of my throat, bending to kiss me before filling me once more with his cock. The night and the city were our witness as we fucked high above them. The Winter stars watched us there on Learco's terrace with envy. We were the whole of the world. We were every magic that had been before, every power there would ever be.

I came without touching myself, clenching as the spasms of my orgasm shot forth in ecstasy. Cernun cried out as he wrapped his hands around my head and filled my mouth. Learco growled as he finished inside me, pumping still—though slower now—to milk the last of his cum from his still hard, still throbbing member.

We collapsed into a pile before the fire. Our bodies twined with one another's, seeking out new canvases of touch, of pleasure. Our auras blanketed our nude and spent bodies.

I didn't want to move. The fire was so warm as it flickered its white and blue, red and yellow flames across my body. Cernun's leg draped across mine as he spooned me from behind.

"You know we have to get up, right?" he whispered. "Save the city from a witch serial killer and all."

"I know," I moaned.

I stretched across the carpet as Learco hung up his phone. He smirked as he tossed me my pants and finished buttoning up his shirt.

"There's been no sign of Madison," he said. "And the only complaints of a witch acting strangely turned out to be a husband in East Point being secretive as he planned a Valentine's surprise for his wife."

"And Jason?"

The concern on Cernun's face as he pulled his sweater over his head was palpable. I finished buttoning my jeans and clutched his hand in comfort. The DMFM certainly had their way of muddying the waters, but their actions—as violent and destructive as they were—served mostly as distractions to the real danger. Still, their numbers were growing, and we couldn't afford to overlook them any longer.

"Agents are keeping an eye on his hotel," Learco said. "But the moving of the body and the histrionics at play with their firebomb at both HEX and the library have convinced most people, and the news media, that the entire thing was simply a scare tactic by Defend Mankind From Magic to move citizens to their side."

I had a feeling a spell or two from within the MAW headquarters was also at play there, though they would never admit it. Spell casting to change a human—physically or mentally—was strictly forbidden by the Moral Authority of Witches. But most of us knew they rarely played by their own rules. It was one of the things the DMFM used against us.

"His speech and their rally that was scheduled for Saturday has been cancelled, and Jason booked a flight back to Albuquerque tomorrow," Learco continued. "So, we can at least rest easy in that."

"He's going back to regroup with Brian, Todd, and Mavis,"

Cernun sighed. "Or to be reprimanded for his little stunt."

Behind Cernun's worry, a glimmer of amusement sprung forward at the idea of his youngest adoptive brother being admonished by the others. But they were the ones we really had to fret about. Masterful manipulators, they could take Jason's inept attempt at exposing witch-kind as demons and turn it into something fruitful when given enough time.

We needed to find the killer and stop them so no more witches met that horrible fate and so that the DMFM had no more bodies to use in their plans. And we only had—I checked the clock on my phone—six hours to do it.

"We're back to square one," Learco groaned.

"We're not though," I said, and my lovers leaned forward expectantly. "The next victim is Madison. I'm sure of it."

The clarity that came in the afterglow of sex was its own kind of magic. I saw the ghastly image of Madison's face—scared and alone—which had swirled through the ravages of Balor's mind when he pulled me there. I hadn't paid much attention to the sight before, thinking it more of the mind games the leader of the Dark Fae was playing on me, but now I was certain of what it meant. Madison was slowly succumbing to the wildness that had taken three other witches.

And though I didn't know how to find them, I knew how to stop it when we did.

"You're sure about this?"

I nodded in the affirmative as we stood in the porte-cochère of his building, waiting for the second car to arrive. His sedan already idled in the drop off lane with the driver as Rafael directed the taxis and Broomers attempting to pull in to find another way around.

"I am," I assured him for the tenth time in the past half hour. "I know Madison is his next victim, and I know exactly where they would go. I saw it when I was in his mind. It was all there, and barely cohesive, but I just… knew."

"And you know this isn't just a trick? Another one of his mind games?"

"It's not. He kept saying shit like 'I've grown so tired of waiting' and 'I should see myself through.' At first, I thought he was just complaining about us not finding a way to secure our bargain yet. But then I realized, he's been trying to come through on his own. He wants to inhabit our world, even if it's in a witch's body."

"And he's ripping them to shreds when he tries," Cernun frowned.

A second black four door slipped silently behind the first. Learco shifted into boss mode.

"Alright," he said. "Leland Hyde will meet you outside Angel's apartment building. No one has entered, though there are confirmations of sound coming from within her unit. Based off your vision, we can assume it's Madison. Leland is on site, but only as a courtesy. I am still the ranking official here. He has been instructed not to go in unless I send him."

His austere expression faltered a bit as his eyes flitted between us.

"Are you sure you two will be alright in there until I arrive?" he asked.

Our argument may not have been fixed, sex aside, but his concern and trust in that moment spoke volumes to his care.

"We'll be fine," Cernun said.

"Definitely," I agreed. "We're just going in to be there for Madison. To give them some sort of comfort. Balor won't be there physically. And his energy will be focused on breaking through. Besides, we should still have a few hours before all hell breaks loose."

Learco scrunched his lips tight, but he nodded. He shook his head and stared off at the streetlights with a hearty sigh.

"I'll be there as soon as I can," he said. "Hopefully, whatever Salem faxed down will be the answer."

Cernun's shifted eyebrows asked the same question I was thinking.

"The spells contained in our archive rooms are too dangerous to send digitally, even encrypted. So we still rely on a phone line and a fax machine—"

"In a secret room with a fingerprint and an eye scan for access," I joked, but Learco didn't smile.

"—And a spelled lock," he added.

I was grateful to the agents who'd spent the last few hours poring over the more extensive archives up there in Massachusetts for these spells. I knew how dangerous they could be in the wrong hands. Or, at least I was starting to realize as much. Even if a larger portion of me believed the magic of our ancestors should be public knowledge. Learco had been especially apprehensive about this part of the plan. But hey, if we were going to fight an ancient Dark Fae, we needed ancient magics to do so. He'd insisted, and with Leland's approval, they'd sent everything—even the mentions deemed merely fairytales or flights of fancy. Though it was unlikely many—if any—of the MAW agents believed in Faerie Magic as they faxed things over, Learco would know what to look for as he sorted through the pages.

He side-eyed the waiting vehicles, then kissed us both on the lips before he moved to open his car door.

"I'll have Leland and a team meet you there," he called as he disappeared inside. "Good luck."

Leland Hyde tapped his expensive loafers against the curb outside of Angel's apartment building. His arms crossed his chest atop his well-formed belly, and his face held a stern expression, only supplanted by the glimmer of amusement in his eyes. He nodded when he saw us, freezing his eyes on Cernun.

"Cernun Kyteler," he said, extending his hand as he'd done when meeting me. "The famed third leg of this Eiffel Tower, here."

Cernun gave him a firm handshake and chuckled at the joke. He always did have a thing for crass humor. But, then again, so did I.

He asked, and I answered again—for the eleventh time in half an hour—of my assuredness of the plan.

"The—" I started, then swallowed hard as I looked to Cernun.

We couldn't afford to let Leland Hyde, and, by proxy, the Moral Authority of Witches know about the Fomóraiġ—that they were real, or about our bargain with them. At least not yet.

"The witch who bound my powers—" I continued. "Got those back, by the way. When he did so, I think he inadvertently formed a bridge between our minds. He—uh, I think he wanted to use my magic to complete his plan of transmutation on these witches. Like he needed the extra oomph."

It hovered somewhere between a half-truth and an outright lie, but it was as good as any other explanation.

"Ah, yes. Aiden," Leland said.

I hid my shock as a shudder upon hearing that name. Cernun, to his credit, remained completely neutral.

"Those Gowdies always were obsessed with shapeshifting, huh?" the MAW fixer continued. "All the way back to Isobel's original confession."

I swallowed hard as I smiled. Of course, it made sense to pin this all on Aiden because we couldn't tell them about Balor. He was still at large from last September, and a nationwide MAW hunt was already underway for him. It was quick thinking on Learco's part to pin it on him. A few of the spells in the Gowdie Grimoire they'd commandeered were nearly as awful and insane as those being used on these witches which made it believable. And if the assumption was made that he'd managed to create at least a spark of his own magic, he was the perfect pawn. Plus, it kept the Moral Authority agents from wasting their time and money searching for a suspect who wasn't even in our realm.

It worried me a bit that Aiden had managed to stay undetected for six months now, but with no spell sign to track, and the belief that the Gowdies were little more than parasites keeping him low on the MAW's priority list, I supposed it made sense. Besides, that was a problem for another day—if we managed to make it through defeating Balor without nulling our bargain and being whisked to the Faerie realm and saving Madison without them growing gills.

"When Clarke told me you two were going in alone," Leland continued, "I had my doubts. But as you've both faced him before and lived, I'll defer to him on this. And you are the one who figured this all out. Maybe we consider making your agent status permanent?"

I scoffed loudly, then cleared my throat. Leland had the grace to ignore it.

"I'm just fine with my shop," I said. "But I do want to help my friend."

"Right you are," he said.

The smile fell from his face as he shifted into mission mode in much the same way it did with Learco. It made me wonder if MAW agents were placed under some sort of spelled hypnosis when it came to the tasks they were required to handle, but that, too, was an issue for another day. Leland's body stood a few inches higher as he pulled himself to attention and laid out the plan. His part of it anyway.

"I have eight agents and myself in strategic positions around the apartment building. We know, as the curse is placed days in advance, the likelihood of the Gowdie witch being here now is slim. However, there is the possibility he will try to return to his victim to discern if the spell has worked or not. Once you have entered and confirmed the presence of Madison Ridge, I can have a dozen other agents on hand. No one will enter that apartment other than Clarke when he arrives. At his orders, we are leaving this to you. But I will be here—just outside—if you need me. If anything goes wrong, I'll take command."

I got the impression that Leland was not used to being sidelined when it came to the action, but he seemed to kind of enjoy being put in his place. At the very least, it gave him an apparent respect for Learco I had not noticed before.

"Unit Two Oh Five," he said, handing me a key. "We've evacuated the building as a precaution in case you need to use lethal force to bring the corrupter down. Non-witch residents believe it's a gas leak so any explosions will be covered. Tried and true and a bit stereotypical, but it gets the job done."

Now I saw why people, even within the Moral Authority, were so afraid of Leland Hyde. His face fluttered with a near giddiness as he encouraged us to break every MAW law in dealing with whom he thought was just a run of the mill witch. An evil, and though unbeknownst to him powerless one, but a fellow witch all the same. If he took pleasure in the idea of the three of us blowing a soul into the ether, I didn't even want to imagine his approach when a MAW captive was entrusted to him for punishment.

I slipped the key into my pocket and nodded.

"We hope it won't come to that," I said. "If Learco can get his hands on the right counterspell, it shouldn't."

I ignored the disappointment on Leland's face as he punched a code to open the gated entrance to the building.

"In four hours' time," he said, "it becomes whatever it needs to be. Or else we have another mutilated witch's blood on our hands. Excuse me. Your hands."

My breath quivered as it passed my lips. He was right. Time was running out, and if I was wrong about this, Madison would face the same excruciating death as Angel, Daniel, and Jenna had. I couldn't let that happen to my friend. I could not afford to be wrong.

"Fae help you," he said as we entered the building, using the common witch phrase for "good fortune." If only he knew the Fae were the last help we needed right now. Dealing with one very angry, very mad Fomóraiġ would be enough.

The key pushed easily into the lock on Angel's door. I hoped I was right, that Madison was inside. Katrina had been insistent that they felt helpless, like they had somehow failed their friend. As Balor's magic worked its way through them, where else would they go but where their best friend had encountered the same fate?

If they aren't, I tried to convince myself, *we still have four hours to find them. That's a lot of time.*

"They're in there," Cernun said when he noticed my hesitation. "And we've got this."

The strength of his smile steeled me as I pushed open the door.

Angel's flat was nice, despite being trampled through by the boots of countless MAW agents a few days prior when her body was discovered. Modern and white, her furniture was the type built as a solid piece instead of the screwed together items from Sweden found in most college students' homes. Marble figurines of classic Greek Olympians frolicked in the nooks of her entertainment center, and festive pointed hats woven from silk, leather, and eucalyptus rose to Edison bulbs on her sofa end tables.

I had a feeling her parents—the same ones who'd hired a cleaning lady for their college aged daughter and gone to the human media when the MAW did not perform fast enough for their liking—had decorated the place. But Angel had certainly left her mark. If the discarded coats and bras strewn across the furniture had not given that away, the wooden tray with the glass pipe, grinder, and cannabis on the kitchen counter would have. But there was no sign of Madison.

Gulping to clear my throat, I called out their name. I hoped the ennead of MAW agents hadn't frightened them away. No answer came.

The kitchen was small, but serviceable, and I paused briefly to study the photographs magneted there as a tribute to happier times. In one, taken years ago, Angel had her arm wrapped around Madison's shoulder as they stood proudly outside the Freshman Dorms at GA Thaum. All incoming students were required to live on campus the first year. It must have been hard for them when Angel's parents bought her a place and Madison had to stay behind. Angel's smile was warm and inviting. She had an obviously brand-new nostril piercing, still raw and slightly infected, and her straight blonde hair glistened in the flash. Madison looked a bit more awkward, not the confident, self-assured person I now knew. Their chin length dreadlocks had not been died their signature electric blue. But an awakening was busy rumbling behind their eyes.

They both looked so happy, grinning into the camera with that fresh-faced charm of youth that made them ready to take on the world. Now, Angel would never have that chance. But I was going to make damn sure that Madison would.

I called their name again and listened for any response, any rustle or thud or sign that they could hear me. Cernun winced at the silence and pointed to the closed bedroom door.

With the exception of her body, Angel's bedroom appeared just as it had in the crime scene photo Learco showed us. The bed had been stripped, but the mattress held the blackened crimson where her body bled out. Her bedroom furniture, less expensive than her living area and obviously of her own choosing, was splattered from the spray where the bones snapped and pushed through her skin. The room smelled of wet copper and iron, tasted like a penny pressed under a tongue. Blackout curtains were drawn tightly closed, but a small bedside lamp gave the space a surreal glow.

"Madison?" I questioned softly.

A faint rustle of movement sounded from the other side of the bed. Cernun flicked on the overhead light. We stepped carefully, more worried than afraid of what we would find.

"Are you the demons come to take me?"

Cernun buckled at hearing words so similar to his brother's, and I grasped his elbow in comfort. His hand wrapped mine as we assessed the scene, their state of being, from the foot of the bed.

"Madison," I said, my voice cracking now as the words tried to form. "It's Cernun and Darragh. We've come to help you."

"So, you aren't the wild ones?" they asked, tilting their head as they peered straight through us.

Madison sat on the floor beside the bed, back against the wall and knees drawn close to their chest. Their pupils were dilated as they rocked back and forth. Their hands moved independently, as if casting a spell they weren't quite sure how to perform.

"I'll go let Leland know we found them, and things are under control," Cernun said, letting go of my hand and gripping firm to my shoulder. "Are you okay here?"

"I'll be fine," I said, darting my eyes from his to Madison as his arm slipped down my bicep. "But hurry."

He nodded as he turned to leave, Madison's eyes following him to the door even though they did not appear to be focused on any one thing in the room—anything in this realm.

"Demon, be gone!" they yelled. "Leave so that the wild may come through."

They squinted as they turned back to me and added, "You, too, clever witch."

My breath hung in my throat as I heard Balor's words in their mouth. I had figured it may be a possibility, but I was hoping it wasn't true. We had nearly four hours until the transformation—the killing shift of muscle and bone—began. Still, Balor was already settling into their mind, filling it with himself, with his madness, as he attempted to push through into our world.

I snatched a picture pinned to the bulletin board above Angel's desk and used my thumb to brush what I could of the dried blood from across the image. I stepped forward carefully and knelt in front of my friend. I showed them the photo, smiling through my fear as I attempted to reach them. I knew the swirling mania they faced, red and yellow and ghastly. I knew how hard it was to see beyond to reality, to the self.

"Do you recognize this photo?" I asked. "See? That's MA'AM. The Magical Artifacts and Antiquities Museum where you used to work before you came to work for me."

Their eyes swam across the picture, but there was no recognition behind them.

"And that's you." I pushed further. "Madison Ridge. Badass enby. Third year at Georgia Thaum. Witch, not animal. You work at my store—you work at HEX."

"Me?" they asked. I worried it was not a question of who they were but of personage in general as the mad mind of the Dark Fae leader wove through them.

Balor's hold on them was strong. I needed to try harder, to push through the madness to their pain in hopes it would break his hold, even if just a little. I winced at the thought of hurting them, but I had to try.

"This picture," I said. "It was taken by your friend, Angel. Do you remember Angel? This is Angel's room that we're in."

Madison blinked. Tears welled in the corners of their eyes. Their breath came in tatters from between their trembling lips. Their connection to their pain was grounding them, I bit my lip as I pushed it further.

"You once told me you had a crush on her," I said, "but in the end you were the very best of friends. You were always there for each other."

"No! I—I didn't believe her," they said. "She—this…. It happened to her. It was happening, and I didn't believe her. I told her to sleep it off, and I left."

Their eyes locked onto the mattress. Their hand searched along its seam.

"She died alone. And now, so will I."

"You are not dying," I promised.

Their hand recoiled as I touched them, but their eyes met mine fully for the first time.

"Darragh?"

"That's right," I nodded. "And you're Madison Ridge. Come on, we're going to figure out a way to stop this."

They shivered as I took their hand but didn't pull away this time. Their body, though, remained locked into place. Their free hand still wove through the coming spell, fingers twisting as their wrist snapped to and fro against their will.

Most magic—at least nowadays—was performed through thought, word, and intent. Sure we had our poultices and our potions. We had our offerings and ceremony and flourishes, but the core behind it all was the focus. This, however, was something different. Something primal. A pulling of the strings of the elements without ever invoking them by name. This was not working through the natural world to guide the fundamental principles of the elements to a wanted goal; this was laboring to control them, to change them in spite of the native order, to create something from nothing. Madison did not even need to understand what their hand was doing in order to enact Balor's wishes. It was terrifying.

I grabbed hold of their free hand to stop its motion. Their eyes went wide and dark.

"Off!" they snarled, rising to their feet and dragging me up with them.

In an instant they were free of my grip, breath measured as their palms met my ribcage and forced me back against the dresser on the other side of the room. A sharp pain split me as the wooden corner hit the center of my back. Angel's belongings scattered to the floor.

I yelped, more out of surprise than the hurt, as Madison's fists dropped to their side. Even balled up, their fingers twitched with Balor's spell.

"You simple farmer," they growled, but they were Balor's words in their voice. "You churlish, despicable witch. You will not stop my coming."

I swallowed hard as I brought a protective circle around me with my thoughts. But it didn't matter. Balor, through Madison, flicked it away with a touch. They stepped forward, unsure and wobbly as whatever was left of Madison in there fought against him, determined to rip my head from my body. I held my hands between us as I backed slowly away. My shoulder hit the doorframe as I passed through, but I couldn't afford to take my eyes off the advancing Fomóraiġ, even if he was cloaked in the skin of my friend. They were still in there, I told myself. He had not fully taken them. They could regain control. And I would not stop until they did.

"I will be of this world!" Balor bellowed in Madison's voice. "I shall take this witch and a thousand other souls if needed to enter this realm."

"What about our bargain?" I asked, hoping to calm him down. His madness was overtaking him. It was overtaking Madison.

"Our bargain, clever witch," he growled through them, "does not preclude my own advances. It stands, even if you do not. I felt you earlier, you know. Rooting around in my head. A pest. A worm."

Their palms met my chest once more, throwing me backwards over the arm of the couch. I lay there helpless as they glared down upon me. But it wasn't their eyes really watching me. My chest burned with the air knocked out of my lungs.

"A beetle on its back," they scoffed. But it wasn't them. I had to remember it wasn't them. "An insect grown too big for its shell. Here, let me help you out of it."

I gasped as Madison's fingers worked their way into fists. My eyes pleaded with theirs to stop, to realize who they were. Not Balor, but my friend. I swallowed hard as they reared back to pummel me.

CHAPTER 14

"Gbe kuro!"

"Imigh le!"

The crash of Learco and Cernun entering the apartment opened my eyes just in time to see their calls to "move away" from me in Yoruba and Irish push Madison's body from over me and to the wall of the living room. I sat up swiftly as their head crashed against the drywall and they slipped limply to the floor. I truly hoped they weren't hurt, but if we didn't act fast, a bump to the back of their head would be the least of our worries.

"It's definitely Balor," I said, standing to embrace my lovers as they rushed to my side. "He's determined to break through the barriers between our worlds. And he doesn't care how many witches he destroys while trying."

My heart sank as I looked at Madison's crumpled body. I couldn't let that happen to them. I refused to let another soul die at the hands of the Dark Fae. We had to stop Balor, here and now, from taking Madison or any other witch's lives. I hoped I read the subconscious thoughts in his mind correctly, that I had strung together the muddied, disjointed ideas in the right ways. If I was wrong, Madison was dead. And I had a feeling I'd be next on the list.

"Did Salem fax down anything useful?" I asked.

Learco winced and bit his lip.

"Potentially," he said. "But you're not going to like it."

He pulled the pages from his bag—there were a lot!—and tossed them on the coffee table between us. I reached for them timidly and sighed as I shuffled through the first few pages. They were written by hand in a dialect and language that seemed both familiar and unplaceable. The pages had browned, leaving the fax rendition gray and darkened in its black and white approximation. Entire words and phrases blurred into oblivion. That worried me more than not being sure of what language they were in. If we didn't get the spell completely right, if we called the heat of fire when we needed the cool of water, we could wind up killing Madison ourselves in a way that was just as painful and gruesome.

I handed a few of the pages to Cernun, but he shook his head to tell me he didn't understand them either.

"I had the translators at HQ take a stab at them," Learco said. "These books are eight, nine hundred years old. Some of these dialects have not been used in centuries. Other words appear to be a completely made-up code for the witches of that time. But what they could discern is this:"

Learco's eyes scrunched with worry as I peered at him from over the papers. I held my breath. The man did not worry easily— not about magical things anyway—so seeing his tongue click against the back of his teeth of he tested his words was unnerving.

"Our kind—witches—did once possess the power of shifting."

My mouth dropped open. Madison was right! That our ancestor's abilities to transmogrify their form had been lost to time—or the annals of Moral Authority servitude—was downright criminal. But the answer was here is my hands. Our magic could be restored! Learco raised his hand to the growing smile stretching across my face.

"Only under certain circumstances," he continued. "Those pages—they're littered with entries from various witches over hundreds of years relishing in their shifts from man to beast. I mean, the stories are incredible. These witches could change their bodies into those of elk or wolves or foxes. Fully sentient, fully aware as they ran on all fours through the midnight forests."

"That's amazing!" Cernun interjected, taking the words right out of my mouth.

My mind flashed to what that could feel like. The freedom of form, of being not only connected to the elements, but to animal kind as well. It must have felt like salvation, letting go of the binds of the human world and being wholly one with the woods.

"They could only change at night, and by dawn the spell would break. Some warn that the call of nature was great, but morning always brought with it release."

I nodded. All magic had its limitations. We were witches, not gods after all. But still, the possibility of feeling the night-darkened landscape beneath my paws or my hooves—I wondered what animal I would transform into—was breathtaking. And, if I was right, it also gave us the chance of freeing Madison from Balor's grip. Not only that, but it could stop him from harming another witch in that same way ever again.

"So, what?" I asked. "We just forgot how to do this? Lost the spells to history?"

Learco sighed. It was a heavier sigh than I anticipated. He should have been just as excited as I was at this discovery.

"I'm not sure," he admitted. "It's not something the Moral Authority, at least on record, claims credit for discarding."

"But we all know how that goes," Cernun scoffed.

"We do," Learco nodded. "Still, as far as we know, this magic ended well before our inception. Our current working theory, with less than an hour's thought, is that the tales of werewolves, of witch's familiars all spring from those days when witch kind would turn themselves to beasts beneath the light of the moon. And that those fears—human's of were-beasts; our kind of being accused of witchcraft due to the presence of a familiar—lessened the practice until it was all but gone."

Learco's eyes glazed over as he stared at the papers in my hand. There was something he wasn't telling me yet. I could see it in the blankness of his expression, in the quiver of his chapped lower lip. I gathered the pages and placed them back on the coffee table as I leaned forward to look him in the eye.

"We're out of the broom closet now," I said. "The world knows about our magic. And despite jerks like the DMFM—Sorry, Cernun—"

"Don't apologize for those idiots," he smirked.

"Despite them, we are free to embrace all the things that make us witches. Having a power like this back in the world should be celebrated. It's a part of our heritage. A part of our souls."

I was laying it on thick, but I did not want Learco's MAW training to cloud his eyes to the wondrous possibilities these pages contained. Not only could this ritual save Madison's life, it opened endless possibilities for witches everywhere to fully embody their powers in ways we had not experienced in centuries. The MAW chose to focus on the dangers of our powers reawakened. But me, I saw the possibilities they held. And they were breathtaking.

Reticence formed a thick line on Learco's forehead, even as I waxed poetically about the implications these papers held.

"All that aside," I finished, "this helps Madison, here and now. If their body can shift, I truly believe they'll be able to withstand Balor's advances without it killing them."

My eyes fell to Madison, still crumpled in a heap on the floor. Their locs spread out like electric sea snakes; their shoulders slumped. But their breath was slow and steady, showing me they were okay—for now at least. And there were still hours to go before Balor's transformation would fully take hold to cleave them into a gory, mutated mess.

I blinked away the imagined carnage and turned back to Learco with a wistful, scrunched brow.

"It's not about the magic itself," he said, voice heavy with concern and teetering somewhere between Director and Lover. "These are the issues: The transmogrifying spell must be performed by the witch who wishes to alter."

Okay. No big deal. I'd gotten through to Madison once, despite Balor's advances. Though it was brief, they had regained a temporary control of themselves. I could do it again. Hopefully long enough to teach them the rite and have them perform it. We'd overcome larger obstacles in the past.

"But the kicker," Learco sighed, "is that the spell requires the presence of the Fomóraiġ. My agents think that's euphemistic. Like a prayer. Like calling a god for assistance. But—"

"But we know the Dark Fae are real," Cernun said.

The revelation fell upon me like a massive oak in a thunderstorm. Shit. So that was why our kind had ceased shifting. Whatever magic had dislocated the Fae from our realm had taken the power with them. As much as I envied the potential of feeling the wind in my fur and the starlight on my muzzle, it was a small price to pay for keeping the Fomóraiġ away from our reality. The utter chaos, the pain that Balor had caused as just one of their ilk attempting to break through—or break me—from the other side was bad enough. I didn't even want to consider the destruction he would create if he were unleashed.

Fuck. There had to be another way.

"Can we tweak the spell?" Cernun asked what I was thinking. "Make it elemental instead of Fae?"

"I'm not sure," Learco admitted. "I don't think so. The ritual is there, on the last page. And even that is an amalgamation of six different retellings. It's got roots in our magic, but the conjuring is… different." His gaze set on Madison. "And I doubt we even have time for the trial and error required in reworking the ceremony."

I pulled the back page from the pile and looked it over. Learco had been kind enough to scrawl the English translation of the words in his practiced, controlled writing style. Overall, it was relatively simple. I could see the intent, the goal that our magic required, but the working of ritual itself required the summoning of Faerie Guides in the space of our usual earth, air, fire, water, and spirit.

Cernun grimaced as he studied the page from over my shoulder. His magical upbringing hadn't relied solely on family lore as—well—his family wasn't around to teach him. He used his power from a more innate source, letting the magic itself guide him intuitively to the spell. The other things he'd learned had been a hodgepodge of lessons as he traveled the country as a runaway, unhoused youth. I raised my eyebrows to him in question, hoping he'd be able to see a way the two of us couldn't, but he shook his head.

Frowning, I scanned the page again as an idea settled into me. It was a long shot, but it had potential. At least I hoped it did. I spoke through it in my mind to see if it could work, to try to convince myself it would. Balor: he was fire, right? The flames of the sun, of heat and carnage, burned brightly in his single eye. And Manannán was the ruler of the sea, so he could be substituted for water. Would the spell work if we switched out the Fomóraig for the elements they held supposed jurisdiction over? Could earth bound magic accomplish such a shifting of reality?

I focused on the second column Learco had created on the page. Like in most Books of Shadows, where the first indicated the incantation—the words spoken to enact and focus the spell—the second offering held the physical directions. My mother, in our family's Book, had always drawn little doodles to accompany the instructions to "light the red candle now" or "gesture skyward with flourish." But here, the motions which accompanied the words were more intricate, like hands on a loom, weaving thought together into practice. It reminded me of something.

I glanced toward Madison's still prone body. Their face remained shrouded by their hair, but their shoulders carried a tension that had not been there before. My eyes met their fingers, pointing and twisting as they had when I'd found them in the bedroom. Shit. They were awake. And Balor still had his hold.

I slipped the page with the ritual into my pocket and leapt to my feet to take up stance between Cernun and Learco, nodding to the motion of Madison's hands. Our breaths froze in the silence of the room. The only sound was Madison's fingernails clicking against the hardwood floor.

"Mads?" I tried, hoping for the best. The spell wouldn't matter one bit if we couldn't get through to them long enough for them to learn it. To perform it. And we needed them conscious—and in control of their body—for that.

Madison rose to their feet, craning their neck to stretch it as their body shifted to a wide-legged stance before us. Balor, using Madison's voice, cackled.

"The vessel need not be conscious for the spell to work," he moaned. "In fact, it's rather more pleasant when they are not."

Never ceasing the snarling of Madison's hands, he pushed their hair out of his eyes and grinned as he cocked their head at us.

"The Kyteler and the Clarke," he hissed. "You've brought the coven together again. Are you here to fulfill your bargain and help me through?"

We stood our ground on the other side of Angel's living room, but I knew I gripped Cernun and Learco's hands a bit too hard.

"This is not how you come through to our reality."

Learco said it as if it were a fact, firm and secure, like his position as Director carried the gravitas of finality. But he knew, unlike his agents or most of the public, Balor would not so easily capitulate to his demands.

"I've. Grown. So. Tired. Of. Waiting."

Balor punctuated each word with a step, with a simple gesture which flung another piece of furniture aside. It was odd seeing such an unfettered rage of power emanate from Madison's body. But it was obvious to all three of us who was in control.

The glass coffee table shattered as it hit the wall. One of Angel's marble figurines burst through the window and landed on the street below.

"Clarke?" Leland bellowed from the sidewalk.

"We've got this!" Learco replied, then to us he added, "Keep Madison away from the windows. He's got a twenty-one-gun salute aimed up here and spells to back that up. He won't hesitate to take them down if he feel's they're a threat to me. Even if he believes they're under Aiden's control."

I nodded. Madison would already be dead if Leland Hyde knew the truth: that it was a Dark Fae in control of their body and not some lowly Gowdie. Swallowing hard, I slipped away from the safety of my boyfriends and made a bee line for the kitchen. I swiped the photo I'd seen earlier—the one of Angel and Madison together—from the fridge and brandished it before me like a shield.

"I know you're still in there, Madison," I called. "Fight him! Remember who you are. Remember me. Remember Angel!"

They turned to face me. The hatred in their eyes softened as they studied the picture. Their lip quivered with an uneasy sorrow. They stepped toward me slowly, looking past the picture into my eyes.

"Darragh?" they asked timidly, but I knew it was an act. The quiver in their lips stretched into a wicked growl. "Stupid farmer. This witch is mine. As you will soon be too."

The photograph burned to ash in my fingers, and I dropped the singed remnants to the floor. I hadn't expected it to work, but my distraction had given Learco enough time to slip to the other side of the room.

We had Madison surrounded. And though Balor's power may have been great enough to break my protective circle on its own, there was a chance the combined power of my coven could hold him. We at least had to try.

A circle formed without the calling of the elements was invariably weak. It did not hold the keys of the world to bolster its protective qualities. But Learco and Cernun were some of the strongest witches I'd ever met. And, even if I didn't believe it, they said the same about me. Our arms stretched as we willed the bubble into being. It swirled in a mesh of green, gold, and blue—the colors of our auras—like a physical manifestation of the power we each contained.

From its center, Madison howled, then began to whimper like a caged animal.

"Get out of our friend," Cernun roared.

Balor ceased his simpering and glanced sideways at the man. The way he contorted Madison's face was unbearable. Seeing all that evil, all that bile on their sweet features unnerved me to my core, but I held firm on our circle.

Balor smacked Madison's lips and shook their head. Their shoulders shrugged with a heavy sigh as their fingers continued to work through his spell. They raised their arms and flicked outward as if swatting a fly.

Our circle broke, rippling outward with a seismic force that knocked each of us backward. Panting, the breath knocked from my chest, I scrambled to my feet. A hard, thick ball, sweating with golden energy whizzed in front of Madison's face and slammed into the television, breaking it in two. Cernun hadn't intended to hit Madison—if he had, he would have—but it distracted Balor enough to cease his steady stepping toward me.

Not many witches could heave masses of their materialized power in such a way. The three of us had not even known we could until we learned it from Samara Byrne when she was trying to kill us. Manifesting our energy to actual matter hurt like hell, but it was a powerful distraction.

"*Di nkan!*" Learco yelled, and a thick swath of air enwrapped Madison's arms and legs to bind them. Their limbs pressed together but their fingers continued their movement.

Cernun and I added our own binding spells, but Balor broke through all three with an annoyed roll of Madison's eyes.

"Churlish witches," he cackled. "You are weak, simple little things. Gnats. The lot of you." A fire raged in Madison's features. Their dark skin sweated, glistening in the ambient light created as my coven pulled more power into being. Balor was gaining more and more control by the minute. "I suppose that's why you break so easily," he growled.

A flick of his wrist sent me flying across the room. I landed in the pile of broken glass left behind by the coffee table. Learco extended his hand to help me up as I fished a shard from my palm. My blood was hot as it ran down my fingers, dripping to pool on the floor by my feet.

Madison licked their lips. I could almost see Balor's row of saw-edged, shark-like teeth behind them.

"You cannot best me," he said. "I could kill you where you stand, squash you like the earthworms you are. But I would rather first watch the agony on your helpless faces as I take your friend. I will make this body mine, and then I will take your lives."

I gasped as Madison cried out in pain—I was sure it was Madison this time—and dropped to their knees. Their head swung back as their limbs jutted to their side. Saliva gurgled in their throat as a cracking sound joined the noise of ripping flesh and their ulna popped through their skin. Even though their arm was broken, their fingers continued the conjuring.

We were out of time. Balor was enacting the spell before the witching hour, consequences be damned. If Madison's form didn't work, breaking and dying as it cycled through all of what was natural to try to contain him, he would simply choose another witch to torture, and then another, until he broke through. We needed to act fast.

"I have an idea," I said. "But you're not going to like it." I echoed Learco's words from earlier.

"I trust you," Cernun said, taking my bleeding hand in his.

"What are you thinking?" Learco asked, ever the voice of reason.

"Balor has Madison," I said. "Or at least a part of them as he attempts to come through. But their consciousness, it must be somewhere..."

"You're not suggesting—?"

"I am. If it takes the presence of the Fomóraiġ to enact the shapeshifting spell, and we can't bring them here, we have to go to where they are. Or, at least, to where one of them are."

My body shook against my own thoughts at the idea of returning there. But I'd been inside Balor's mind twice now and survived. I was beginning to understand how it worked, despite the insanity which moved within it. I was whole when I was there. Detached from my body, true, but my spirit was intact. And my own. There was a chance Madison's would be the same.

Learco bit his lip as he thought through my proposition. It was our best shot at gaining some semblance of control, even if we lost ourselves to Balor's madness in the process. We had no other choice. Finally, Learco looked me in the eye and nodded.

"I trust you, too," he said, taking my other hand in his.

I closed my eyes. I could still hear the writhing of Madison's body as Balor twisted them through. I hoped they wouldn't bleed out before we could finish the spell to take back what was theirs. Wounds created by magic could be healed as long as the body didn't die first.

"Follow me," I whispered.

I focused on the memory of Balor's mind, still etched inside me like a childhood dream my own mind wanted nothing more than to forget. I saw its cliff like the red clay of my youth, precariously placed and crumbling all the time. I saw its swirling red and yellow—swarming like locusts, like wasps, like flames converging upon the world. I let the vision fill me. I willed myself—I willed us there.

"Holy fuck."

I opened my eyes to Cernun's exclamation to find us standing in the ether, toes dangling off the cliff. The ghosts of thought and memory spiraled before us, churning and frothing in the ether.

"This is where you were when you went into that trance?" Learco asked.

I nodded. It was a lot to take in, even in its nothingness. Balor's madness bore down upon us like heavy air. A rotting, sulphuric odor swept the threats of his mind into a clustered mass around us.

"Darragh?"

I spun to see Madison on the other side of the cliff. The electric blue of their locs looked black against the red and yellow void. Tears poured from their eyes, staining their cheeks in reflective streams of sorrow.

"Madison!" I yelled, rushing toward them and taking them into my arms. I squeezed hard, as surprised by their firmness, their solidity, as I was my own.

"Where—where are we?" they asked.

"Look," I said, steeling my voice in the way I'd heard Learco do a hundred times. "We don't have a lot of time. The Fomóraiġ are real. And one of them—Balor—is attempting to take over your body to cross into our world. We are inside his mind."

Madison's breath trembled as they released me from their embrace. They huffed as they stared around us at the seething insanity.

"Is this what happened to Angel?" they asked.

My wince gave them their answer.

"I didn't believe her," they cried. "I thought she was pranking me. I told her to grow up."

"It's okay," I sighed. "What happened to Angel is not your fault. And we're not going to let it happen to you."

I fished the paper I'd slipped into my pocket free and handed it to them. I was lucky it came through with me. Maybe fate was on our side. They looked confused as they scanned over the text.

"Is this the transfiguration spell?"

Their eyes darted from me to Learco as he and Cernun approached us slowly. They winced, remembering the secret they'd asked me to keep from him.

"You have to perform it," Learco said. "Darragh believes—and I do to—that if you shift your body, it will at least keep Balor's attempts from breaking you."

"And chances are, it will toss him out completely," Cernun added. "If you can shift, he can't control you."

"But here's the hard part," Learco said. "I know he has your body. And I know it's in a great deal of pain. But you have to push through all of that. You have to control your motions in the physical world for the transformation to occur in our reality. Otherwise...."

"Otherwise, I'm dead," Madison finished.

They nodded as their eyes fell to the page once more. They sniffled as their tears began to dry.

"I'm sorry I brought you into this," they said. "All of you."

"This isn't your fault," I assured them. "Now. Try the spell, so we can get the fuck out of here!"

I stepped back to give them space as Madison concentrated on the text. Their eyes darted between the incantation and the actions as they attempted to piece it together. A tremor in their fingers waved the page like a flag of surrender.

"Simple farmers!" Balor's favorite insult resounded through the ether. "You could not control me in your world. What makes you believe you can control me from inside?"

The spell disintegrated in Madison's grip, ash sweeping off to join the orgy of the ether as if it had never been there to begin with. As if it was just another memory for Balor to recollect at another time. There were centuries of them there. Faces and thoughts. Moments of triumph. Of betrayal.

But I had been here before. And I was beginning to understand how his mind worked.

I concentrated hard, reaching out with my own mind to pull a thought from his, like a thread from the noisy, unkempt spindle of his history. I tugged until I could see it, until I could feel its emotion overwhelm me.

I saw moments etched into time like commandments. Great battles, the bones and the blood of enemies and friends soaking in to make the fields fertile, to impose new life from their sacrifice. I watched wives warn of impending ends, of violence—so much violence being whittled down to madness. I glimpsed dying breaths form the regenerative force of an idea, of a Fae who was never truly lost.

I reached through the memories, through the flashes, until I found the string I was looking for. I pulled it from the others. Let it wrap around me.

Eight witches, each dressed in long, dark brown robes, not unlike the ones I used as uniform at HEX, stared me down in anger, in violence. But they were staring Balor down. I was seeing the memory from his point of view. Their hands moved in formations similar to those directed by the transformation spell. They were earth-bound witches using Fae magic! This was it! The memory I'd hoped to find. This was when the Fomóraiġ were banished from our reality!

"You think you can use my own thoughts to scare me?" Balor wailed.

Thick, rootlike vines burst forth from the earth, wrapping my arms and dragging me across the quaking ground to the edge of the cliff. My toes teetered at the edge, threatening to slip at any moment. A third vine snaked its way up my body, twining my hips and thumping hard against my chest before it took my neck like a noose and squeezed. My vision blurred, but I could see Cernun and Learco facing the same fate as mine.

But Madison was okay. Balor's vines had not trapped them. He must have needed their consciousness unbound in order to work through their body. I watched their fingers twitch as they tried to remember the spell they had just seen, fumbling through the motions in frustration. If they could remember it, they could stop Balor. That was what mattered. Not me. Not my life.

All of this was to save Madison. To prevent Balor from forcing his way into our world.

"Close your eyes! Let it come!" I called to them before the vine tightened its hold around my throat.

This was it. Our last chance.

I let my own eyes close.

CHAPTER 15

I felt suddenly peaceful, as if all my pain, every ache of my body or my heart, had been lifted from me. A warm, misting comfort rose inside my mind, and pumped, like blood from my heart, through every last inch of my being. My skin tingled in euphoric bliss. I floated—I was floating, wasn't I?—light as a feather on a gentle, all-encompassing wind. Each gust brushed my cheek, fluttered my still-closed eyelashes playfully, and kissed my lips full on. A moment or an eternity; it didn't matter. All there was was here. All there was was now. And now was beautiful.

It wasn't so bad, as far as deaths went.

"Silly spell speaker. You aren't dead."

My eyes shot open, and the world formed around me. Bright and ethereal, like light reflected through water, the horizon took the shape of mountains, of castles, of lore. Beneath me, a rolling field of clover stretched into undulating hills. But I was alone, save for a sole crow eyeing me from atop a nearby boulder. Her feathers, deep and black as Cernun's hair, radiated a prism of color where the light touched them. Her head tilted to take me in, head to toe, with an unbridled curiosity. If she hadn't had a beak, I would have sworn she was smiling.

It was a surreal experience, but I'd seen far stranger things in the past few days. At least this wasn't scary. Or gruesome.

"Is this the void between life and death?" I asked.

My own voice sounded hollow yet high pitched in this realm, and I cleared my throat to find my tenor.

The crow's caw turned into a hearty laugh. It was musical and terrible and enchanting.

"What's all this about death?" the crow called. "It is not yet the time of your demise, Darragh Cullen."

Her feathers ruffled as she stretched her wings and hopped toward me on her rock. Her eyes—a moonless midnight—held a magnificent interest as she watched me watching her. Her voice stretched not only from her throat but from the whole of the atmosphere.

"Who are you?"

My voice was shakier than I'd expected it to be. It floated in jarred triplets from my mouth, a skipping record still intent on finishing the song.

"So many questions," the crow laughed.

And with that, she took flight, becoming a swarming mass of plume and talon, wrapping in on herself with light—so much light—and expanding ever outward until a woman stood before me. Her hair, straight and silken and halfway down her back, held the same radiant glow the crow's feathers had displayed. Emerald eyes crowned her narrow nose, and her garnet smile stretched straight into her cheekbones. Her breasts heaved as she sighed, nipples hard beneath her ash blue gown, and she stretched her limbs as she adjusted to her human-like form. Or Fae form. She was definitely Fae.

"I've had many names," she smiled, licking her lips in delight at my wonder. "I've had many forms. Some call me The Mórrígan. Others Anand. There was a woman in County Kerry once who simply called me God, though my fingers were between her legs at the time."

I bit down hard on the inside of my mouth. My grandmother had loved telling stories of The Mórrígan. Like Hecate to the Greeks or God to the Catholics, she was a triple being—queen, warrior, and fate—who prepared the Tuath Dé—the "tribe of gods"—for war against the Fomóraiġ. They were Fae, all of them, but like humans, like witches, were not above some in fighting as they jockeyed for control of the world.

The Mórrígan was said to have seduced many a warrior and maiden to their death. A shapeshifter and a sonnetist, a single poem from her mouth was said to have driven the Dark Fae from the battlefields and into the sea long before witches had even walked the land, let alone banished the Fomóraiġ from it. Like others of her kind, she was keen on bargains, on tricks, on offering an open hand while her other held a blade.

Shit. The last thing I needed was to get involved with more of the Fae folk.

"You are frightened of my presence," she said. She still moved like the crow, head swiftly tilting to eerie, uncanny angles as she studied me like a trinket. Like prey. "That's wise," she said. "Perhaps there is hope for your kind yet."

I did my best to stifle the growing dread bubbling in my gut. It clashed against my heartbeat, against the serenity of my surroundings. I'd learned it was always best not to show too much fear in the face of the Fae, lest they use it against me.

"How am I here?" I demanded, albeit timidly. "Where are Cernun and Learco?"

The Mórrígan giggled her awful laugh.

"Stretched to three realms," she said, "and still thinking with your heart. Or your penis."

Her amusement infected the land around us, tripping it to a glittering glow even brighter than the brightness of before.

"You are still where you were, as is your coven. Your body cowers before the majesty of darker gods in an earth-bound dwelling. Your mind starves for air in the twines of Balor's mania. But your spirit rests here with me. Something of a triplicate yourself, it would seem."

She moved with the grace of a wind-blown sail as she walked, bare feet soft against the field. Seeing her attentions turned away from me filled me with longing, with absence, as if I needed her gaze upon me to survive. As if all I had ever wanted—all I could ever need—was to bathe in her light. She grinned as she crouched down and plucked a four-leaf clover from the patch.

"I didn't summon you," I said, remembering it was Aiden Gowdie's calling to Balor—and our presence as offerings in his circle—that had gotten us into so much trouble in the first place. I didn't want to be beholden to yet another Fae. "I did not ask for your aide."

The clover vanished from her fingertips as she turned back to face me. There it was: that warmth, that want.

"I saw you in a memory, Darragh Cullen. One not my own or even yours, but that of another. I saw your eyes peer down upon the battlefield through that of one of my Fomorian kin. On the day we made them surrender." Her mouth carved a wicked grin across her face as she thought back to the battle. The clover at our feet grew the dense, red spikes of flowers to mimic the blood-soaked field. "I wanted to know more of the witch who could see our past."

A heat rose within me as she circled me. Her eyes caressed my skin as she studied me, carving over every tendon in my neck, noting every muscle in my back. I flushed as her tongue wet her hungry lips.

"I've learned not to bargain with your kind," I said despite myself. I wanted only to bask in her view, in the light her eyes afforded me.

She laughed once more—melodic and terrible—and I found myself afloat atop the noise.

"You are not here for that," she said, not offended by my aggression. "I do not trifle to barter with your kind. Though you seem a bit… overwhelmed at present. Your presence here allows me simply to study you. Should that time give you occasion to determine the answers which already lay within before your air runs out, so be it."

She was magnanimous, this Fae. Or, at the very least, the power, the pheromones she released into the air tried to convince me she was. She seemed to have an ulterior motive in bringing me here but was of no mind to reveal it. She also seemed to hate Balor as much as I did.

"You know the future," I said. "My fate. Show me!"

She came full circle to stand face to face with me. Her hand cupped my chin and tilted my head as if appraising livestock.

"It's a simple thing to do to see the past," she grinned. "Though not always so easy for those of your realm. The future, in its many, varied strains, is something else entirely. You—at least as you are now—must live it. But I will give you this once more: the answer already lies within you. In here."

Her fingers touched my forehead, and I gasped.

The euphoria vanished as quickly as it had taken me and was replaced by the sick, dripping feeling of pain and anger and derangement. I was back inside Balor's head.

He toyed with us as captives—loosening the grip of the vines which held us precariously over the vast nothingness and then squeezing them once more before we fell—as Madison sobbed. Their fingers twisted as they tried to remember the spell, halting, and balling into fists as they crumbled to their knees. Tears streamed down their face. Their body bent, chest heaving with strained breath, as Balor's transformation in reality began to affect their consciousness here.

"You can do this, Madison!" I gasped when I could collect enough air to fill my lungs.

Balor's maniacal laughter echoed through the ether, exciting the ghosts of his memory into a torrent of movement. We were losing ground, and it was falling fast. I could not let myself consider what would happen to us if Balor fully succumbed to the madness which seemed to grow ever greater as he pushed further into the transformation. At best, we'd be dead—lost and eviscerated as if we had never been. But that was a pleasant thought compared to the alternative of being lost forever in the Dark Fae's head, a plaything for him to rattle whenever he so chose to remember us.

"I can't!" Madison cried. "It hurts! Fuck, it hurts!"

I watched in horror, helpless in the binds of Balor's vines, as Madison rose from the ground, arms akimbo, and snapped suddenly backward. He was letting their physical pain transfer through now as he positioned us—me, Learco, and Cernun—to watch. Exactly as he said he would do. Before he killed us.

We were in his mind. He could do anything he wanted. Manifest anything he wanted. Shit. I thought I could control it, but I'd walked all of us right into his trap. In my hubris, I'd doomed us all. I felt the dizzying nausea of insanity creeping into me. The longer we were in his head, the more of him—his madness, his horror—would fill us until there was nothing left.

"I'm sorry," I whispered, turning left and then right to face Learco and Cernun. "I thought—I thought this was the way…"

My words trailed off as Balor's vines pulsed against my throat. He was enjoying toying with us almost as much as he loved the torture he was inflicting on Madison. A cyclone raged around us, redder and redder as the softer yellow grew dark.

"Do not give up!" Cernun growled. He grunted as he struggled with the vines against his chest. They squeezed at his form as if they were made for his body.

But his body wasn't here. None of ours were. The Mórrígan had told me so. As before and as with Madison, our minds, our spirits had entered Balor's head, not our physical beings. We were at the will of his thoughts, true, but we still had our own.

"The spell is in our heads," I gasped.

Unlike Madison, we didn't need to break through our subconscious to our physical selves to stop Balor's transformation from destroying our bodies. At least not yet. We could change here. In our minds. In his.

"The spell," I called again. "We all saw it, saw the translation. It's in our minds. Find it in your thoughts. Manifest that memory."

"Fuck," Learco yelped, but he nodded.

I closed my eyes. I felt the vines constricting around me. But it wasn't me. Not really. Not entirely. I let my mind shift from the pain I felt, focusing on the white piece of paper, the last page in the stack. One moment in my past. One brief stop in time. I could pull it, as I had with Balor's thoughts, from my own memory. I could make it real, make it present. I just needed a glimpse.

My fingers twitched beneath the vines to pull the at the filament of thought.

"See the past," I thought loudly as Cernun and Learco's ruminations echoed back on mine.

There it was! In my memory, upon viewing the page, even the ancient script made sense. It was a language Balor knew, and his understanding of it was creeping deep into my mind. His madness too. We had to work quickly.

"Invoke thee now, you spirits of the ether-land," I read, grimacing as I looked ahead to see the name of the Dark Fae whose head I was inside. It would be risky, calling him from within, drawing his attention to us. But it had to be done. My fingers bent to new positions. "Hear this, my plea of transformation. Be my guide through the muscle and sinew of man. Lead me through to transformation. I call thee, Manannán, of the sea, whose renewing waters may wash me in the flow of transition. I call thee, Danu, mother of earth, whose soil meets death with life and rebirth. I call thee, Anand, whose flight of air upon the wings of the raven brings with it the winds of change. I call thee, Balor, of the sun and fire, whose flames clear the past for what is to come. My spirit enters to this union willingly. I accept unto me the form of my alteration as it comes. So mote it be."

An exhilaration spread through me. My stomach churned. A charge, like ungrounded electricity, shot through my body, twisting and contorting all that I was into something fresh, something new. I'd expected it to be painful, but it wasn't. Instead, I felt the pull of the air above, the root of the earth below. Fire and water raged through my being, regenerative and soothing, melting and cooling me like sand into glass, forming that which had always been within. I shifted—expanded and contracted. I slipped free of Balor's vines.

My legs felt heavy against the clay of his mind. And powerful, like they could send me leaping into the clouds were I not careful. My nose—or I guess snout now—crinkled at the metallic, acidic aroma which plagued Balor's thoughts. I could sense it so much better now. I also had an intense desire to fuck, but I couldn't really blame that on suddenly finding myself a hare. I peered down at the reddish-brown fur of my paws and felt my heavy ears twist as they perked to the whispering whoosh of the Dark Fae's madness.

To my left, where Learco had been, a magnificent peacock rustled his array of tail feathers. Jewels of sapphire and emerald— as bright as The Mórrígan's eyes—waved against the red and yellow of the ether. And to my right, Cernun huffed as he scratched his ram hoof against the cliff. Two curled horns defied the weight of his head, and his lush, black, curly wool hung soft against his powerful frame.

We had done it! At least mentally, the transformation spell had allowed us to shift into beasts! Our new forms slipped easily from Balor's vines before he had the opportunity to reconfigure their shape.

I planted my paws against the red clay of Balor's mind and stretched to find my equilibrium. I felt wild and free. For a moment, I found myself lost in the sensation. What it must have felt like for our ancestors! To embody that which was feral, basking in the moonlit forest as the wind ruffled their fur or feathers, and the trees whispered secrets to the night. Even here I heard the faint tingle of that call, but it was supplanted by the rage of Balor's fire.

My ears pricked as the sounds of Madison's anguish broke through my reverie. I understood now why the spell needed the help of the Fomóraiġ and lasted for but one night. It would be too easy to become lost in the untamed, to never find my way back to myself. I shook it off and set my eye on Madison. My legs quivered as I felt my desire roll through them, curling from hip to toe as I vaulted forward. Damn! I could get used to that.

I felt long and graceful as the raw kinetic energy of my body slipped far beyond its compact frame. I was alive—truly—guided by instinct and whim. I wondered if Cernun and Learco could hear the call to forget radiating through them. We could become one with nature; let go of our cares, our worries. No more bills or Faeries, no fires seeking to destroy our lives, no Moral Authority or DMFM. Just a peaceful existence, romping through the wilderness, a denizen of the woods, one with the forest.

Except there were no trees, no underbrush. Only a vast, swirling mass of flame and discord. A body contorted, high above the ground, twisting in agony. A beautiful fowl, lithe and majestic, stood to my side. And another beast rutted his great weight against the ground. They were Learco and Cernun—my lovers, my coven. And I was Darragh Cullen. I remembered. I knew who I was.

Madison's head twisted on their spine, eyes filling with wonder in place of the pain that had ransacked them as they took in our animal forms.

"You've got this," I thought, hoping somehow my words would reach them. "We've got you. We believe in you."

I saw the wonder form determination in their irises. Their wailing, that horrible witch noise, ceased in heaves and gasps, even as their body still broke with Balor's spell. But their fingers: they began to twist in a new, familiar way. My whiskers quivered as I recognized the spell. They were doing it! They had fought their way through! I hoped the motions had translated to the real world.

I wanted to stay. I needed to make sure they were okay, that they were successful, but the Dark Fae's mania was beginning to mix with the lure of the wild. It was up to Madison now, at least on this side of the spell. I reached to grasp Learco's talons, Cernun's hoof.

I shuddered as we flashed back to reality. Back in my own skin, I already missed the inherent inhibition of my animal self. I swallowed hard as I looked at my hands, the functionality of my digits, the rarity of my opposable thumbs feeling suddenly less efficient than the short-haired pads of my paws. My nose crinkled as it had before, but the smells were less intense, less alive. There was an overwhelming urge to weep, to mourn the loss of freedom. I closed my eyes sadly as I pulled back into myself.

"You will not escape me!" Balor panted through Madison's throat.

I lifted my head slowly.

Before us, Madison's body was a heap of bruise and puncture. Blood pooled in oceans at their bended knees while skin tore to make room for feather, for scale. Yet even as their body fought its natural containment, even as bones snapped free of their skeleton, their fingers twitched.

I recognized the workings. Madison had made it through! They were working the transformation spell on both sides of the plane!

Still, Balor glared at us from behind their eyes.

"Clever witches," he moaned. His own transfiguration was taking its toll on him, even as he pushed Madison's body to its brink. "To attempt to use our power to best me. Lucky once. But not again once I come through."

Cernun's thick hand wrapped my shoulder as he helped me to my feet. Fuck, I would have missed his touch. The feel of his hand against my neck, the rush of Learco's palm against mine brought me back fully from my animal state. I exhaled sharply then breathed the haggard air into my own lungs. This was me, I told myself. And I had a job to do.

"We have to keep him distracted as Madison works," Learco whispered. "And hope to fate they finish in time."

I nodded. But Fate had more in mind than distraction. She had told me so herself. Fate was not content to cease Balor's hold on this one body, she wanted to stop him from attempting such a scourge on any other witch. My mouth twitched as I remembered The Mórrígan's words. I looked back on the past—not mine, but Balor's. I knew what I had to do.

A smiled stretched my lips as I raised my eyebrows to my coven.

"Circle," I said. "A real one this time."

We joined hands and called the corners. My worries that our lack of offerings to hold their attention would weaken our hold vanished as the elements rushed to our sides. Earth, Air, Fire, Water, and Spirit swirled in the waves of our power, fascinated enough by the workings of Fae magic to hold strong in our will.

There weren't eight of us—there were only three. But we were three badass witches. And our connection to one another—not just as a coven but in love—made us stronger. We could do this! We could take Balor down.

"Follow me," I cried as I worked the banishment spell I'd seen in Balor's memory. The rush of the ancients pushed through me as if guiding me in primordial wisdom long forgotten. I could feel them guide my hands through the complex mix of Fae and Natural power, drawing on both to cleave his world from ours. I knew Learco and Cernun felt it too.

A thought occurred to me, as if whispered into my ear by The Mórrígan. Balor's physical self had long been banished from our reality. It was his mind we needed to stop. And banishing that would prevent him from attempting this again with another witch.

"Bind the mind," I whispered, and Cernun growled.

We dared a step closer, pushing more of our will upon him. I could tell from the motions of their fingers that Madison was nearing the completion of their own transformation spell. We had to push Balor out. It was now or never. I breathed in the electric pull of our power. And I pushed.

Our circle dropped as a wave of energy pulsed from us, forcing its way through Madison's body. They or Balor—I wasn't sure which—wailed as the surge hit them, and they crumpled to the floor as Learco, Cernun, and I dropped to our knees. My lungs were hard and spent. I was exhausted by the depths of power the banishment spell had taken from me. I closed my eyes as I hoped to the no longer listening elements that our magic had worked.

"They're breathing, but it's slow," Cernun said as his eyes

scanned the broken mass which had once held Madison's shape. "They're no longer transforming. But the wounds…"

He didn't need to finish his sentence. My mouth went dry as I took in their lacerations. It was just too much for their body, any body, to take. I had failed them. I didn't try to blink the tears from my eyes.

"Hey!" Learco insisted, grabbing my hands and forcing me to focus on him. "You stopped Balor. This will never happen to another witch at his hands because of you."

"But I couldn't save them."

His beautiful brown eyes turned down as he let go of my hands and pulled me against his chest. He breath heaved against me, forcing my own lungs to action, my own heart to beat once more.

"One thing the Moral Authority has taught me," he whispered, "is that nothing comes without sacrifice. Madison was a good kid. They'd be proud to have played a part in stopping that monster."

"They wouldn't have wanted to die."

Learco let out a surprised laugh as he answered. "No. But they wouldn't blame you for their death either."

"Uh… guys," Cernun stammered.

I followed his gaze to find Madison's head shifting as their fingers pushed through the pain to complete the ritual. Their usual brown eyes—now the emerald green of The Mórrígan's—twinkled as they met mine. Somehow, this would make me indebted to her—to another fucking Faerie—but I didn't care. Not in that moment.

Cernun stepped back to join us as Madison's body began to morph. Their wounds healed before our eyes. Thick streams of blood were replaced by scars, by skin, by fur. The transformation was incredible. Slow but then fast. Immediate and agonizingly paused. A wonder not witnessed in ages.

"Holy shit," I babbled as the shapeshifting concluded.

A sleek house cat sat before us, slightly larger than most and with electric blue fur, but they licked their paws like any other feline. Their whiskers twitched, and their tail bristled. Madison mewed as they leapt the pool of their own blood to wind my feet and rub against my ankles. Their body was whole! Their limbs intact, and every single one of their wounds was gone! The spell worked exactly as I hoped it would!

"Fuck yeah, Mads!" I said as I knelt to the floor. I let my palm run the length of their head, down their back, and wrapped my fingers to massage their tail. I hoped it wasn't weird, my petting them, but they didn't seem to mind. "It really worked. Now it's time to change back."

Madison purred loudly as they crossed the room and leapt to the kitchen counter. Their tail twitched around them as they sat and stared me in the eye.

CHAPTER 16

"Come back to bed," I moaned.

The first rays of the sun, still misty and gray, were just beginning to peek through the slit in the curtains. It had been a full day since we defeated Balor and saved Madison. Or at least somewhat saved them.

Cernun shushed me as he checked his watch.

"I can't," he said in a low enough tone to not completely jar me from my half slumber. "The guys have been at HEX since six. I'm already over an hour late."

"Grrr," I pouted playfully. "Look at you always doing nice things for me. Fine. Go. Be on your way."

He laughed as he leaned to kiss my forehead.

"Happy Valentine's Day," he whispered.

I beamed him my best sleepy smile as I felt the call of the mattress, the comfort of the sheets, overtake me. He chuckled at my squinted eyes, my head bobbing back toward my pillow.

"Go ahead and sleep in." I felt the gentle landing of four feather-light paws at the foot of the mattress. "If Madison will let you."

The neon blue of their fur glimmered in the new morning light as they yowled at me to meet the day. And feed them breakfast.

Tufts of medium length fur appeared like a lion's mane around their snout, and their long whiskers twitched with their mewing.

When they hadn't responded to my urging them to change back into their witch form, I had hoped the ending of the night would complete the spell and end the transformation, as it had for our ancestors. But already the full dance of the sun and moon had completed, and they still wore their fur coat.

Cernun had his work boots on and was halfway out the door when he turned back to me with a grin.

"Dinner at yours tonight?" he asked. "We should be wrapping up the renovations today. I'm excited for you to see it."

"And just when I was getting accustomed to waking up in your bed," I joked, stretching wide as Madison kneaded the comforter across my lap. I was worried about them not changing back, but I tried not to let it show. I remembered all too well that desire to stay, to become feral, to let the wild overtake me. The comfort it offered. The safety. Still, I smiled as they maneuvered themselves to rest in the tiny beam of roving light from the window.

"The bed's always here," Cernun smiled.

"Will Learco be there?" I asked, and the joyous look on my boyfriend's face faltered, giving me the answer before he even spoke.

"He hasn't confirmed," he sighed. "But it's possible."

I'd really hoped that the three of us coming together to defeat Balor and save Madison would have helped put our argument behind us. He'd even told me he trusted me as we worked through ancient magics none of us knew a damn thing about. But he'd been largely absent since we parted ways outside of Angel's apartment building; him returning with Leland and a bevy of agents—those not left behind to clean up the scene—to the MAW HQ to issue a report, and Cernun and I headed to Grant Park with "Angel's forgotten kitten" in our arms. I tried to tell myself he was just busy—defeating a witch serial killer who couldn't be fingered as Fomóraiġ was a lot to cover up—but I knew it was more than that.

I listened to the gentle sounds of Cernun leaving—the soft gasp of wood on frame, the twist of metal guiding pins to lock—before I pulled myself to a seated position on the edge of the mattress.

"Breakfast?" I asked, and Madison mewed their approval as they leapt to the floor and padded out the door, tail swishing high in the air.

I spooned a hearty mixture of tuna, flaked salmon, quinoa, and mashed peas into a white bowl on the countertop. It was a recipe I'd found online—vet approved—with ingredients from the Dekalb Farmers Market since I hadn't felt right feeding them kibble. Their fangs glistened as they smacked their lips and waited for me to finish serving up their meal.

"You eat better than I do now," I joked, and the engine in their chest rumbled as they began their feast.

I finally had the hang of Cernun's espresso machine, and I smiled as the lush espresso-warmth of my cold iced latte filled my gullet. I leaned against the doorframe and looked out over the backyard garden, already imagining how exuberant and verdant it would become in the Spring and allowed myself a moment to really smile.

We had defeated Balor—this time, anyway—and it hadn't triggered a renegotiation of our previous bargain which would have allowed him to take our spirits as playthings into his realm. I liked to think it was because I'd gotten him to admit when he had me trapped in his mind that his current actions and our bargain were not related, but I had a sinking suspicion there was more to it than that. The Mórrígan's interest had been piqued, and she had provided favors. There was more to come there, too, but that was a problem for a different day.

Finished with their meal, Madison yowled as they wound my ankles. I pushed open the screen door and grinned as they leapt from the deck to prowl the yard, pouncing as the drops of dew caught the light of the rising sun. The electric blue of their coat looked both natural and fantastical as they frolicked between the raised beds.

"I'll figure out how to bring you back," I promised, and they tilted their green eyes at me before a beetle distracted them and sent them crouching to attack.

Cernun was waiting for me on the sidewalk when my Broomer pulled up shortly before 6PM. The street was filled with lovers nestled close to one another as they made their way to their dinner reservations or drinks within the restaurants and bars along the strip. Valentine's Day was surprisingly busy, even for places like Aunt Paulina's, who offered a casual, more authentic alternative to the pomp and circumstance of the "nicer" places Downtown or in Buckhead. Especially the ones with cold beer and on par cocktails at half the cost.

In my arms, Madison yowled and batted at the crisp petals of the roses Cernun was blushing behind. The potted bush—he knew I wasn't a fan of cut plants save for my spelling ingredients—burst with red flowers, and I had a feeling he'd spelled them against the chill to keep them bright for my arrival.

"They're beautiful," I smiled, then, remembering that my apartment—while it had great lighting—was not really the place for an outdoor shrub, added, "They'll look fantastic in your garden."

"Perhaps," he grinned and leaned around the bush to kiss me.

Madison used the opportunity to jump from my arms and purred loudly as they batted against the front door of my shop.

"They're as excited to see it as I am," I quipped.

Cernun placed the potted roses on the sidewalk and pulled the spelled skeleton key—the one that had been used to ward the building ever since Uncle Gardner had bought it—from his pocket. He passed it to me with a ceremonious bow. The metal felt good in my grip, like a missing piece of myself was being restored. It slipped easily into the lock, and I pushed through the threshold. Madison rushed ahead of me as I flipped on the lights, whiskers jumping as they sniffed the new interior.

Cernun and his crew had outdone themselves. Not only had they built new display tables to replace the ones burnt in the fire, the surviving shelves had been waxed and refinished to the former glory, before storefront guided sun and the oils of a thousand customer's fingertips had left the wood dull and lifeless. The cash wrap, once centered on the sales floor, now snaked the back wall next to the stockroom entrance to allow more floorspace for customers and easier access to the back for employees. A custom-built display to showcase Stacey's poultice bags now proudly proclaimed her name in carved wood, and hexagonal shelves adorned the far wall from floor to ceiling, awaiting the displays of spell books and journals I'd always wanted. The MAW couldn't restrict me from selling an almanac or two and some gardening tips. And if I ensured all the books about the Fae Folk and their ways were labeled as Fantasy, that should be A-OK as well. I wanted them there though. I had a feeling us witches would need them in the coming years. Maybe I'd even throw in a series or two of romance books just to round out the collection.

"I increased the storage beneath the display carts so you could clear out more of the backroom and keep it out here," Cernun beamed excitedly as he pulled open the drawers to show the added space. "I figured you may want to expand the area around Gardner's old spelling table to add classes to your offerings."

It was an idea I'd been mulling around for a while now, despite my failures with Aiden, but I had never mentioned it to him before. It's like the witch could read my mind. I smiled as I kissed his cheek.

"It's beautiful," I said, the word coming nowhere close to encompassing my feelings.

Cernun pushed past me into the space and bent to flip a brake switch beneath one of the tables.

"The new displays are on wheels now," he said. "So you can move them around easier if you need to…. Oh! And wait 'til you see this!"

He galloped to stand by the backdoor and was nearly glowing as he reached the turn the ancient knob that hadn't worked since before I took over the shop. Above us, the gold and crystalline chandelier—the only original fixture since Uncle Gardner had put in track lighting in the 80s—sprang to life. Flames flickered at the wicks of the white candles—40 of them—and the crystal towers glistened in the glow.

"They're spelled flames," he said, sensing my sudden concern. "So nothing will catch on fire. Learco's MAW agents were still hovering around looking for anything to tie this to the DMFM, so I had them help me with the spell."

"You're amazing," I chuckled as Madison hopped atop the counter and batted at the screen of the cash register. They purred their approval as their tail wrapped their body.

"Just wait until you see the piece de resistance," Cernun smiled, biting his lip seductively.

"After dinner," I growled, eyes locked tight on the bulge in his pants. "I need you energized."

I locked the door behind us as Cernun waited by the back room, hand extended for mine. Madison bounded ahead of us as we made our way up the stairs.

I inhaled deeply as I entered my apartment. The scent of burnt wood and hatred left behind by the fire had been replaced with the fresh aroma of citrus and rosemary. My eyes scanned my sofa and my bookshelves, the stack of unanswered mail on the counter I'd been meaning to get to, and the large, woven rug that guarded the inlaid pentacle used for spelling on the living room floor. As much as I had enjoyed being at Cernun's house, it felt good to be home.

A timer dinged from the oven as Madison leapt to claim the upholstered armchair by the window I used for reading as their own.

"Time to baste," Cernun smiled as he grabbed the bulbed tube from the counter and bent to check his cooking. "Since I already did the pork chops the other night, I had to go for option number two."

My mouth grew tight in a smile as I shook my head.

"Mom's Rosemary-Stuffed Roast Chicken," I said. "You know, she won't even tell me the right seasoning mix for that, right? Says I have to learn how to roast good broccoli before I can roast a good bird."

She also said it was only passed down to the Keeper of the Kitchen, a made-up title her great-great-grandfather had determined to anoint those in our family who kept the hearth fires burning for their loved ones. Knowing that meant they had welcomed Cernun in, and considered him to be forever, warmed me even more than the grin and the "I'll never tell" on his lips.

I noticed he had set the table for three, and I raised my eyebrow.

"Just in case," he winced, and I nodded.

I slipped out of my coat and moved to place the potted rose next to the chair by the window until I could determine a more suitable home or replant it over at Cernun's. Madison's eyes were closed as they purred contentedly on the cushion, and their tail only twitched a little as I adjusted the plant. I poured myself a glass of whisky, really wishing for one of Aunt Paulina's Old Fashioneds, and pulled a bottle of beer from the fridge for Cernun.

"Thank you," I said, realizing I hadn't said it before.

"For dinner? That's nothing," he demurred.

"For dinner, yes. And for everything you did down at HEX. And for always having my back and loving me unconditionally."

"Aww, shucks," he said, and leaned across the kitchen island to kiss me. His lips were warm and soft on mine, and I trembled at the way the stubble of his beard tickled my cheek.

"Room for one more?" Learco asked from the doorway.

I'd been so wrapped up in Cernun's lips, I hadn't even heard him come in.

"Always," Cernun grinned.

I smiled as I grabbed the bag he offered—filled with wine, an unlabeled and resealed bottle, and Cernun's go-to beer—and placed it on the counter.

"I had Paul mix up a full batch of his Old Fashioneds for you," he blushed. "Well, Rafael did. But it's from me."

I grinned as I finished the whisky in my glass to ready it for what I really wanted.

"Let me pour you some wine," I smiled, and he followed me to the bar. "I'm glad you're here."

A flush brushed the mahogany of his cheeks as he nodded and said, "I wouldn't miss Valentine's Day."

The wine poured slowly, its red currents sloshing like a wind-torn sea as they coated the inside of the glass. I watched it fill as if it didn't want the moment to end. I knew the feeling.

"I'm truly sorry," I said, handing him the glass by the stem and fighting the look of sorrow in my eyes. "I know you said you trust me, but that was in the heat and intensity of the ritual, so if you aren't ready for this… if you need more time, I fully understand."

"Thank you," Learco smiled timidly as he took a sip of his wine in slow motion, as if he didn't want the moment to end either. "I do trust you, Darragh. I know you mean to do the right thing. But no more secrets. Even if you think it's for my own good."

"Deal!" I said. Then, "Sorry" as I laughed at the smirk on his face at my using of Balor's words. Hey, we had to laugh about it sometime, right? Otherwise, the weight of it was just too heavy. Even though we had stopped him from coming through on his own, the clock was ticking on our own bargain. We all knew it. And, boy, was he going to be angry when we faced him again!

Cernun smiled at us knowingly as he called us to my rarely used dining table to eat. He'd made a delectable meal. In addition to the roast chicken, a salad of early greens was topped with slivers of fennel and radicchio, and I could smell the spicy richness of the blood orange dressing he'd already tossed through. Charred sweet potatoes that looked suspiciously like my grandfather's called to me from the serving dish, and a basket of handmade rolls still steamed.

"Thigh, please," I said as Cernun carved, and I raised my glass in honor of the chef.

It just felt right, the three of us sitting around the table to enjoy a feast of the saints. It felt like home.

"Just to get the business out of the way," Learco said, clearing his throat as he spooned salad to his plate, "I've now got the Chicago and the Portland offices scanning their archival rooms for any other mentions of transformation or transfiguration spells. If any of them find anything, we may be able to help Madison change back."

I watched them sleeping happily on the soft cushion of my favorite chair. That was great news. Though I also had a sinking suspicion they'd turn back when they were ready. If they remembered how.

"If those don't work, we can go international. Leland Hyde thinks that 'Aiden' may have escaped through the sewers somehow, so the manhunt is still on for him; and Madison's parents believe they have taken a semester abroad in Prague until we can get this part of things cleared up."

"Prague, huh?" Cernun asked, mocking Learco's practiced, boss-man demeanor as he spoke. "Wouldn't Catalonia have been more apt?"

"Or Kathmandu," I piled on.

"Purrrr-u?" Cernun offered, and Learco rolled his eyes.

"I'm getting surprisingly good at covering up the messes of the Fomóraiġ," he sighed. "I don't know if that's a good thing or a bad thing."

"Not just the Fomóraiġ," I winced. "Now we've got the Tuath Dé."

I told him of my encounter with The Mórrígan as we ate, and of how I believed it was her doing that aided Madison in completing the rite. Even Cernun, who'd heard the story thrice now already, listened with bated breath. Another of the Fae folk interacting with us could not be a good thing, no matter how friendly and magnanimous she seemed.

"I did find mention of her in that book I borrowed from Verne," I said. "And though she has a reputation for total annihilation of her enemies, it says she's really generous to those she takes favor to. So there's that."

"How many other gods are we going to encounter while we're shacking up with you?" Cernun laughed.

Learco frowned as he considered the destructive possibilities.

"Hey now," I warned, reaching across the table to cup his hand. "Save that for work on Monday. We've got tonight and all day tomorrow for me to show you how truly sorry I am. Lots of lost time to make up for."

He shook it off and smoldered at me, mind meeting mine in the gutter.

"That reminds me!" Cernun cried, leaping from his seat and crossing to the bedroom. "The piece de resistance! Grab your coats."

"I thought the point was less clothing," I smirked as I slipped into my wool waistcoat and followed him to my bedroom window.

Learco was behind me with Madison timid on his tail as I followed Cernun up the fire escape to the roof of my building. The city twinkled in the clear Winter night. Madison paused on the top step and peered down the street. I could barely make it out, but I'm sure their cat eyes saw much more than mine as Katrina wiped down one of the window tables and gathered her tips into her apron. The longing in their yowl let me know that Madison was still in there, somewhere beneath the feline instinct. There was hope in that at least.

"Ta da!" Cernun bellowed, and I turned swiftly to take in the wondrous scene of my rooftop.

"I had the guys build out the boxes with whatever wood we could reclaim from the old fixtures," he beamed. "And the greenhouse was on order for a while now."

My mouth gaped as I stepped forward. Four more rose bushes that matched the potted one downstairs glowed in the moonlight in one of the eight planting boxes now lining the space between a greenhouse and the parapet walls. I could smell the rich loam of the soil as it waited for life, and I smiled at the seedlings already started on the center table through the glass.

"Learco got the permits pushed through with the city so it's totally legal for you to grow here too. And supply the shop if you want."

"It's amazing!" I whispered, my breath still taken away by the sight, by their love.

I turned to kiss them both, pulling them into me with a ferocious growl as my lips searched out their own. Madison mewed a goodbye as they leapt back down the fire escape to the warmth of my apartment below. But our bodies could keep us warm. Our clothes became a mattress, our auras a wrap, as the Winter moon of Saint Valentine shined down upon our nude figures, twined together in the night.

GREAT HEX

**BOOK THREE
IN THE
HEX'D SERIES**

**COMING SOON
FROM**

ACKNOWLEDGMENTS

I would like to thank Sean for his encouragement, his sounding ear, and putting up with my wistful—hopefully—stares as I blanked out of conversations when scenes and characters were getting the better of me or telling me where they wanted to go. Living with a writer can be difficult, supporting one harder still, but you do so with grace.

So much heartfelt gratitude also belongs to Melissa T. whose editing eye and unrelenting enthusiasm remain unmatched. Thank you for your support and for making me better, no matter where the writing takes me.

To Seven for their friendship, long talks, and unabashed honesty through their journey. I hope this story—and those to come—can even begin to scratch the surface of the discovery of self you've allowed me to be a party to.

And to my parents: all four of them. Thank you for believing in me, encouraging me, and allowing me to follow the sentences where they want me to go.

Founded in Atlanta, Georgia in 2023, **PARLYAREE PRESS** is dedicated to publishing writing that expands, reveals, and interrogates the mainstream. We seek out fiction, creative nonfiction, and poetry that exists in the liminal space between what was and what will be.

The cant of circus performers, freaks, queers, and thespians, Parlyaree is the invented language required to tell the stories of those othered, to keep their secrets, to keep them safe. It is a polyglot of experiences that may only be told in one's own voice. Parlyaree—as an invented language—borrows from what was to create something new.

That is what excites us at Parlyaree Press. Stories that transform; essays that reimagine; poetry that takes us behind the stanza to the core of our being and back again; language that plays as much as it conveys.

Writers: tell us your secrets.
Readers: reimagine your worlds.

Founded in Adrina, Georgia in 2025, PARKYARD PRESS is dedicated to publishing writing that challenges norms and interrogates the mainstream. We seek out literary, creative nonfiction, and poetry that exists in the liminal space between what was and what will be.

Immersive often performative, brave, queer, and timeless, Parkyard is the forward language required to pull the words of those unqualified to keep their craft, to keep their craft. It is a merging of experiences that may only be held in each year. Parkyard is an unqualified language where... remains committed to something new.

These vital voices at Parkyard Press furnish the imminent essay that reimagines poetry that marches behind the vanguard of ever-being unheard, again, language that plays... to remain.

Where will us your series.
Readers remains committed.